THE EX FILES

MORGAN ELIZABETH

To Alex who taught me how to change a tire in the parking lot of our first apartment, probably with that creepy guy watching. I love you.

THE EX FILES

By: Morgan Elizabeth
Book 1 in the Ocean View Series

NOTES FROM THE AUTHOR

Dear Reader,

I can't express how much it means to me that you chose to grab my book off of your to be read list and spend some time with my characters. Thank you from the bottom of my heart for making my dreams come true.

The Ex Files contains mentions of weight, diets, infidelity, and family estrangement. Please always put yourself first when reading - it's meant to be our happy place.

Love always,

Morgan

PLAYLIST

Say Anything (Else) - Cartel
Nothing New - Taylor Swift
Strangers by Nature - Adele
Breadwinner - Kacey Musgrave's
I Don't Wanna Live Forever - Zayn
That's What You Get - Paramore
THAT'S WHAT I WANT - Lil Nas X
Paper Rings -Taylor Swift

PROLOGUE

SOMETIMES YOU CAN LOOK BACK AND FIND THE EXACT MOMENT you made one impulsive decision that changed the entire scope of your life.

Today, I made two.

One was deciding not to get gas at the station near my apartment before work, meaning I had to drive through construction to get to my meeting later that day.

The second was RSVPing 'plus one' to my father's wedding.

ONE

-Cassie-

"Okay, I'm leaving, Gabrielle!" I say over my shoulder as I walk towards the office door. It's small, but I never imagined I'd be here when I started The Ex Files from the top bunk in my dorm room. Seven years later, I finally have a lease on a small office in town with an assistant and a roster of clients, all relying on me to change their lives.

"Cassie, wait!" said assistant calls at me. Turning towards her, I smile. My assistant, Gabrielle, is tiny and cute in a nerdy way with thick-rimmed glasses and blunt bangs á la Zooey Deschanel. Her long hair is usually pulled into a messy knot with a pen sticking out like it is now. She wears a mix of retro skirts and quirky tee shirts that would look tacky or forced on anyone else, but on her is adorable. When she reaches me, I'm pulling the strap of my bag over my shoulder and grabbing the keys to my new car. In her hands is a stack of paper she keeps on a clipboard for moments like these.

Our office is tiny, not even sectioning into different offices, just small work areas, but she follows me around like Andi in *The Devil Wears Prada.*

"What's up? I have a date at five." I glance and see I have about an hour to get to the Italian restaurant he booked across the city. Thankfully, I have a collection of dresses, outfits, and makeup here, so there's no need to go to my apartment before heading out. Still, I'll be cutting it close enough. I'll need to avoid rush hour traffic and take back roads to get there.

"At Teresa's, right? On Westport?" She glances down at her notes, and I nod. "With Jason Falcone? The marketing exec?" I nod once more. "Okay, perfect. This is date two?"

It is, and the first went wonderfully, meaning I'm actually looking forward to this one. Mr. Falcone was a true gentleman, pulling out chairs and holding doors and answering all of my questions with an ease I rarely see. He should be easy to pair with someone, and I already have a few clients in mind. It's rare I don't get at least a glimmer of something on the first date, the tiniest sliver of the 'real' man all men hide behind the facade they think women want to see. They all love to play the nice guy, the gentleman. But each one has some other version hiding. Deciding whether that actual version is a walking red flag or a good guy with some flaws is why women trust me with their potential soulmates.

"Yes, it should go well, and then we can get him on the schedule. I'm hopeful I can get some notes for you before the morning." She nods before continuing to look at her clipboard, this time gnawing her lip. Gabrielle has worked for me for about ten months, two months longer than I've held this lease. She's attentive and always on top of things, but she hates drama and conflict. This means one of two things. An unhappy client or...

"One more thing—your father called." My gut sinks. I'm not surprised; I've been avoiding him for weeks now, and he probably needs my answer. "He asked me to confirm you're not bringing a guest." She cringes at the words, hating to put them out there, but it's not her fault. Dear Old Dad is getting married for the third time to some beautiful young thing I'm pretty sure is either my age or younger than me. Every time I talk with him, which isn't often, to be fair, I get the question I'm dreading: are you bringing someone to the wedding?

It's valid. With wedding planning, you need to know who's coming and who isn't. But in this case? It's not what he's asking but what he means. The question is common and mundane from anyone else, but not with my father. Not with his side of the family looking down on me for years, seeing me as lesser. Too thick, too loud, low class. Always single because I can't find a man. The daughter of the woman who was too stupid to see the truth. If I show up alone, I just know I'll get the questions, the judgment, the snide remarks, the quiet whispers.

The thought of showing up alone and facing the firing squad judging me makes me queasy.

But I don't date.

Ever.

Why bother when every man is the same, hiding the shit parts and fluffing up the appealing ones to capture your heart. They all work to pull you in deep, so when their true colors come out, you can just brush it under the rug and coast on the sweet memories.

I've seen it time and time again. It might be a surprise, my being so cynical about love and relationships and men while being a matchmaker, but it's what makes me the best at what I do. The men I meet, the men I vet? I *know* them. Dig deep to find their weaknesses, the ugly spots. Then, I shine a spotlight on them and reveal the hidden truths so that each woman I pair is fully equipped to handle them, pairing up the right bright spots with the right shadows in each personality to make a beautiful masterpiece that can coexist perfectly. It's why I'm the only person who goes on the dates, asks the questions, takes the notes. It's why The Ex Files is literally *my file of exes I've dated.*

I can stay unattached, see through the bullshit. And while love always ends in heartache for someone, I supply my clients with a more complete picture of who they're hitching themselves to in order to avoid even more of a disaster.

But dating someone beyond my requisite two dates? No. I've seen enough of the aftermath to know love isn't in the cards for me. The rubble it leaves in its wake isn't worth the risk. Hence my conundrum.

"I'll handle that on... Monday. Or Tuesday."

"Cassie..." she trails off, but I know what she's saying. This isn't the first call I've dodged. It's just the first one *today*. I need to give an answer, if only so my new mommy doesn't call personally, making it awkward for Gabrielle, who will probably break out in stress hives trying to dodge the drama.

Am I bringing someone, or am I once again showing up alone? Without a man on my arm. The perfect target for pesky questions I do not want to answer.

The scales in my head balance my options. Show up alone and hear the whispers pointing out my flaws, all the reasons I can't keep a man—*just like that mother of hers'*—or... find a solution.

The truth of the matter is, I want nothing less than to show up at the wedding alone. The thought makes me queasy, knowing I'll be facing questions about my single status, about when I'll have kids. Relatives I see less than once a year will mumble under their breath about how maybe I could keep a man if I lost some weight or tried harder, about how I'm not getting any younger. And, shit, it's not like I'm fifty. I'm twenty-nine. And I'm building my own business, happy with my life the way it is. I don't need to add a man and make things more complicated.

Plus, I've learned with time, a man will offer nothing other than whiplash and heartache.

An orgasm or two would be nice, my inner sex fiend whispers. The inner sex fiend who hasn't been satisfied in much, much too long. Some people have a devil and an angel battling on their shoulders, whispering in their ears.

Because I'm a crazy person, I have a sex fiend and an uptight librarian who keeps me grounded. I mentally stuff a sock in the sex fiend's mouth and shut her into the dark closet I keep her in. I have a perfectly capable collection of battery-operated boyfriends, *thankyouverymuch*. What more could a man offer me?

Precisely, the librarian says. The one who always uses common sense to remind me men bring nothing but pain and suffering. The one who looks alarmingly like my mother.

I sigh.

A man would offer me the chance to show up my father, though, and quiet the judgmental family who hates me. The librarian shrugs because even she can't argue that fact.

So, in that moment, I make the fatal move of deciding something based solely on emotion, not on intelligence or planning or my rules or my carefully crafted life plan. No, this one is a pure, idiotic impulse.

"When he calls next, tell him I'm bringing a date." Gabrielle's eyes widen with shock before she nods, jotting down a note. Before she can say another word, I wave goodbye and walk out the door, wondering what the fuck I've just done.

TWO

-Luke-

My phone rings from where it sits on my toolbox, the vibrations rattling on the red metal and catching my attention more than the ringer. Glancing at it, my sister Quinn's smiling face is staring at me with *Quinny calling* written across the screen. She added her own contact years ago, using the name I called her when I was just three or four.

I'm covered in grime and in the middle of a job, but my dad taught me no matter what, when family calls, you answer. Family is more important than any job, any repair, *anything*, so I peel off the grease-covered latex gloves, toss them into the can next to the car I'm working on, and tap the screen to answer.

"What's your email address?" Quinn asks before I even say hello.

"Well, hello to you too, Quinny. I'm great, thank you." The sound of her eyes rolling can practically be heard over the line. The thing about being the little brother is I live to annoy my sisters. It's basically the main thing I was born to do. And with two older sisters, one five years older and one ten, I've had more than a few opportunities to do just that.

"Yeah, Luke, hi, how are you? Still as boring as yesterday? And the day before? Great. Now, what's your email?"

"Why?"

"Why what?"

"Why do you need my email?" She hesitates, piquing my interest. My two older sisters are both happily married with kids of their own to bully and baby, but they each still call me nearly every day to check in. Unfortunately, they're also the nosiest women I've ever encountered. As the youngest of three, I've learned this kind of silence can be one of two things.

One, she's trying to save my feelings. This is rare because, again, she's my older sister. In the same way I live to annoy her, she lives to bring me down a few notches. Whereas my oldest sister, Tara, still babies me and lives to give me motherly advice, Quinn taunts me.

Alternately, there's option two and the situation I'm pretty sure I'm in now: she doesn't want to answer my question because she knows I won't like it.

"Quinn..." I say in a warning.

"I'm creating a profile for you."

"What kind of profile?" I already know. I know where this is going. It's where nearly all of our conversations end these days.

"A dating profile." Ding ding ding.

"Jesus, Q, no." This has been going on for three years now. The day I hit 30, my sisters decided I needed a wife and kids to keep my life exciting and happy. But I disagree. I'm satisfied with my life. Happy to be working on cars, living simple, going out for beers with friends, and just... being. Eventually, I want all of it, what they have— the family, the kids, the white picket fence. But profiles and apps and countless first dates sound painful. I'm just waiting for the moment the perfect woman falls into my lap.

That's not too much to ask for, right?

"Luke—"

"No, Quinn. I'm not going on some weird catfish crazy swipe right app. It's not for me."

"Luke, seriously, listen—"

"When I decide to find someone, I'll do it the old-fashioned way. I'm not looking for hookups, and I know you mean well, I do, but you're so far out of the dating scene. You lucked out, found Ty back before the apps and complicated dating. It's just a lot of trial and error, and I don't want to spend months having first dates that lead nowhere."

"Luke, shut up for two seconds, God. It's not an app, and you don't have to do anything at all. You'll only be set up with good matches looking for something serious. If you don't want to go on a date after that, don't. Hell, you're so boring there's a chance you won't make it past the screening before anything happens."

"Screening?"

"If you'd shut up for two minutes, I would have told you it's not an app, and you do nothing. Just go on two dates and then you'll get set up. Unless you fail because you're secretly a waving red flag. But I'm telling you now, if that happens, Tara and I are going to kick your ass." I sigh, having heard this before. I was raised in a loving household with happily married parents and two older sisters. My dad taught me how to wine and dine, throw a ball, and get my hands dirty in an engine, but my mom and sisters taught me how to treat a woman.

They showed me the ropes: from holding doors open to how to treat a woman when she's emotional to making them feel good about themselves to the right way to break up.

Once, Quinn heard I'd broken up with a high school girlfriend via text message. When my mom picked me up that day, all three were in the car. We sped home and they ripped me a new one, telling me they wouldn't endure having *that* kind of man in their family.

When I tried to get my dad on my side, he'd sat me down.

"Son, one day you'll have someone in your life, and you'll realize you'd do anything to keep her happy, even if it means letting her sit your son down and bustin' his balls with feminist chats and conversations on how to treat a woman. There are worse things, bud. Just accept it. If not for whatever future lady you have in your life, then for your old man who doesn't want to hear his wife bitchin' all night about the piece of scum son they're raising."

"I heard that, Jeffrey!" my mom had called from the other room, my sisters giggling after her, and my dad just rolled his eyes, but the smile was genuine. Because he loved her, and he'd endure this to get her, to keep her happy.

I never made that mistake again, always having any conversation of consequence face to face. It was one of many lessons I never forgot over the years.

"Fine, I'll bite. What are you talking about?" Over the years, I've also found it's easiest to let my sister get it out now than argue. At the end of the day, I'll still have to sit through her speech, but the process is more painful if I delay it.

"I have this friend—do you remember Jaime?" I don't, but if I admit it, I'll get an hour-long summary of Jaime, her relation to my sister, and every interaction I have ever had with the woman, even if it was as minute as attending the same holiday party seven years ago.

"Sure."

"Okay, well, Jaime met this guy through this matchmaker—"

"Oh, hell no. Absolutely not."

"Shut up and let me finish. So, she met him through the matchmaker, and they've been married for years. Perfect couple, like they were meant to be from day one."

"Quinn, I don't—" I try to cut in, but she keeps on.

"So Jaime's sister went to school with this girl, and I have the inside scoop. Usually, she finds the men to match through dating websites. Crazy, right? She dates them and vets them and then matches them up. It's genius, really. Like cutting out the middleman to avoid the catfishes and creeps and red flags. But because she knows this girl, she told me I could just fill out an application, and if you pass her inspection, you're in." Like always, the words fly through the phone line with her excitement. You need a trained ear to catch Quinn's every word on the first try.

"I don't want to meet some matchmaker, Quinn."

"Look, you just need to go on two dates with her. Easy peasy. Call it an early Valentine's Day gift to your favorite big sister."

"Christmas was just three weeks ago."

"I don't know why you're being so difficult when all I'm trying to do is improve your life, Luke."

"Well, you're trying to send me off with some unknown match-maker, so..."

"She's not unknown. She's a friend of Jaime's."

"I don't know Jaime!"

"You just said you did, though!" Quinn yells, and I pull the phone from my ear with the shriek.

"I lied!"

"There's no need to yell, Luke." I sigh, knowing arguing here is pointless. So instead, I make my tone neutral and calming.

"Quinn, you called me and told me I'm, for some reason, going on dates with a matchmaker to get more dates with other people? Because I'm apparently lonely? I'm happy with my life, Q. I appreciate the gesture. I don't need anyone."

"We're worried about you." Her voice has gotten soft and concerned, a tone I recognize. Shit. I need to fix this before it gets sticky.

"No need to worry about me, honey."

"You're always working. You come alone to everything. Shit, I don't know the last time you brought a woman home. Wasn't it weird at Christmas?" It was, not that I'll admit it. Christmas dinner at our parents' was the same as it's always been, but also not at all. My sisters are married with kids, both with husbands who were chatting about family vacations and wiggly teeth, and I just... sat there. I couldn't relate. For the first time in my life, I didn't feel connected to my close-knit family. As my sisters grow into their own families, I'm feeling left behind. "We just want you to be happy, Luke."

"Who's we?" I don't know why I'm saying this. It's basically opening the door to her, giving her hope I'll say yes to this mess.

"Tara, Mom, and me."

"You pulled Mom into this?"

"It was her idea. She said it's killing her to see her *baby boy* lonely." The teasing tone is back.

"You guys need to stop. I'm not lonely." I don't bother arguing the baby boy crack. As both the youngest and the only boy, I am one hundred percent my mother's baby boy.

Some days, it's fine, like when I always get the biggest slice of cake or how I got away with way more than my sisters as a kid. Other times, like this, it's the absolute worst.

"Yes, you are, Luke. You don't have to admit it to me, but you're not that guy. The guy to live alone for the rest of his life, unattached. You love family. But it's not going to just fall into your lap, babe. You need to actually go out and find it. I know you're happy, but soon everyone around you is going to be attached and you'll be alone. I don't want that for you."

Quinn's always known me best of all, regardless of her endless need to mess with me. Right now proves it. I've lived my life with little to no change: gone out to games with friends, spent long days on the pier, kept the same daily routine for years. And year after year, I continue to do it without issue. But it's predictable. It's the same. And sometimes, even though I refuse to admit it to my nosey ass sisters, it's lonely. "Just give it a chance, Luke."

"I don't know. It seems so weird. Why don't I just... I don't know. Download some apps. Go on dates."

"So you're admitting it. You want someone." *Shit.*

"I'm not saying I'm unhappy or lonely." I pause, planning my next words carefully. But, you're not wrong—I want a family, eventually. And you're right, I'm not getting younger. I'm not just going to stumble upon the perfect woman on the side of the road."

"Perfect! So let's make it happen. Let's find you a woman! I want a sister!"

"You have a sister."

"A new one, with more fun clothes. Tara just wears leggings and gym clothes all day." I laugh. She's not wrong, though I'm sure Tara wouldn't like her calling her out like that.

"Let me try it on my own. I'll join some of those sites, download the apps."

"No apps. They're cesspools."

"I love trashy women," I say with a smile, knowing her response before she even says it.

"That's what got you into this mess. Trashy women who aren't looking for something real." Once again, not wrong. "Please. Just go on the two dates. If it blows, you can cancel after that. I won't hold it against you."

"And if I don't say yes?"

"If you don't say yes, I'll tell Mom you're lonely and sad you haven't met the love of your life yet." *Jesus Christ.*

"No, don't do that. She'll hook me up with everyone's niece and granddaughter from here to Philly." Quinn laughs an evil laugh I've heard many, many times over the years. I sigh, resignation clear in the sound. "I'll do it. Send the details."

"Yes! I promise you won't regret it!" she says, but I doubt it. Things like this always blow up in my face. But before I can argue, my work phone rings from beside me and I have to answer.

"That's work, gotta go, Q."

"Got it, love you, bro."

"Love you too." I disconnect before answering to hear I need to take the truck out and tow a car two towns over. I clean up before I leave, but something about our call, about the impending shitshow, has me distracted the whole drive there.

THREE

-Cassie-

"You have *got* to be kidding me!" My brand new BMW made an unsettling sound on the back roads before my tire pressure light came on, blinking to tell me my rear passenger tire was dangerously low on air. I tried to rumble on, praying I'd reach a turnoff, a gas station, *something* on the windy, deserted road, but eventually knew any further and I'd be screwing up my car. So topping off my shit sandwich of an evening, I only have ten minutes to change a tire, drive back to the city, and get to this date. I'm squatting in my red-bottomed heels on the side of the road and inspecting the clearly flat tire as if I know what to do with it.

Spoiler: I don't.

This is the *last thing I need right now.*

After leaving the office, I realized I was dangerously low on gas and needed to stop at a station. Everyone knows there are two people on this planet: those who fill their tank when they hit the halfway mark and those who fill up ten miles after the gas light goes on.

I am in group two and regretting it. If I had just filled up on my way into the office, this would have been avoided.

I vow from now on I'll fill up at the halfway mark. Hell, maybe the three-quarters mark. Whatever it takes.

To get to the gas station closest to the office, I was forced to drive through a construction zone, adding seven minutes to my drive and, from what I can tell, a nail to my tire.

Why me?

I kick my tire, then curse when the movement reverberates through my open-toed shoes and up my leg with sharp pain. Ripping open the front door, I lean over to find my bag and pull out my phone to call Roadside Assistance, the contents of my bag spilling out across the console as I do. Adios, lip gloss I'll never find again.

When I glance at my phone, my misery grows.

No bars.

"ARE YOU FUCKING KIDDING ME!?" I shout to the sky, fighting the tears that want to fall. Stupid, *stupid* tears every woman sheds when the world seems to be against her and the walls are closing in.

This is not me, frazzled and emotional. I don't cry. I don't let my feelings control me. I live by rules, by plans. Structure and systems keep me safe, stable, and away from emotional turmoil. But the message from my dad, my stupid, *stupid* panicked decision to tell him I'm coming with a date? It all has me a mess. The entire drive, my mind sorted through options to get out of the wedding, from faking an illness to hiring an escort in order to make it out of this in one piece. And now I have... I glance at my phone again... seven minutes to drive *fifteen* minutes to meet with a potential new match.

Taking a deep breath, I run through solutions. I need to be sensible with this, to lay out my options so I can think with a rational mind. This road seems empty with not a house or car in sight, so I can't rely on a good Samaritan stopping to help. It's long and windy, with steep hills and empty fields on either side. *The perfect location for a slasher movie,* my pessimistic librarian says from my shoulder, staring down her nose at me and tsking because I'm so unprepared.

Shaking her off, I remind myself I can do this. I'm a problem solver. It's what I do for a living, right? I just need to figure out my options and choose one.

Option one: put on the spare and go.

Problem: I don't know where the spare is in this car, much less how to actually change a tire. Add it to my very long list of 'things I need to learn how to do' alongside finally using the app I bought to learn Spanish, installing the new fancy shower head I got six months ago, and making the perfect omelet.

Option one is out.

Option two: call Gabrielle and cancel the date.

Problem: No bars, and I *never* cancel a date. Ever. My business relies on my promptness, my reliability. People are looking for love and have faced enough disappointment as it is. I refuse to add to it and pin my professional reputation on it.

Option three: walk up the hill a bit and pray to God I'll get a bar so I can make a call to the expensive roadside service program I was talked into joining when I bought my car.

I guess we'll go with that one.

Pulling my shoulders back, I head towards the top of the hill the road leads to, trying to avoid potholes and pebbles in my regrettably high heels and monitoring my cell's range. My breath puffs in clouds in the freezing January air, reflecting the light of the rapidly setting sun. Panic creeps in again as night falls, but when I reach the peak of the hill, it dissipates with relief.

My prayers are answered when, if I hold my phone up and at the perfect angle, two beautiful bars appear in the upper right-hand corner, occasionally flickering to just one. But it's all I need.

It's the most gorgeous sight I've ever seen.

Immediately, I pull out the small laminated card with the Roadside Assistance number on it and dial, praying the connection will hold.

"Hello, this is Roadside Assistance; how may I help you?" the cheery woman on the other line answers.

"Yes, hi, this is Cassandra Reynolds. I have a flat, and I need to get it fixed."

"We can do that. Can I get your account number?" I give her the numbers and information and then wait while she inputs it. "Thank you, Ms. Reynolds. Before I can send someone out, I'll need you to tell me the name of the road you're on and any nearby crossroads?" *Shit.*

"Uhm, I'm not so sure?"

"We'll need to get your location in order to dispatch a truck to you for help." Gone is her cheeriness, annoyance in its place. It's very "what an idiot, how the hell does she not know where she is?" and I cringe, trying not to be frustrated.

"Well, I don't know where I am. I'm somewhere on County Road 324, right outside Ocean View, but that goes for miles."

"Are there any landmarks in sight?" The words fill me with an uneasy dread because *no, there are no fucking landmarks, and how are they going to find me, and am I going to be stuck here forever? And if I am, who will know? Gabrielle will probably notice when I don't show up tomorrow, and the date might call the office, but he might not. My mother is off on some single woman's retreat, and my father is getting married, and I have no one at all who will notice I'm gone!*

"No, nothing. Just.. uhm... trees and grass." And even that isn't much. With winter here, everything looks dark and desolate. The tiny bit of sun is fading, the winter night is setting in, and the panic rising in my voice is unmistakable. This is confirmed when her voice goes from annoyed to calming and reassuring.

"No problem, we'll figure this out, Ms. Reynolds. Can you turn on the coordinates in the app so we can pinpoint your location?" Relief. There's a plan B. I won't be completely screwed, freezing in my car and found, mummified years later. The headlines will read, "Local Matchmaker Found on CR 324 Years Later: No One Knew She Was Gone!"

The app. I need to open the app. Simple enough. I mentally make a note to bring Gabrielle a latte in the morning as a thank you for forcing me to download the app when I bought this car. Pulling my phone from my ear, I hit the speaker button before tapping to my apps.

"Okay, I'm in the app. What do I do next?" My eyes keep looking up at the bars, which keep flicking from two to one. My gut drops. *Just hold on, little bars! A few minutes, I'm begging you!*

"You're going to go to the Find My Location tab and accept the location tracking." As I do it, the line starts to crackle, the bars flickering to one and staying there.

"I think I'm losing service," I say in a panic.

"Just click the location services. Once it's activated, someone will be dispatched." As I tap the bar accepting the terms of the tracking, my phone crackles more and then beeps. The call has dropped.

Staring at my phone in horror, all I see is a rotating loading circle above "Track my Location." *Shit shit shit!* I jump in my heels, phone raised in the air, trying desperately to get the service I need to send my location. The last thing I see is the rotating circle before it's gone, and "No service" flashes on my screen. It feels like at the exact moment, the night drops around me, everything going black.

"Well fuck," I say to myself. Taking a deep breath, I realize all I can do now is pray it sent and try not to cry as I carefully walk down the hill in the heels, promising I will forever carry a pair of flats in my car and learn to change a tire as soon as I'm out of this mess.

Let's just hope I won't become a local news headline before I can make that happen.

FOUR

-Luke-

I'M STILL THINKING ABOUT MY SISTER'S CALL AS I DRIVE BACK from towing a car to a customer's house outside of the city. The loud rumble of the tow truck is near deafening as I go, perfect for attempting to drown out the thoughts of my sisters and mother worrying for me. I *hate* making them worry, almost as much as I hate being treated like the hopeless boy who needs their help to make my life complete.

It's not working.

Should I be looking for a woman to settle down with? It's not like I'm running rampant and hooking up with random women every weekend. Sure, I occasionally go out with Ben or Chris and the guys, and sometimes I leave with a woman, but even that has been few and far between lately.

And then I try to figure out the last time I went out with my friends other than Ben and Chris, who are also happily single. Sure, we text regularly, but now that most of my friends have married off, random guys' nights are becoming less and less popular. They have kids to find sitters for and partners to cross-check plans with. My large group of friends has migrated into a group of couples with me watching from the outside. When did that happen?

Fuck, have I somehow missed the memo that I was supposed to start looking for someone? Between work and hobbies and family, it's just never been something I felt the need to focus on. Maybe Quinn is right. Perhaps I need to focus on the future and who I want to spend it with before it's too late, before I'm the lonely single friend that gets invited to birthday parties out of pity.

These are the thoughts flying through my mind as I crest the hill on CR 324. At the valley between the two hills on the windy road sits a small white car pulled to the side, interior lights near blinding in the dark night. Slowing the truck, I pull over to check if there's anyone in it and if they need help. From here, I can glimpse into the car, where a pretty woman with dark hair tumbling over the shoulders of a white coat sits. The coat alone looks more expensive than my entire outfit combined, face made up perfectly, except for the rivers of black that stain her face and down her cheeks. Jesus. Hopping out and jogging over to her window, I tap on it, but it's unnecessary. Her frantic eyes are on me.

"Hey, miss, can I-"

"Oh, finally!" She steps out, black shiny high-heeled shoes leaving the car first as she opens the door and steps out. I recognize the iconic red bottoms the interior light reflects off and the logo on the cuff of her jacket. Money. She has it. I would know. While I chose to work a blue-collar job, we grew up on the wealthy side of town, never wanting for anything.

"I'm sorry, I—" I try to figure out what's going on, how she got here, why she's been crying, but she cuts me off once again, the words curt and clipped.

"Come, it's this one. God, I can't believe it took this long. I sent the dispatch request nearly two hours ago." She sounds... angry. At me? I look at my phone to see if maybe Jeff sent me a text for a disabled vehicle pick up, but nothing. There's no service on this stretch of road. I've driven it enough to know service for the next two miles is spotty at best.

It's clear she thinks I'm someone else sent to help her. It's also clear that whoever was *supposed* to help her wasn't coming.

"Ma'am, I think you're confused—" I try to explain the mix-up. Either way, I'd be happy to help, but again, she cuts me off, looking over her shoulder as she walks around her car. Glossy dark waves sway with the movement.

"I seriously thought I'd be stuck here all night. This service is terrible. I can't believe I paid so much for it." I should be annoyed or angry even, but something about her indignation, as misguided as it is, is entertaining. So instead, I decide to play along.

"I do apologize, Ms..."

"Reynolds. Cassie. It's right here." She points to a flat rear tire, but I can't look at it. Her hand has moved aside her white coat, and even in the dark, I can see her figure is phenomenal in a dark dress hugging generous curves but still covering her demurely, a mix of vixen and modest. Ending at her knee, shapely legs lead to those heels that have me thinking about... "Hello?" The annoyed voice bursts through my thoughts.

"Huh?" My eyes shoot to her face, which looks even more frustrated than before, if possible.

"I said, can you fix this? I need to get out of here. I already missed an appointment, and I'll need to reschedule. I *never* miss appointments."

An appointment. What kind of appointment could she have to go to dressed like that?

Squatting beside the tire, the issue is clear—a silver nail glints in the moonlight and tells me the reason for the flat.

"Do you have a spare?"

"I have no clue. I think so?" Looking up at her, she's gnawing on her lip. Instead of frustrated, she now seems embarrassed and stressed. "Honestly, I just got this car a few weeks ago and barely know how to turn on the heat. I keep telling myself I'm going to learn how to change a tire, but I never get to it because, you know, life and work and life and Netflix. But now I'm really regretting it because I was pretty sure I was going to be stuck here forever and freeze, and then I'd be found a like a human ice pop and no one would—"

"Alright, sweetheart, calm down. You're gonna be okay. No human ice pops on my watch." I'm fighting the desire to laugh at her rambling as I stand and go to the trunk, tapping it twice gently with the side of my first. "Can you pop this?"

"Can you not hit my car, please?"

"Just a love tap, trust me. Doesn't hurt it." I wink at her, and she rolls her eyes at me but doesn't argue, instead walking to the driver's side to pull the latch, popping the truck. Digging in, I pull out the spare and jack before getting down to where the flat is. "Wanna learn?" I ask, staring at her in the dark. It's hard to see her face, but the moon illuminates her head, shaking, declining the offer. "Suit yourself." I loosen the lug nuts along the rim, setting up the jack and continuing to remove the flat before replacing it with the spare. "So you're gonna want to bring this to a garage as soon as possible, get this flat fixed. You shouldn't drive far on your spare." She looks confused.

"You guys don't do that here? What the fuck am I paying for monthly?" she grumbles, and maybe this has gone too far. I can't blame her for her frustration, especially if she's been stuck out here waiting for a truck for two hours. I know how overpriced the dealers' services are, and I also know that they are incredibly unreliable.

"Ma'am, I don't—"

"Cassie. Please, call me Cassie. It's fine. I get it. You don't make the rules. Just get it on. I'm freezing." She's looking up impatiently at the empty road now, rubbing her hands over her arms. Her demeanor has changed again, going from relieved to frustrated she's still stuck here. Like I've become an inconvenience for her. What is *with* this chick? Finally, I'm done playing the game. I stop and look up at her, the wrench clattering to the ground.

"Look, I don't know who you think—"

"I know I'm being a bitch," she says, cutting me off, and the look in her eyes has me forgetting what I was going to say. Regret and anxiety and... sadness are there. "Honestly, I spent hours out here, not sure if you'd ever come. I missed a meeting and left him there, no notice. No one knows where I am. I've been... I've been through it tonight, and my emotions are still a bit crazy. I'm cold, hungry, and I *really* have to pee. But that's no excuse to talk to you like that."

"No one knows where you are?" I pick up the cold metal wrench and get back to tightening the nuts, making sure they're even and secure.

"Well, my assistant would probably notice in the morning that I was gone, but...." Once again, I pause to look at her. She's beautiful. And through the frustrated, bitchy mask, I think she's kinda sweet. She has to have someone waiting for her at home.

"No man?"

"What?"

"No man to keep tabs on you?"

"I don't need a man to keep tabs on me."

"You were stuck for an indefinite amount of time in the middle of nowhere with no cell service. If you had a good man, he'd have found you." She never answers my question, nor does she argue, even though the stark look on her face says she disagrees with me, but drops it. Smiling for some strange reason, I go back to finishing my job. Finally, her voice breaks the silence.

"Wow. It's pretty out here." The soft breath of her voice has me stopping again, but when I glance at her, she's not looking at me. Instead, her head is tipped up, taking in the clear night sky dotted with stars.

"Stars are bright."

"Yeah. I never... I'm usually in the city. No stars out there. The lights and the boardwalk are too bright."

"We're just far enough to catch the stars out here. You want to see them for real, though, go up to the mountains. Poconos. Bright as can be out there." She pauses, staying quiet as we both stare up at the twinkling stars.

"My dad's getting married out there in a few weeks."

"Yeah?" I tighten the last bolts and brush off my hands before I stand.

"Yeah." The words are clipped, annoyed.

"Sound pissed about it."

"Not... not pissed. Just not excited. A messy divorce, weird family dynamics. The normal, you know?" I look at her as I lift the flat into her trunk, but her eyes are still to the sky. The truth is, I don't know. I have friends who understand, even cousins. But not my family. My parents love each other more today than they did years ago, still kissing in the kitchen just because, my dad still grabbing my mom's ass when they think no one's looking. My sisters are both head over heels in love with good men they made adorable kids with. But you don't say that to a stranger who may or may not be having an existential crisis in the middle of nowhere.

"Yeah." It's all I can say as I pack away the jack, flat tire, and tools before wiping my hands on the jumpsuit I'm still wearing. I need to drop the truck back off at the garage before heading home to change. When I slam the trunk closed, she comes out of her daze and looks at me.

"Ugh, I'm so sorry. I'm out here losing my mind, telling you all my problems, and having a meltdown while you're just trying to get your job done." She laughs, the sound self-deprecating. Now that my eyes have adjusted to the dark more, I can see her better. She's cute though, curvy, with a pretty face that I'm sure in better light is drop-dead gorgeous, despite the black stains on her cheeks. And now that her anxiety and frustration have ebbed, I think she might also have a decent sense of humor.

"No problem, Cassie." Pretty name too. "So here's the card for the garage. Jeff, the owner, won't rip you off. Tell him Luke said you're cool and you'll be taken care of." Thinking back on my conversation with Quinn, I decide to shoot my shot. When the world drops an opportunity in your lap, you know?

"Hey, look, I know this is weird, but—"

"Oh, that's super sweet, but I am so not the right woman." She digs in the purse on the passenger seat. "So, do I owe you anything? Or is this included in the service?" I blink at her, confused. Was I just turned down? Or did I read the situation so totally wrong? Something tells me I didn't, but...

"Service?"

"Roadside Assistance? Do you need my membership card?" A hand waves a laminated card at me, and I remember. She doesn't think this is good luck and I'm doing this to be nice. She thinks I work for some kind of roadside service company. I huff out a laugh and try to explain.

"No, I—"

"Great, well, that should be good, right? I can go?" She walks around the car to the driver's side, heels sinking in the not-quite frozen grass and nearly tripping. I lean forward to catch her if she falls, but she grabs the door and gets her footing before climbing in and starting the car. "Thanks so much for everything. Here's something for your help," she says, handing me a few folded bills before shutting her door.

As she drives off, I stare at her taillights, wondering *what the fuck just happened.*

FIVE

-Cassie-

WALKING INTO THE OFFICE THE FOLLOWING DAY WITH A LATTE for Gabrielle and me, I'm a mess. My body aches from the shivering and crying jags—yes, jags, plural—I had in the car, my favorite shoes are scuffed beyond repair, and I have to call somewhere to see if they can fix my tire. On top of that, I had a nasty voicemail from the client who was stood up last night waiting in my inbox when I finally got in cell range.

Well, at least he outed himself quickly. No need to waste my time on the required two dates if that's how he acts when he doesn't get his way.

After all, that's the name of the game, my job. To find all red flags and save women from wasting time on them.

The Ex Files started in my college dorm to help a friend avoid getting catfished.

She'd been on a dating app and found a guy she thought seemed great, but a few red flags were flaring. So I looked into him, being an internet super sleuth, and decided she was right—some things weren't adding up. But because you never know when the love of your life could stumble in, she was hesitant to call it quits before it even started.

Instead, I matched with him and went on a date to vet him for her before she gave up on him. Turns out he was actually a great guy, he just didn't have any clue how to fill out a dating profile without setting red flags off. That's how Taylor met her current husband.

That should have been that, but word quickly got out that I could 'test' out men for my friends and friends of friends and friends of friends of friends. Soon I was being paid in gift cards and my favorite wine. It didn't take long for word of mouth to turn into a full-time matchmaking business where I match women looking for love with men I've already 'dated'—men from my 'Ex Files.'

The process is simple. I charge a consultation fee to learn more about the woman and then a flat fee for a guaranteed six dates over six months. During this time, I shuffle through my Ex Files and set up dates I genuinely believe will be a perfect match. So far, I have about a ninety-eight percent success rate. That other two percent is usually women who didn't know what they wanted, weren't ready to commit, or had red flags of their own. My entire client base has been grown from word of mouth, happy customers sharing my information with friends. And really, my walls plastered with marriage, engagements, and baby announcements say it all.

I'm really effing good at my job.

Finding the men is a whole other process. For about five years now, I have used several accounts across multiple dating websites to find men looking for love. Once they match with the persona's I've created, I tell them about my business and ask if they'd be interested in joining my Ex Files. If they agree, we go on two dates.

Date one, I choose the restaurant and the activity. The second, if I decide they're decent and worthy of moving to the next stage, the guy has to plan. One meal, one activity. I find forcing them to do some of the work tells me even more than my arsenal of questions does sometimes. Each date lasts at least four hours, during which I work to learn more about them, shuffle through the facts and exaggerations, and get past the mask they're wearing.

Because if there's one thing I've learned about men, it's that they all have some kind of facade they've created to draw you in.

The only rules I have are simple:

1. Two dates and two dates only.

2. I never take them to my place and never go to theirs.

3. I never ever kiss a client.

4. Never ever, *ever* get attached.

Thankfully, I've never had an issue with these rules.

Because they're all hiding something, even if it's not a horrible personality or a secret life. And that's the one thing I cannot tolerate.

I've seen what happens when you fall for a man who lives beneath a facade.

So I've made it my mission to save women the trouble of getting caught up with a man who can't commit, a man who doesn't want to be faithful. Whether it's someone who just wants some fun or something more devious, more harmful in the long run, I shield my clients from that kind of heartache.

Walking through the front door, I smile at Gabrielle.

"Good morning, Cassandra!"

"Cassie, Gabrielle," I say as I drop the latte cup on her desk. It took me nearly seven months to convince her not to call me Ms. Reynolds. The name reminds me of the promise of a happy family that came crashing down years ago. So now I'm working to break her of the more formal 'Cassandra.' Only my father calls me that, and because of it, I hate it.

"Right. Cassie. Thank you for this," she says, tipping the cup to me. "Should I reschedule Mr. Factor's meeting?" The date I missed last night.

"Absolutely not. He screened himself out. A man who can't handle a missed appointment without screaming profanities into a woman's voicemail isn't worthy of our clientele." Walking over to my desk, I shuffle through papers. The office isn't large—just a single suite in one of the many business complexes, a desk for myself and my assistant. I rarely ever have to meet a client in the office, and it's mostly just a hub for files, calls, and a place for Gabrielle and me to be in the same room.

Before I got my office space, it was rare that I left my apartment for anything other than for meetings. So I'd be lying if I said one of the biggest factors to moving into an office was just getting out of my home each day.

"Oh, my goodness! You're kidding me!"

"Nope. Can you please send him an email stating I was unable to meet him due to an unforeseen emergency and I will *not* need to reschedule? If he calls, please send him to me. I'd love to have a frank conversation with him." She chuckles, knowing how my 'frank discussions' go. "When you get a moment, can you please pull up the customer service number for the roadside assistance company? The guy who helped me last night said they don't replace the flat, but I could have sworn the sales associate listed that in their services." She nods before digging through files as I sit down and get to work, running through applications, answering emails, and making love happen.

An hour later, she's in front of my desk with a sticky note. "Here you go, Cassie." On it in grade-school-teacher perfect handwriting is the number I requested.

"Thanks, Gabrielle." I grab it and dial the number, walking towards the hall to take it outside.

"Hello, Roadside Assistance; how may I direct your call?"

"Hi, I have a question about my account. Last night, I was sent a truck for a flat, but the serviceman told me that you don't change the tire, just put on my spare, and I need to take it to a separate garage to get it properly replaced. I was under the impression all of that was covered." I try to think of the papers I signed when buying the car, and the salesman sold me on the expensive maintenance and assistance plan. *What have I been paying for?*

"That's correct. We supply our customers with top-tier help from beginning to end. Even if we were unable to change the tire, you'd be going to one of our certified locations for whatever is needed. Can you give me your name so I can look up your account?"

"Yes, it's Cassandra Reynolds. The man told me I could go to a, uh..." I dig through my clutch I brought out if they needed my account number and find the business card. "A Jeff's Garage? On Beach and Third?"

"That's not one of our service centers." I hear clicking before she makes a confused noise. "Ma'am, do you have your account number on hand?"

"Yes." I look at the card before rattling off the numbers. She makes another confused sound.

"And this is regarding a service call made last night? January 21st?"

"Correct. I was on Country Road 324. I called around 5 pm."

"Yes, I see the call. And you say someone came and put on your spare tire?"

"Yes. What seems to be the problem?"

"Ma'am, we never sent a truck out to you." Ringing starts in my ears.

"You did. He came and changed my tire. He came in a tow truck."

"None of our techs work from a tow truck. If we need to tow a customer, we dispatch a separate service."

"But he did. He was. I called!"

"I see a call logged at 5:03 last night, but it seems connection was lost before we could capture your location. We were unable to reach you or know where you were."

"But I..." I stand there, confused, playing over the night in my mind. He pulled over and asked if I needed help. I told him he took too long and... *Oh God,* he looked *confused.* It was dark, but I remember that much played on his face, the confusion. The truck. It was white. White and... I concentrate, trying to picture it in my mind, what it looked like. I was in such a state I didn't even pay attention, didn't even take it in.

My mind pulls up the image—bright green lettering. Curvy words reading... *Jeff's Garage and Towing*.

Well, fuck.

It wasn't Roadside Assistance.

He wasn't two hours late. He just happened to be in the right place at the right time.

He changed my tire to be friendly, and I was... *rude*. All of my self-taught lessons on etiquette flash in my mind with painful clarity as I remember shoving money in his hand as a tip when he tried to ask me out. *I'm going to hell. That's it.* A sweet, admittedly attractive man saved me, full-on knight-in-greasy-coveralls'ed me, and I *tipped him*.

No wonder I'm single. Both the uptight librarian and my inner sex fiend nod, arms crossed over their chests with disappointment.

"Ms. Reynolds?" The woman chirps through the line, reminding me I'm, once again, being rude. Shit.

"Yes, sorry. There must have... must have been a miscommunication. Thank you for your time." Before she can say anything else, I move the phone from my ear and swipe to end the call, staring at the business card in my hand. The address isn't far from my office building, just a mile or so.

I need to apologize.

———

Unfortunately, that doesn't happen today, as when I get back to my desk, Mr. Factor requires a word from me and further proves there is an obvious reason he's still single and struggles to find a woman. And it didn't even take the second date.

It also further cements for the millionth time my theory that all men have a real face under the mask they wear to attract women.

Sometimes it works. Some even get past my questions and dating process, but most? Most out themselves before long.

But sometimes, in rare cases, it takes years—decades, even—for the true face to show.

Take my father, for example.

He was married to my mother for twenty years. The entirety of my childhood was filled with mental snapshots of a happy family, a couple in love, and their darling daughter. A family that struggled some, sure. Christmases weren't extravagant. Clothes were hand-me-downs. But it was filled with warmth all the same—or so I thought. Sometimes I get glimpses, memories that make their way through my childish rose-colored glasses. Memories of my dad poking fun at my mom's dinner choices or my mom trying to make things perfect for him. Despite that, my childhood was fine.

The day I left for college, my father packed his bags, leaving my mother broken beyond repair when she learned for the past fifteen years he had a woman just an hour away and had been unfaithful for nearly the entire twenty years of their marriage. It turns out he only stayed with my mom to have a fallback and avoid paying child support until I was 18. The woman he had on the side, some high-class former Stepford wife, only lasted two more years before she, too, was left in the dust. Now he's planning to marry wife number three next month. During the divorce, it was revealed we never had to struggle those years. We didn't need hand-me-downs or to skip the Disney World trips. My father made and came from enough money to support not one but two families, and once he got rid of the baggage holding him down, he could live up to the life his wealthy family wanted for him.

The wealthy family I never knew; the wealthy family who left him a hefty trust when his grandparents passed when I was two.

My father spent twenty years living a lie to keep from sharing that money with his daughter and wife. He saw my mom as trash, someone who couldn't offer him any of the exclusive life he believed he deserved once that trust was signed over to him. I'll never live up to his standards, just like whichever wife du jour won't someday.

I shake my head to break the thought, the memories from the cobwebs of my mind as I swipe through the tiny clothes rack in the corner of the office. Choosing a sleek black and white bodycon dress, I take it off the hanger and move towards the small bathroom to change.

"Hey, Cassandra?" Gabrielle calls from outside the bathroom.

"Cassie!" I correct her again. My mind is already in an unhappy place, so the formality rubs me wrong. It's a trait I seem to have with others, to make them feel like they need to address me properly. Sometimes on lonely, rainy days in my apartment, when I've watched all of my saved *Housewives* episodes and have nothing else to scroll through, I wonder if it's my own doing, if I'm my own worst enemy. If I've gone too far with my propriety and tailored etiquette, making myself seem cold and standoffish.

"Yes, sorry, Cassie." She pauses there, not answering as I wiggle the tight dress up my hips, reminding me I need to order a salad tonight and reschedule those missed sessions with my trainer. Again. Preferably before the wedding next month, which will be filled with waifish, malnourished women who live to be eye candy for men with more money than taste, women who need to live to a standard or be shooed out for a thinner, younger version.

"What's up?"

"Oh, yes. I'm going to head out, okay?" I check my watch and see it's four. On Wednesdays, she leaves early to watch her sister's kids.

"Of course, thanks, Gabrielle."

"I sent your location to my phone, so I'll be able to see if you made it okay. I also scheduled you for tomorrow at eleven to go to the garage and have your tire fixed." Personal assistant isn't technically in her description, but she does it well.

"You're a blessing. Give your nephews my love!" The words come out before I think to hold them in, and they feel foreign. Not only have I never met these kids before, but we rarely talk about personal life. It's like the mix of dwelling on my history and being stranded in the cold last night has me going through a midlife crisis and questioning everything.

Mid-life crisis? I'm not even thirty. Quarter-life crisis? Will I live to be... one hundred and twenty?

If I do, I'll probably do it alone, which sounds pretty damn miserable.

What is *wrong* with me today?

"Uh, sure, Cassie. See you tomorrow?" I sigh before nodding, then remember she can't see through the bathroom door.

"Yes, see you then. Have a good night." I'm too embarrassed at this point to walk out of the bathroom until I hear the front door click shut and the lock turn. It's one of the few rules we have for the office: it's always locked. Two women in an office in this city, though small and mostly safe, is asking for trouble. Opening the door to grab my shoes, I decide just to run a brush through my long hair and put an extra layer of gloss on before leaving for the restaurant five minutes downtown.

Another day, another date

SIX

-Luke-

I CANNOT BELIEVE MY SISTER TALKED ME INTO THIS.

As I walk down the cold streets wearing the too fancy sweater, jacket, and pants my sisters bought me for the holidays, it's all I can think. But beneath that, I'm still wearing my leather work boots. Dress shoes are for men who want to impress, and that's not me. If I don't pass this matchmaking chick's test being the way I am, I'm out. Why would I want to be matched up with someone based on some fictional version of myself? Quinn and Tara will understand that, at the very least.

I am blessed with a family who loves me for who I am, and I will *never* take that for granted. When my father, son to wealthy old-money parents, married his high school sweetheart, daughter to public school teachers, it could have gone wrong. It could have gotten ugly, with harsh words exchanged and feelings hurt. Instead, my grandmother on my father's side, Meema, sat at my maternal grandmother Nanny's side while she sewed my mother's wedding dress by hand, teaching her to sew on the tiny pearls to the veil, the same veil both of my sisters wore as they too walked down the aisle. My nanny was too proud to admit they didn't have the funds to pay for an extravagant wedding to accomplish the 'bride's family foots the bill' tradition. So instead, my grandmothers worked together to make near everything themselves, ending in a handmade event still bragged about to this day.

When my oldest sister was born, she was showered in not just things but with love, and that love never ended. Now my entire family comes together for every event, celebrating holidays and birthdays and first teeth lost in a mix of love and food and shared memories. Everyone comes as they are, whether that's wearing pearls or dirty work boots. While I come from money, while it was always the intention of my family for me, the only son, to take over the family's finance business, no one batted an eye when I decided to work on cars, work for someone else, and earn a 'normal' paycheck. No one has ever made me feel anything but proud of my choices.

With that in mind, I live my life with one true rule: be me and nothing else. Take me or leave me.

Maybe *that's* why I'm still single.

This is my thought when I enter the hip Thai fusion restaurant I'd typically avoid like the plague. Still, when I told Tara where we were going, she gave me a long list of what I'd like and what I should try, knowing the complex menus that don't also feature a burger and fries as a fallback are too overwhelming for me. I think Q and Tara are more excited about this date than I have ever been about anything, with my receiving no less than three calls from each during the day to ask what time I was going, what I was wearing, and reminding me to be on my best behavior. That's when I reminded them I will be who I am and nothing less.

"Welcome, do you have a reservation?" the cute, young girl dressed in all black asks when I walk up to the hostess stand.

"Yeah, I'm meeting someone here, Cassandra...." I look at the screen of my phone where my sister texted me the matchmaker's name. I probably should have memorized it, especially if I'll be spending at least four hours with her today.

Four hours. That's probably the longest I've spent with a woman not in my bed in... God. Years. Should I be embarrassed by that? Does that make me a piece of shit? Probably.

"Oh, Cassie! Yes, follow me." Since the 'rules' state she sets up this first 'date,' I assume she probably has a rotating list of restaurants she goes to, dates she plans with the intent of learning the most from random men as humanly possible. It's strange how something that should be intimate, a first date, probably feels clinical and textbook to her. I can't help but wonder if she goes on non-business-related dates or if they all feel the same to her at the end of the day. I wonder how her man feels about this if she has one. Or if maybe it's a case of, "If you can't do, teach."

These thoughts tumble through my mind, which rarely stops moving, as I follow the hostess to the back of the restaurant. Then, slowly, a woman comes into focus, sitting alone at a table with a notebook next to her.

And for the second time in twenty-four hours, the chaos in my mind quiets.

It's her.

SEVEN

-Cassie-

"IT'S YOU," I SAY WHEN HE COMES INTO MY LINE OF SIGHT. CAN I catch a damn break this week?

He's not in the uniform he wore yesterday, instead, in a sweater and jacket I recognize as a popular menswear designer. His hands are in his pockets, casually pushing back the bottom of his jacket. Regardless of his classy clothes, when my head to toe hits his toe, beaten leather boots are peeking out. As much as I want to dock points for a faux pas—the mix of workwear and date wear?—it's oddly endearing on him, and he makes it work.

But it's not the outfit or the boots that make me remember. In the dark, with only headlights and the moon to light the roadway, I wasn't able to see that. No, it's the smile I notice.

It's big and bright and casual. So warm. Shiny white teeth sit in a perfect line, making me want to use my lips to cover the small gap between my own my parents couldn't afford to fix when I was a teen. And he's got a *dimple*. A dimple!

His head is topped with what can only be described as an

achingly adorable mess of dark hair he clearly made little attempt to slick back. As one hand leaves his pocket and combs the hair back, it becomes obvious that's the extent of the styling he gives it. Big blue eyes are framed with thick, long eyelashes all gorgeous men seem to be blessed with, leaving us women to coat ours with mascara and falsies until we have an emotional day and cry them off in the driver's seat of our car when we're stranded on the side of the road.

Why is he here?

Something in my gut knows it's not a coincidence—he's my date.

But why? Why the hell does he need my services?

There has to be something wrong with this man.

There is no reason for him to be single.

Much less single and looking.

He's not here for me. He's not my client.

"It's *you*," he says in reply, and I'm confused for a split second before I remember that's what I just said.

"What are you doing here?"

"I'm Luke Dawson. Your date, I believe."

"No, you're not. You're—" But when I look down at the printout of basic information Gabrielle left on my desk, there he is. Hair slightly more styled, smile a bit forced, a tux pulling tight against his chest. He's there, smiling at me and looking nothing like the man I met last night. Except he does. "But you..." I stumble on words before I just stare at him with my mouth slightly open like I'm a star-struck teenage girl and he's the lead singer of some boy band.

"Is everything okay, Cassie?" Sara, the sweet hostess who knows me since I come here for dates often, asks. It pops me out of my daze, thankfully.

"Uh, yeah. Sorry. Yes, Sara, thanks." I shake my head before gesturing a hand at the seat across from me. "Sit."

"Are you always like this?"

"Like what?"

"Bossy." He says the words with a smirk like he's telling a joke instead of poking fun of me, but it's not a joke I'm in on. I *hate* that kind of joke. It's the kind of joke my cousins and aunts on my dad's side share when I have to see them. The whispered under breath kind.

"I'm not bossy."

"You are right now."

"No, I'm not." He laughs, the sound rich and comfortable.

"Okay, sweetheart. You're not bossy." He removes his jacket, setting it on the back of the chair before sitting down. "So, the appointment you missed?"

"A date."

"And you're a..."

"A matchmaker."

"Got it." He settles in his seat and orders a drink from Sara before smiling at me again. This... he's entertained by this.

"I think this is a bad idea."

"Why?"

"Because of yesterday... I was..." I'm stuck on my words, looking for him to fill the gaps, but he just stares at me, an eyebrow raised and waiting. "*I was rude,*" I say, a near whisper.

"You were frantic and stressed out. Totally reasonable. I don't hold it against you."

"But I acted like you were a mechanic."

"I *am* a mechanic."

"No, you're not." He scoffs with a laugh.

"Yes, I am."

"But you don't dress like a mechanic." I can feel my brows furrowed in confusion, and I should smooth them out like my mom always reminds me to so I don't get wrinkles, but I'm *so lost*. I feel like I'm watching season three of a show without any insight into the first two seasons.

"My sisters bought me these clothes."

"They're... nice." Another handsome laugh.

"Yeah. I can dress up with the best of them." That much is clear as broad shoulders fill out the grey sweater that's just tight enough to outline his well-defined chest, which is absolutely mouth-watering. This man is a dream.

"I see that." The words fall from my mouth and my face burns with warmth. *What is happening to me?!* But the deep laugh he lets out, tipping his chin back with a scarred hand on his stomach, makes the embarrassment almost worth it. When he finally comes down from his laugh, he looks at me with a smile on his lips.

"Okay, so before I get too far into this, can you tell me what this is all about? Like how it works? I get I'm dating you, but not... really." My eyebrows move together in confusion.

"Didn't my assistant tell you the process?" A hand moves through his hair, the hand rough and worn with a small gash on the side of his pinky finger. My mind immediately wants to ask where it came from, wants to know what his hands feel like, if they're calloused, and how they'd feel on my—

"—my sister." He stops talking, but it's clear when I'm staring at him with my mouth agape I missed a good chunk of what he just said.

Shit. What is wrong *with me?* This man has me so frazzled, which is not like me. Not at all. My job is to be attentive, read body language, learn everything there is to know about the person sitting across from me. Not... daydream about them.

"I'm sorry, I missed that. I was... distracted." My eyes flit to his lifted arm, his hand now behind his neck, and I note his nervous tic is a hand through his hair and settling on his neck. He revealed something. Something I should have caught. I begin to chastise myself but almost get distracted again when my eyes land on his wide bicep, stretching the fabric of his sweater in a way I don't often see on my dates.

The men I meet with are typically well-dressed, financially stable, with well-paying jobs. They keep on top of their appearance with clean-shaven faces, perfectly styled hair, and regular visits to the gym. Luke is sporting a five o'clock shadow, and he seems as comfortable in the expensive, familiar brands he's wearing as he did in his coverall last night. His body, clearly built and lean, isn't crafted in a gym. Last night, he lifted those tires like they were for a Barbie car, not a full-sized sedan.

He is an enigma, and I cannot decode him.

I've never been more uneasy on a date in seven years.

"I said, it wasn't me who set this up. It was my sister." My eyebrows push together once more before I remind myself that it will only make wrinkles my family will point out. I smooth my features.

"Your sister?"

"Yeah. She, uh. She has a friend of a friend who used your services? My sisters are tired of me being single. I'm the only one left. Both sisters are married off. They think I need someone."

"Do you?"

"Do I what?"

"Need someone?" He pauses for a moment, contemplating the idea. This typically would be a check in the cons column because any man who sits across from me should say yes, they need someone, they're ready for someone. But Luke doesn't seem the impulsive type. Instead, he seems the type to carefully craft an answer, not because he wants to say what you want to hear, but because he wants to get his words out without botching his true feelings.

"Yes, and no." I raise an eyebrow. "Okay, I don't need someone to be happy. I'm happy with my life now. Good family, good friends. Like my job."

"Like helping damsels on the side of the road?" He laughs, and the sound flows through me.

"Yeah, that." I smile at him, and *what is happening to me?* "But do I sometimes wish I had someone to go to dinner with? Does it suck being the only one at the family Christmas that shows up alone?" There's a pause, and this I've seen before. The pause that a man uses to decide if he wants to share more or stop. I'm impressed when he continues, opening up to vulnerability. "Does it scare me seeing everyone I know pair up and being left behind? Yeah. So no, I don't need someone, but I'd like one."

"Good answer," I say, holding his gaze the way I've learned intimidates men. Once again, he passes when he tips his head to me with a smile, almost in a challenge. I reach a hand out and grab my wine, taking a deep gulp. I think I'm going to need this.

"So, did I pass your inspection?"

"You passed the entrance exam. But we're just getting started," I say and pull my notebook closer to me. On top is my sheet of questions I always ask, pinned beneath his application. I have them memorized by heart, but it's become a security blanket of sorts.

"You didn't explain yet. What does this process look like?" Somehow, I now feel like I'm being interviewed instead of the other way around. I've never had to explain my process to a man. He's always agreed to my process well before we get to a date.

"We'll go on two dates. Each will be a meal and an activity. This one is planned by myself; the next is in your hands. I'll get to know you, your tastes, likes, wishes, and hopes, and hopefully, by the end of the second date, I'll feel confident in setting you up with one of my clients. You'll get added to my files so we can pair you."

"Ah, so that's why it's called Ex Files. So it's a file of men you've already dated?"

"Exactly." I smile. The number of times I've had to explain what I thought was an obvious name is exhaustive.

"I thought you might have a thing for Scully and Mulder."

"Nope, just a silly name I thought of in college that stuck."

"Your job has been to date men since college?"

"It's more than that, but yes."

"What does your man think about this gig?" he asks, sitting back in his chair and resting his hands on his chest. It's like he's sitting around a bonfire instead of at a nice restaurant. Part of me is horrified and fighting the urge to look around and see who might have caught his blip in etiquette, but part of me... part of me is jealous he's so at ease with himself.

"My man?"

"Yeah. A gorgeous woman like you has to have a man of some kind. He cool with you going out every night and dating a new man?"

"I don't have a man."

"You don't?" I shake my head, glancing down at the salads on the menu as if I haven't seen them a million times. "You're telling me the matchmaker is single?"

"My mom calls me a single Pringle." *Why did I just say that?* His laugh booms, and heads turn our way as my cheeks burn with heat.

"Single Pringle! Q would love that." He leans forward before leaning back again, this time with his beer. "So, why are you single? If anyone is qualified to find themselves a suitable man, it would be you."

"That's not how this works."

"What?"

"I ask you questions. *That's* how this works. It's how I decide if you're a good fit."

"That doesn't sound like a date."

"It is. It's *my* date."

"But how would you know the important things? Like if I'm able to ask intuitive questions or care about women. If I can hold a conversation?"

"I don't think you'll have a problem holding a conversation."

"Yeah, it's you who bulldozes people, isn't it? How long did it take you to figure out I wasn't the Roadside Assistance tech?" Blood burns on my cheeks once again, but he's still smiling. At least he's not holding it against me.

"I figured it out today."

"I tried to tell you, you know." I do know, of course. I've replayed the situation more than once, over-analyzing the entire embarrassing experience until I was nauseated. More than once, he tried to stop me on my tirade and let me know he was not Roadside Assistance, instead of some random guy in the right place at the right time.

"I know. I was rude and didn't let you speak. I feel bad about it, if it helps, but in my defense, I was in a state."

"The mascara was a dead giveaway." I groan, remembering the black tear tracks I scrubbed off when I got home. Those two hours alone in the cold tested me more than I'd like to admit. Realizing I had no one who would notice my absence quickly was worse than any midlife crisis I've heard of. Because really, what am I doing with my life? I have no friends, no reliable family, no boyfriend. And while I don't think by any stretch of the imagination a woman needs a man in her life to be happy, the thought that the road I'm walking down now means I'll remain single and lonely... it's not making me feel like I'm enjoying life to its fullest.

"I kind of hoped that you couldn't see that in the dark."

"A blind man could have seen it, sweetheart." The term of endearment, one he used last night as well, sends a warm shiver down my spine. Instead of answering, I sip my wine. "So, questions. I'll answer whatever, but for each you ask, I get one." I stare at him for long moments, deciding how to answer.

On one hand, absolutely not. This is not how this works, and he doesn't need to know anything about me. On the other, I'm pretty sure if I decline his offer, this is over. He won't answer any more questions. And I can tell myself all day long I want him to answer these questions for research, for work, but the reality is I'm dying to know more about him for some sick reason.

"Fine." He smiles bright, joyous, and happy, free of any frustration or heaviness. I wonder how much of his personality is that: just happy to be here, glad to be alive. He seems to be that kind of person. I wonder what that's like, to live like that?

"First question." I brace for some kind of intrusive, personal question. "Cookies or cupcakes?" My brows crinkle.

"What?"

"Cookies or cupcakes. Which is better? I like cookies, but my mom also makes the world's best chocolate chip cookies. I'm the only boy and the youngest, so anytime I go home, there's a plate waiting for me." The smile is there again, unashamed and open. It's another interesting detail, one I'd typically jot down in my notes, but for some reason, I don't feel like taking notes on this date. Instead, I slip my notepad into my bag before smiling at him.

"That's not a real question."

"It's not? Well, it's the one I'm using. Now, answer."

"Cupcakes."

"From where?" It comes immediately, and for a moment, I think it should count as a second, but I let it fly.

"The Italian bakery on Fifth. Luigi's."

"Good cannoli."

"You like their cannoli, next time you're there, try the cannoli cupcakes. Life-changing."

"I'll make sure I do."

"Okay, my turn. What did you want to be when you were a kid?" He smiles as I repeat the same question I ask all potential matches.

"You're predictable, huh? A mechanic. I always wanted to be a mechanic."

"Yeah? You knew then?"

"Always. My dad works in finance, good money. He wanted me to follow him. But... I wanted this."

"Were they angry? That you didn't want to follow in their foot-steps or get a more prestigious job?" I think of my father, in his own high-paying career, who finds my 'hobby' to be 'cute.'

"Not at all. My parents just want us to be happy, no matter what. So now I get the best of both worlds—I get to fix cars like I love, and my mom and sisters make sure I still get to wear nice things. In exchange for being on the hook for any car repair they need. But I don't mind." The dimple comes out again.

"That's... great. Rare. Parents supporting you in whatever."

"I'm lucky." I nod, thinking about how I wish so profoundly I, too, was that kind of lucky. "Okay, my turn. Favorite gas station food?" I laugh but answer, and the night goes like this for two more hours as we eat our dinner then dessert. He asks silly questions about 80s movies and favorite drinks while I slowly knock out the questions I've memorized at this point. Eventually, I start adding in my own, asking things like his most embarrassing childhood memory or what his sisters would describe him as (spoiled, which made me laugh and sounded so typically big sister).

He comes from a sweet, loving, and incredibly close family. Each Sunday, he still has dinner at his parents' with his sisters, their husbands, and his nieces. He's kind, backing off when it's clear I don't want to answer something. In return, I dig at him playfully when he blushes at some of my personal questions.

It feels... normal.

Too normal.

Not like a work date at all.

This becomes even more clear when the bill arrives and my hand swipes it out quickly, slipping in the company card without even looking at the total.

"You're not paying," Luke says with angry eyes focused on my hands holding the leather envelope.

"It's part of the process. I pay for the first date."

"This is basically one giant interview, right?"

"I guess?"

"So wouldn't I fuckin' fail the 'is he a good guy' test if I made you pay for our first date?"

"That's not—"

"Take my card." His hand holding a credit card goes out as his eyes are locked to mine as the poor waitress stands there, unsure what to do.

"Luke."

"Cassandra." I stare at him, and I want to fight, but he's not wrong. And usually, the men I date do try to pay, but this one... this man tells me he won't acquiesce when I tell him no. Something tells me he will stand his ground however long it takes, and something about that sends a shiver of pleasure down my spine.

"Fine. But I'm still paying for the activity." He rolls his eyes, and I can almost hear his thoughts as the waitress runs off with his card and the bill: *We'll see about that.*

When our server returns, handing the bill back to Luke to sign, two wrapped fortune cookies are on top.

"You have to make a wish," I say, grabbing my own before popping the plastic. Next, I pull out the orange cookie, snapping it out and slipping the paper from its cookie prison.

"What?"

"Make a wish. I had a client show me this years ago, and I do it every time now." I read my fortune cookie aloud. "'To truly find your-self, you should play hide and seek alone.'" I stare at it for long moments as Luke busts out laughing. I follow him before putting it down. "That one stunk. What does yours say?" He's cracking his own open and pulling the paper out to read.

"'*Your love life will soon be happy and harmonious.*'" He looks at me with a smile. "Wow, you work quick, huh?" I laugh.

"Okay, so now you have to kiss it and fold it into a heart, making a wish."

"Then what?"

"Well... it's supposed to come true. I don't know. It's just a fun superstition."

"Well, you kiss mine. Your lipstick is much prettier," he says with a smile. "I'll do yours. Show me how." Shaking my head, I want to argue, but the one glass of wine with the light salad has me feeling unnaturally light and airy. Or maybe it's the company. I snatch the paper from him, pressing a kiss to it and seeing the faint mark from the long-lasting red lipstick I put on before I got here.

"Okay, so you take it like this, then fold it like this and this..." I look up and smile at him playing along, folding my fortune the same way I'm showing him. Then, tuck it in and..." I lift the tiny heart. "Voila! You have a fortune cookie wish." He smiles back at me, snatching the red and white paper from me before pocketing it.

"You're fun, Cassie." He says this before standing, getting his jacket on, and leading me out of the restaurant to continue our night.

———

"I'm not going in there."

"What?"

"I'm not going in there." We're standing outside the art museum a few blocks from the Thai restaurant, the night air already cutting through my jacket. We're about five blocks from the ocean, and the wind is always freezing on this side of town.

"This is the activity we're doing."

"Nope."

"What do you mean, 'nope.' That's not how this works. I plan dinner and the activity. You go."

"You've never been on a date with me." When he says this, he's not looking at me with my hands on my hips and ready to argue. He seems the type to enjoy it, to argue for the fun of it. He's digging in his pocket while he reaches for my hand, pulling me away from the museum.

"Luke!"

"Not going to some uptight art museum. Not on a first date, not ever."

"What if the woman I match you up with likes art museums?"

"Did I already pass the exam? You know I'm getting added to your roster?" He's smiling over his shoulder as I move to catch up with him as he guides me along the crowded streets. It's dark, but it's easy to see where we're going with the streetlights and lights from restaurants and stores. Towards the boardwalk.

"What? No, I just-"

"Do you like going to art museums?" I can't lie. Because honestly, most of the time, I find them quite dull, but they tell a lot about a person.

"Not particularly, but that's not—"

"Sweetheart, if you set me up with a woman who loves art museums and expects to drag my ass to them regularly, you didn't do your job right." His fingers are twined with mine as he dials something into his cell.

"This is crazy! Where are you taking me?" But his phone is to his ear, and he doesn't answer me.

"Hey, man, what's goin' on? Are you in Ocean View today? Yeah? No way, for sure, we'll be there in uh..." He looks around to find a street sign. "Five, maybe ten? Yeah. Hold a spot for us. Nah, got a date." He laughs that attractive deep chuckle once more. "Go fuck yourself, man. Yeah, see you then." He swipes to hang up before putting it back into his pocket and dragging me towards an unknown location.

"What is going on!?"

"Going somewhere more fun."

"This is not how this works!"

"Yeah, well, it's how I work. And how I work is, I don't go to museums."

"But your application said you were cultured and you enjoy art."

"Already covered this. My sister did that. Who the fuck knows what else she said?"

"This is ridiculous, Luke. I can't just go to some unknown location with you." The panic is rising now. Truly, this isn't a great idea. "Plus, no one will know where I am. This isn't safe. I have protocols!" It's not that I don't trust this man because I do for some bizarre reason. But this is *not my plan*, and I do *not* like when things don't follow my plan. He hears the panic and stops in his tracks at the sound, turning to look at me. Now he's standing in front of me, hands on my shoulders and reading every thought I'm sure is crossing my face. I can only hope he doesn't see *every* thought there, especially ones I wouldn't want to be broadcasted to him specifically.

"Okay, sweetheart. That makes sense. You text your girl. You tell her you're going to Tommy's Tavern on the boardwalk, the entrance off 34th, for trivia night. Tell her we're meetin' my friends there, one is my best friend, Chris Jacobs." I stare at him, and although the plans are changing, I nod, although this train is so far off my well-planned track. I don't know why. But I dig through my bag and find my phone, doing as he asked and sending Gabrielle a text to tell her the change in my plans. Then we head down to trivia night with Luke's friends.

EIGHT

-Luke-

"Hey, man!" I shout over the sound of the crowded pub's raucous laughter. There's something about the sound of a crowded bar, overflowing with laughter and talking and glasses clinking, that is comforting. Ahead of me stands one of my best friends, Chris. He grew up down the street from me before he moved up north. He still comes down pretty regularly, and earlier today, he asked if I would be free to meet up. Next to him stands a pretty redhead I don't recognize.

"Dawson! You made it! Good to see you, man!" We hug and pat backs in the way good friends do when they're trying to pretend they don't actually like to embrace.

"Yeah, man. We were close by. This is Cassie, my date." Cassie is standing there, her arms holding her coat closed in front of her, shoulders lifted high and clearly not comfortable. I throw an arm around her shoulder and pull her to me, the fit perfect. I should be surprised, but I'm not. Everything about her makes sense. "Cass, this is Chris, an old friend." I look to the redhead. "This your girl?" Chris laughs before putting an arm around her.

"Oh yeah, this is my girl, Jordan." When her eyes bug out, and I don't recognize her name as one of the many he's always bragging about, I'm admittedly confused. But then a hand slaps Chris' head before another guy tugs the woman into his chest, where she instantly makes herself more comfortable.

"Fuck off, Jacobs. Find your own woman or you're fired." The woman, Jordan, lets out a sweet giggle before turning to put an arm around the man's waist.

"Come on, Bossman, Let me live the dream for a moment."

"You better shut the fuck up, Chris, or Tanner will beat your ass. You know he's protective," a man to Chris' left says, and my eyes shift to him, dark hair and tattoos creeping under the rolled sleeves of his shirt.

"Hey, Ben, how's it goin'?" I reach a hand out to shake his, keeping Cassie at my side.

"Good to see you, Luke. Do you remember my brother, Tanner?" He gestures to the other man, tall and broad with dark hair with sun-bleached tips. The Coleman brothers grew up north of Ocean View, both working their family construction site where Chris works now. Ben left before he could be forced to take over, following his dream of becoming a tattoo artist, while his brother got the business. Ben and I are close friends, so I've heard stories about the undue stress their father puts on Tanner and how completely consumed by the family business he's been. But, as I shake his hand and take in his less stressed appearance, it's clear Tanner has figured things out, and the woman next to him is probably the reason.

"Hey, I'm Luke, and this is Cassie," I say to the woman.

"Jordan," she says with a sweet smile, and now the story kind of comes back to me. She used to date some sort of country star before she moved to the town Chris works in. It turns out the guy was abusive, and when he followed her back to Springbrook Hills, Tanner stepped in and kept her safe. So now she lives there with Tanner and works as the office manager.

"Nice to meet you," Cassie says quietly, her nervous voice just barely able to be heard over the noise. It sounds... strange on her. This confident, professional woman. Like being in an unplanned, causal atmosphere is her kryptonite. Her hand on my shirt is gripping tight, bunching the fabric. My hand on her arm squeezes marginally before rubbing my thumb up and down in what I hope is a calming manner. She relaxes a fraction, and something about that pleases me, the ability to calm this force of a woman.

"So it's trivia night?" I ask once introductions are over and we're settled at the small table, each with a drink.

"Yeah, man, Team Firecrotch—" Chris says, but before he can finish his sentence, Tanner smacks him upside his head as Jordan glares on.

"I told you we're not callin' it that."

"Right, right, Team Masterminds? Boring," Chris grumbles, and beside me, Cassie giggles and relaxes just a fraction. It's going to be a good night.

———

Hours, and what feels like 100 trivia questions, later, we're on the last question, tied with two other teams. Cassie has finally relaxed, giggling with Jordan, who's just about as gone as her, and elbowing Chris every time he makes some kind of semi-rude wisecrack, which is basically every five seconds. Gone are her strange propriety and perfect etiquette, and in their place is this beautiful, hilarious woman.

"Okay, teams, one last question for the win! Who said this famous line: 'Does Barry Manilow know that you raid his wardrobe?'" the announcer asks, and teams across the bar huddle their heads.

"That's *Clerks*, right?" Chris asks, and Ben rolls his eyes.

"Is that the only movie you know?" Cassie snorts a quiet laugh to my left, and I look over at her. She's on her second drink here, plus the one at the restaurant, and she's finally relaxed. She looks at ease and happy. Beautiful.

"What's *Clerks*?" Jordan asks.

"Jesus, Tan, you're with a woman who's never seen *Clerks*?" Ben looks at his brother with disgust on his face.

"Cut her some slack. She was raised in Vegas. Ask her trivia about Elvis or Sigfried and Roy and we're good."

"*The Breakfast Club*," Cassie says quietly.

"Oh shit, yeah. But who said it?" Chris asks.

"Andrew," I answer. "The Jock. He said it to the Nerd." Ben nods.

"Yeah, write that, Jordan," he says, agreeing with me.

"No, you're wrong," Cassie says, and I look at her. She's smiling at me with a 'you're a dumbass, and I'm going to prove it' face, and it's *adorable*.

"What?"

"It was Bender. Judd Nelson. He was arguing with Mr. Vernon. Beginning of the movie."

"I don't think you're right."

"Trust me, I am. My mom made me watch every Molly Ringwald movie at least one hundred times when I was a kid. I can recite the entire movie from memory." She blushes, the color overtaking her tan skin, and even though she's embarrassed, she holds firm.

"Go with Cassie's answer, Princess," Tanner tells his girl, and I'm thankful. Even if she's wrong, she looks pleased to have her answer written down.

"Okay, time's up, boards up!" the announcer shouts as a buzzer goes off. "The answer was 'Bender in *The Breakfast Club*'! Team Masterminds seems to be the only one with the full answer and wins!" Everyone around us cheers, exuberance infectious as Cassie throws her hands in the air and jumps, her tits jumping in that tight black and white dress, hair flying everywhere. Gone is the uptight matchmaker from earlier, and in her place is a gorgeous woman who is ecstatic her team won.

At that moment, I make my decision.

I'm going to keep her.

I'm going to keep this woman.

Fuck her matching me up.

That spark flared last night. After spending a night across from her, watching her get frustrated with me when I wouldn't play her game, I watched her guard fall—tiny bits at a time. As I watched her interact with my friends, watching her slowly relax, that spark spread, catching first on the tinder and burning to a warm blaze.

I just need her to realize that she's burning up, too.

NINE

-Cassie-

"You're not driving home," he says as we walk down the street toward where we parked. Tonight was... fun. It's a surprise when I allow the words to pop into my mind. *Fun.*

God, when was the last time I had fun? The last time I enjoyed myself and had a good time.

When had my life gotten so *boring?*

"Why am I so boring?" The words tumble from me in a rush before I slap my hand over my mouth like I've revealed a secret I've held in for too long. However, something tells me this isn't a secret to anyone but me. He laughs at my faux pas before untwining his fingers with mine and moving them to my waist to pull me to him. The distinctive heat from all five fingers burns through the fabric to my skin.

"You're boring?"

"Like you don't know."

"You didn't seem very boring tonight." That's sweet of him to say.

"That's sweet of you to say." *Why does my voice sound like that?*

Breathy and... adoring. Shit. Am I drunk? "Am I drunk?" Once again, the words in my brain seem to have a direct path to my mouth as they spew out without hitting a filter.

"I think you might be, sweetheart," he says with a gleaming smile on his face.

"You have a nice smile." Well, at least this time, I didn't think it first, the words bypassing any kind of brainwaves before slipping out. "I didn't mean to say that." He looks at me as we walk, the handsome smile growing. "Well, I did. It is nice. But I didn't mean to say it out loud. To you."

"Ahh, got it. Watch your step." He gently guides me around a crack in the sidewalk, and I semi-recognize where we are as we walk toward the Thai restaurant and nearby parking lot.

"This is not how this goes. At all."

"What goes?"

"Dates."

"I haven't been on too many dates, but I think ending it with a pretty, tipsy woman in your arms is exactly how it goes."

"Not my kind of dates."

"Sounds like your kind of dates suck."

"They do." He laughs again. "Shit, no, they don't. They're great." I try to recover, to remember my professionalism and why we're actually here. "I love my job."

"What do you love about it?" Again, the words tumble before I can stop them.

"Helping women avoid the inevitable."

"What's inevitable?"

"Seemingly great men showing their true colors." His pace slows, and he's looking at me, waiting for more. "It's not that women don't lie too." I've been doing this long enough to know that's the next part of his interrogation. When I reveal the true intention of The Ex Files, it always seems that men, usually the ones with something to hide, if I'm honest, start to rail on me about double standards. And they're not wrong. Women lie all the time. About their weight and if they like something and if the casserole their coworker brought in is tasty. But... "But men are better at it. Men can keep it up for like... ever."

"Who hid it from you?" Even in my drunken state, I don't give it all away. I *never* give it all away.

"When I was in college, I had a friend, came to school a virgin. She was saving herself, you know? A dangerous game, if you ask me. Saving yourself for some kind of knight in shining armor. Anyway, freshman year, she started dating some guy, a senior. Gave us all the ick, but we couldn't talk her out of it. So she gave it to him. She found out the whole thing had been a bet with his frat a week later. Like an even shittier version of *She's All That*. She dropped out that semester never came back to school. It broke her. Men can do that. Trick a woman into losing themselves and then break them."

"That's it? I mean, it's fucked, of course, but that kind of thing happens all the time. And it wasn't you. That's what made you so cynical?" It's not, of course, but he doesn't need to know everything about me.

"Can't reveal all of my secrets, Mr. Dawson. But you've gotten more than like... anyone I know. Are you a detective? Are you just pretending to be a mechanic? Maybe you're undercover, trying to catch some creepy bad guys. Maybe that's why you're so good at getting me to talk." I stop in the middle of the sidewalk and close one eye to get him to stay still while I inspect him. He laughs before using that warm hand to keep me going.

"Come on, sweetheart, let's get you home."

"Why do you keep calling me that? Sweetheart?"

"Don't know. Fits. You're sweet."

"No, I'm not. I'm *boring*." I pop the 'b' with more emphasis than needed. "I don't *do* anything. This is the most fun I've had in... a really long time." We're in the parking lot now, and he stops us in front of my car. My hands go into my bag to find my keys.

"I'm glad you had a good time, Cassie. Is there anything you need in your car?" He takes my bag from my arm, reaching in and quickly locating my keys. I try to get them back.

"Give me that. I need my keys."

"No, Cass. I'm driving."

"I can do it. Or I can call a cab or—" He cuts me off, eyes having gone from playful to stern.

"I'm taking you home."

"But that's against the rules." An eyebrow quirks.

"Whose rules?"

"Mine. It's rule number two."

"How many rules are there?"

"Four."

"You gonna share those?" Like seems to be common with the man, he looks amused by me.

Still, I recite the four rules I've lived by for seven years without hesitation. Rules I created to maintain my own sense of sanity, to create distance. To keep me safe. "One, I go on two dates and two dates only. Two, we never go to my place, and I never go to theirs. Three, never ever, ever kiss a client. And four, which, really, is a good life rule, never ever ever get attached." He stares at me, and for a second, I wonder if I shared too much. "It's dangerous business, getting attached."

"Well, I'm a rule breaker, sweetheart. You're gonna learn that. I'm taking you home."

"Look, I've had fun. More fun than... I don't know the last time I had this much fun. Your friends are awesome. Trivia was a blast. But I gotta go home. I have work in the morning. And I cannot get into a car with a client and have them take me home. No way, Jose. I think I'd give my assistant a nervous breakdown if I did, especially after last night." I'm not too tipsy to know that getting into a car with a relative stranger is a terrible idea, especially if no one knows you're doing it. Even if you feel strangely comfortable and safe with said stranger.

"Makes sense. You send her a text now, tell her I'm taking you home. That I'm walking you to your door and leaving, and you'll text her when you lock the door behind you, safe and alone in your apartment." I stare at him, confused. It seems... strangely rational.

"I don't know, Luke...."

"Just need to know you got home safe, yeah? This is a test, right? Would a good man let you take a cab home in this state?" Once again, rational. Too rational, maybe.

"I guess not...."

"What's your address?" I stare at him before giving it to him, then pull my phone out to send a text to Gabrielle. When the clock blinks 2:15 at me, I blink back at it, unsure how it got this late.

"Is this right?" I say, looking up at him after I hit send.

"Is what right?"

"The time. Is it two?"

"Yup." He grabs my hand once more and starts to guide me away.

"In the morning?" Another deep laugh, one resonating in my gut in a way it shouldn't.

"Yeah, Cass. In the morning." We stop a few spots down at a nice, newish black pickup truck. Not the tow truck he was driving yesterday,

"It's not a tow truck." His laugh is intoxifying, making me feel even more lightheaded with the deep timbre.

"Not my daily driver, babe. Plus, that's the garage's truck, not mine. This is mine."

"What about my car?" Common sense returns, thankfully, and I remember I really shouldn't leave my new car in a restaurant parking lot overnight.

"I'll get it to you before you wake up. Just show me where to park it when I drop you off."

"I don't know—"

"Move cars for a living. I'm capable, promise." I stare at him, but my vision is swimming, a mix of exhaustion and drink and something I refuse to acknowledge making my head light and loopy.

"Fine." I agree with this stupid, stupid plan. *Who the hell am I, and where is my uptight librarian with her common sense?* I think. Oh, yeah. I drank three Long Island iced teas and played bar trivia with strangers turned almost, sort of, kind of friends. When he opens the door for me (gentleman points that I hope I remember to put in my notes), I just stare at the seat, considering how on earth I'll get up there without breaking my neck.

But then warm hands burn through my jacket once more, and he's lifting me by my waist, placing me on the passenger seat. Then he leans over, head nearly in my lap and my drunk mind going places it *can not even think about being* before he clicks the seatbelt in place. Then, standing straight, one hand runs down the length of the belt to adjust it, grazing my body the whole way and, goddammit, if my entire body doesn't shiver in response.

The jerk's lips quirk up just a hair before he steps back and slams the truck door, and drives me to my apartment.

TEN

-Luke-

WHEN WE GET TO CASSIE'S APARTMENT AND PARK, SHE'S
sobered a bit, and now her eyes have an adorably tired look as I open
the passenger door and help her out. My hands hold her in place as
she steadies on her heels, and it feels right. Holding her.

"Come on, sweetheart. Where's the entrance?" She points in the
direction, and I twine her fingers with mine and walk towards the
elevator. "Which floor?" I ask, staring at the numbered dots.

"Seven." I nod before pressing the button and making it light
before we start lifting. When the elevator dings and the doors open,
she looks... nervous, her bottom lip pulled between tiny white teeth
as we step out into the hall. It's a nice apartment building. Not
luxury, which is a small surprise considering how she dresses and
acts, but nice all the same.

"Which way?" Once again, she points to the left.

"17A." Walking that way together, fingers still entwined, I'm
shocked by the disappointment coursing through my system. Disappointment that the night is over. And not because I want to follow

her into her apartment. It's a disappointment because this won't end the way most men hope a great date with a beautiful woman ends. Because I like being with her. I like spending time with her, even when she's uptight and in interviewer mode. I like her when she's tipsy and giggling with Jordan, who is a blast, it seems. I like seeing her with my childhood friend and rolling her eyes at his obvious and endless come-ons. I liked it when Chris tried every line on her, and she didn't get offended or annoyed. Instead, she just laughed it off or gave him advice on how to improve his game.

I *like* her.

And I need to convince her to give me a chance with *her*, not some random woman she thinks would work.

"This is me," she says as we stop in front of a big metal door, a small welcome in front of the door that says 'hello' in some kind of fancy, girly font. Below is a second, larger checked rug, which makes no sense to me at all. Why have two? My mind comes off that useless thought because even though I have sisters, I will never understand a woman's brain regarding fashion or decor. "I had... I had a lot of fun tonight, Luke. Thank you. I can't remember when I had this much fun. Please tell everyone thank you for being so kind and welcoming to me."

"They all loved you." She smiles, but for some reason, it's like she doesn't believe me, doesn't trust the words I'm saying. "So when is our next date?"

"What?"

"I get two, right? To prove myself?" I don't tell her that I'm proving myself to *her*, not to her business. That's for later.

"Oh, yeah. Uhm. You can call the office when you know your schedule. I can fit you in." *That* rubs me wrong.

Fit me in. Why does the thought of her dating other men, even in a clinical, professional way, make me fucking furious?

"Saturday," I say. It's Tuesday. Well, Wednesday now. That gives me three days to plan.

"What?"

"Our next date. Saturday."

"This Saturday?"

"Yeah, sweetheart, this Saturday." She pauses like she's not sure what to say.

"I don't do dates on Saturdays."

"That wasn't in your rules."

"I keep to weekdays."

"Well, then you don't have anything scheduled for Saturday." She moves to argue with me, but instead, I lean forward and take her keys, unwinding the key to her car to move it before sliding the remaining key into her lock.

"Ten?"

"Ten."

"At night?" I laugh. How does her brain work?

"In the morning."

"That's too early for dinner." Her eyebrows are scrunched together, her mind working to try and figure out what is going on.

"My date, my rules. I'll text you details."

"You really don't have to, I can—" But she doesn't finish.

She can't finish.

Because she's pushed against the apartment door, metal cool beneath my hand pressed to the small of her back. My lips are a millimeter from hers. The air between us is electric like it's been since last night, since the day we met on the side of the road.

But I wait.

I let her lead.

I can't fuck this up with her.

I *won't* fuck this up with her.

And then it happens.

She closes the tiny gap, her full lips pressing to mine and tasting like Coca-Cola and liquor and the coconut chapstick she put on no less than ten times tonight, and I *groan*. I groan at the taste, at her permission, at her taking that leap.

And then I kiss her, smooth lips moving against my own, her

hand coming to rest on on the beard I need to shave before work in just a few hours. My hand on her back pulls her closer, and her other hand lifts to go around my neck, pulling me closer as her tiny tongue reaches out to taste my lip, touching mine with just the barest, feather-light touch, and God, God, all I want is to take this further. To go further. To follow her into that apartment.

But I won't.

Something tells me it would scare her off, and I can't let that happen. So instead, I slow the kiss, pressing mine to hers one last time before pressing my forehead to hers.

"Good night, Cassie. I'll see you Saturday. Text your assistant." I press my lips to her forehead, and then I turn my back, and I leave, not looking over my shoulder to see her standing there, watching me go.

ELEVEN

-Cassie-

It's days like these I wish I had girlfriends.

I did once, when I was in college. Ones I set up, ones who moved on with men and created new friend groups with other happily coupled people. But the thing they don't tell you about growing up is that there is always the threat of growing apart.

And somehow, through it all, we grew apart.

Because the other thing they don't tell you is that when your friends get married and have kids, they have less time. And when they have less time, what time they do have they spend with other couples, other new parents. Soon, you're the lone single friend who has nothing in common with them, and slowly, slowly, you drift apart until you're just another name on their Christmas card list.

So when I roll out of bed on Wednesday to get ready for work, my mind still drowsy with drink and a late-night, I have no one to make the call all girls need to make when a man shakes their world.

And that is the *only* way to explain what on *earth* happened last night.

Lucas Dawson shook up my perfectly curated world in a way I never saw coming.

The four rules I created when I built my business dating men to vet them for other women were to protect myself.

If I set those rules, follow the structure, don't deviate from them, I can't get hurt.

If I keep myself detached, never fall for the bullshit of a man, I'll always be able to see past the hearts and flowers and deceit. Never get so caught up in the beauty of falling in love that I miss all the warning signs.

After twenty years together, my dad left my mother and completely wrecked her. They married when she was twenty-three and started dating when she was twenty. He was all she knew her entire life. She accepted his long business trips, the forgetting of birthdays and anniversaries. She took on raising me more or less alone, handling midnight puke fests and my sneaking out and boys breaking my heart with a grin, knowing we were a picture-perfect family, the one she always daydreamed of having as a young girl.

As a young girl, *I* daydreamed of the same, of staying home to raise the kids and being the stay-at-home mom while my husband goes out and works hard and comes home to a smiling wife and a hot meal. That was my plan. Hell, in my senior yearbook, I wrote that I would get my MRS. My main purpose for going to school was to find a man, fall in love, and get married.

But when that picture-perfect world came crashing down, my mom did too. Even now, ten years later, every moment of her life is a reflection of the letdown, of the deceit. It's a rare moment when I visit her and she doesn't break down crying.

Still, the truth of the matter is that when I look at my childhood, I see them. Glimpses of red flags, tiny moments where an outsider would have questioned. And living it, it seemed normal because it's all I knew. But they stand out to me now that maybe things weren't as beautiful and perfect as I always thought. I see things like my dad extending his trip, missing Christmases, my mom crying late at night in her room alone. My mom working out religiously and telling me that "in order to keep a man, you have to always look your best." It's like she knew all along, whether she realized it or not. Like she always suspected, and like my dad didn't try very hard to hide his deceit.

After the divorce and before I started The Ex Files, I tried dating. Tried bringing boys home, but it always ended in her questioning things, bringing up tiny flaws and possible lies until I had to walk away from the relationship. That's how I learned to spot the red flags before I even brought them home to her.

It's also why I stopped dating. Why I don't even bother anymore. It's almost like getting a job at your favorite restaurant. After a few months, the meals that used to be your guilty pleasure make your stomach turn. So I have no use for dating. I've lost all ability to get the butterflies and nervous giggles when a boy texts you because I've seen the worst of them all.

Except now I'm staring at a text from Lucas Dawson.

He shouldn't have my phone number since we exclusively work with clients through email and our business line. Except I vaguely remember giving my number to Jordan last night, and if I can remember the hierarchy correctly, Jordan was the girlfriend to Tanner, who was the brother to Ben, who was the boss of Chris, the childhood friend of Luke. I think.

So now I'm staring at a simple text sent at six-thirty am with just seven words, but also an unlimited number of ways to overthink and read into.

Luke: *Had a good time last night, sweetheart.*

What the actual fuck is going on.

Instead of replying, I toss the phone into my bag, ignoring both the message and the beyond late hour as I quickly scrub my teeth and throw my hair up into what I hope is a chic-looking bun and not just a rat's nest on top of my head. Instead of attempting any kind of makeup and knowing I have a full arsenal at the office, I step into my comfy and warm but ugly boots after changing into a pair of leggings and a tee shirt and start for the door.

And then I remember.

My car.

Shit. Memories of Luke driving me home flood, of leaving my car at the restaurant, of Luke promising to bring it to me. He took my keys.

Digging in my bag to find my keys, there are only two on the ring —my apartment and office keys and nothing else.

No car key. My mind drifts back to last night, to Luke promising to get my car here before I had to get to work, but it was three by the time he left. Three am, and the man is supposed to be at work by seven. *Fuck.* There's no way my car is here, and now I have no way to get to the office. Still, I need to check before I panic too much.

Phone in hand, I run down the stairs, skipping the elevator and heading straight to the parking garage and my assigned spot.

There she is.

My beautiful white car, parked in my spot, in perfect condition.

So perfect, it takes me a moment to notice...

The tire. The tire has been replaced. The spare no longer sits on the rear passenger side, obviously different than the others and needing replacing. But instead, there's a tire to match the other three.

Luke fixed my tire.

———

It's nearly eleven when I walk into the office, and when I unlock the door, Gabrielle's head pops up, eyes wide as she stares at me. Stress is written across her face, her hair today held with a pink gel pen.

"Hey, Gabrielle," I mutter as I walk in and head for my desk.

"Oh, my God, Cassie! What the—I was—did you?!" She's stuttering, pushing her chair back when she stands and knocking her cup of sparkly, colorful pens over. Her hands move frantically as she picks them up, her eyes still nearly popping out of her face. "Where have you been!?" she asks, and it's strange... she sounds almost... angry.

But, even more, she *looks* angry, standing there with her hands on her hips and *glaring* at me.

It's actually kind of hard to take serious. In her tea-length shirt with little dinosaurs on it, she almost looks like a kindergarten teacher who caught a kid eating glue.

"What?"

"What? *What?* I'll tell you what! Last night I get a text from you saying you're going to some random *bar* with your date. Then nothing. Nothing at all. So I sat there, panicked, wondering if I should call someone or maybe drive down there and see if you were okay, until, at *two in the morning,* you send me another text that he's *driving you home* because you *drank too much.* You! Cassandra! Cassandra, who has a rule about literally everything in life, including a date is limited to one glass of wine, and all dates end by ten." Her words are frantic, smushed together, and shouted quickly, so my already swimming brain pounds a bit with each syllable.

"I don't have a rule for everything." I try to argue her last point. I'm not *that* boring.

"You do! See!" She grabs a pad of paper with loopy numbers written on the left in a variety of different colors. At the top, it says "Cassie's Rules."

"Is that...?"

"It's all of your rules."

"Why do you have a list of rules?" I ask as I grab it out of her hand. The top four are my dating rules, but then...

Dates must end by 10 pm.

A man who mentions his mother more than three times on a date— red flag.

Always have a backup outfit.

If they say their ex was crazy, they are the crazy one.

And on and on. All of the tidbits of things I've said, rules I've laid out.

"In case I ever need to know them." Now she's blushing a bright red, no longer frustrated but almost embarrassed, looking at her desk and avoiding my eye.

"Well. You take great notes," I say, staring and reading over them some more.

Just because he holds the door doesn't make him a gentleman.

Any man who hates dogs = a jerk.

"It's my job." She looks at me. "Where *were* you, Cassie?"

"I slept in." I sigh.

"You slept in?!"

"Yes."

"You?!"

"Yes, Gabrielle."

"Was he... with you?" Her eyes are saucers now, and she hesitates like she doesn't know if she's crossing some kind of line she should stay behind.

"With me?"

"Did he sleep over?" Frustration coats her words, annoyed that I'm not getting to the point sooner.

"God, no, he's a client."

"But you stayed out until two am with him." She's got me there. And then, for some unknown reason, I spill. Maybe it's because I'm still exhausted. Maybe it's because I'm uncaffeinated. Maybe it's because I can't think of a single other woman I could spill this to. And I really, really need to tell this to someone other than myself.

"Uh, and he kissed me." She stares at me, eyes wider than before and mouth hanging open.

"I'm sorry, what?"

"He kissed me?" I say the words like a question, as if I need her to confirm for me.

"He kissed you."

"He kissed me." I nod, and we're both silent. I can't help but wonder if maybe I made a mistake in telling this detail to my employee. Maybe I should have kept it close to me, stayed professional. It's not like we have this kind of relationship, we—

"Oh, my *God!*" The sound is shocking from my quiet, demure assistant, blasting my eardrums as it breaks from her with an uncharacteristic shriek.

"Gabrielle, I—"

"He kissed you!" Her hands are on my shoulders, arms stretched over her desk, her face in mine.

"I know, I was there."

"But that's against the rules. It's, like, one of those most important rules."

"Yeah, well—"

"Should we take him off the list? Should we blacklist him? Should I—"

"Stop, calm down. It wasn't—it isn't—"

"He *kissed you.*"

"I know. And it was...." My mind flits back to it, shockingly clear in my drink-addled memory. That kiss. How do I describe it? I should say it was inappropriate. That it was wrong, that it was unprofessional, that, yes, we need to blacklist him. But then I remember how he didn't kiss me but instead put it in my hands, let me make the move, made sure I was okay with it. So I say, "It was nice."

"Nice?!" She sits in her seat with a flop, eyes wide.

"Yes. It was nice. At least we know he can... kiss. Well." Her lips turn up in a smirk. "You know. For any... future clients." Why does that feel so icky? Why does it churn my belly, those words, the thought of setting him up in the future?

"You're going on another date?" Once again, her voice is shrill and surprised. "But you kissed him!" I make my way to my desk, dropping my bag on top.

"He kissed me." *Not the full truth...*

"Same difference. You're going on a date with him again?"

"That's my job." My back goes to her, digging in my bag before continuing, not wanting to see her reaction to the next bit of info.

"Yeah, but..."

"Saturday."

"Saturday?" She's as confused as she should be. I sit at my desk, shaking the mouse to wake the screen.

"My next date." I busy myself with papers to avoid her eye once again.

"You're going on a date with him on Saturday?"

"Yes."

"You don't do weekend dates."

"I'm making an exception." Once again, she's silent. When I finally find it in me to meet her eyes, the shock is still there, but so is something softer, kinder.

"You like him." There's a smile playing on her lips.

"What? No. He's a client. Nothing more."

"Bullshit." She says the word, but immediately her eyes widen with shock, like she can't believe the word left her lips. "Cassie—"

But instead of getting angry or reprimanding her as she seems to expect, I burst out laughing, the sound flowing from me with an ease I haven't felt in years. And while I try to pretend I'm not sure of the source, of why I feel free, deep down, I know.

I know and it scares the shit out of me.

TWELVE

-Luke-

"How was it?"

"Remind me to thank you and Q one day when this shit settles," I say when my sister Tara calls me on my lunch the day after my date with Cassie. Or, I guess, technically, the same day it ended. I didn't get home until close to four after I dropped off Cassie, brought her car to the shop to fix her tire, and then dropped it back off at her apartment, which means I'm running on close to two hours of sleep. Still, somehow I feel more energized than I have in years.

It's the girl.

Knowing she exists, knowing I *found her,* gives me the energy I need to get through this long day.

My parents met when my dad was a senior in high school and my mom a sophomore. He spotted her while attending his little sister's, my Aunt Tanya's, band concert and knew then. Hunted her down, convinced my grandfather to let her date him, and since that day, they haven't spent more than two days apart. He's told us since we were kids it was love at first sight; he always knew she would be it for him.

And thirty years later, it's held strong.

While I don't necessarily believe love at first sight is a thing, I couldn't get her out of my mind when I pulled over to help Cassie that night. The entire next day, and when I was getting ready for our date, she was on my mind, making me wonder if going was a good idea. It almost felt like cheating, like I was already betraying my dream woman. But I had no way of finding her, had no clue where she might be, so what could it hurt?

And then the hostess walked me back to the small table in that snooty restaurant where she was sitting in that demure but still somehow sexy as fuck dress, and I knew.

She's the girl.

And then we talked, and I learned more about her, even if she didn't want to share, and it was cemented. I learned what she likes and what she doesn't. Not just from her work, but by reading her, taking in how she reacts, how she treats others around her, how she endures my teasing, the teasing of my friends. *She's the girl.* Now my job is to get her to listen to me, to try it out with me. It's clear to me between us is some unseen obstacle I can't quite pinpoint, and I know already it's going to be hard to overcome.

But the work will be worth it...

"Do you think you aced the interview? Think she'll set you up with someone good?" She sounds shocked, which is hilarious to me considering she's part of the trio who forced the date on me. Some annoying little brother part of me loves that she feared I'd screw it up completely.

"Not worried about the interview. I'm going for the matchmaker."

"What?" She laughs, but I don't.

Last night was the best night I've had in years, and not because I was having fun at a bar with old friends. There's something about being in Cassie's presence, talking to her, getting to know her.

Watching her finally relax and interact with my friends... something about it called to me. It was the perfect night.

And then the *kiss*. It took everything in me not to ask to come inside, to follow her into her bed. But my parents raised me better, and she was tipsy. So, when I finally have her, there will be no question if she wants this. Wants us.

"Luke, what do you mean you're *'going for the matchmaker'*?"

"I said what I said."

"Luke, that's not how this—" Her chiding mother tone is out, the same one my mom still uses on us and the one she uses on her own kids now.

"Tara, trust me when I say that's how this is going to work. I've met her before. A few days ago. She was stranded on the side of the road; I helped change her tire. I couldn't get her off my mind but had no way to know who she was, where she was from. I walked into the restaurant, and there she was." She's quiet on the other end of the line. "So I'm going for her. We had a good night. I took her to trivia night with Ben and Chris. You know Chris. She held her own. Made friends with Ben's brother's girl."

"She held her own with Chris?" Tara sounds shocked, but I don't blame her. Chris is abrasive at best, annoying as fuck at worst. He's a ladies' man, loves to flirt, and will turn everything you say into some kind of crude joke. But somehow, Cassie, even with her sometimes uptight personality, was able to bypass his obnoxiousness, turn it around on him, and make it so he's already texting me, asking when he can come down again to 'hang with my girl.'

And God, do I love the sound of that. My girl.

"Shocked me too. She's not laid back by any means. Thought they'd clash."

"Wasn't she supposed to plan the date or something like that?"

"Yup."

"But you took her to trivia night with your friends?"

"She tried to take me to an art museum first," I say in place of an explanation. My sister is silent on the other end for long moments before she bursts out laughing.

"You? An art museum? God bless her."

"That's why we went to trivia night," I say with a smile on my face, remembering her frustrated look when I told her we were not by any means going into a museum. "We walked to the museum, and I instantly took her to Tommy's on the boardwalk." She laughs hard before it simmers into a slight chuckle.

"So you're going for the matchmaker, huh?"

"Yup."

"When are you going to bring her to Sunday dinner?"

"Soon, but she's skittish. I can tell already. I'm going to have to convince her to give it a chance. Give me a chance."

"Well, if there's anyone I know who can do it, it's you." My sisters have always had all the confidence in the world in me, regardless of the fact they love to poke fun at me. So when my phone vibrates against my ear, indicating a text, I pull it away to see a message from Cassie.

Cassie: Thank you very much for moving my car and replacing my tire. Please send an invoice to my assistant, and I can process payment to you.

"Oh, hell no," I murmur as I read the text.

"What?"

"Sorry, Cassie texted me. The matchmaker. She wants to pay me."

"Pay you? For what?" I laugh, knowing her mind is going to some dirty places.

"Calm down. I replaced her tire last night before I brought it back. She had a spare on."

"Ahh, and your gentleman complex kicked in. Dad did well with you."

"Yeah, yeah, but I don't think she's the kind to easily accept something like that graciously."

"Well, sounds like you have your work cut out for you." In the background, two kids screaming can be heard before my sister's muffled voice yells at them to keep it down. "Alright, I gotta go before your niece and nephew kill each other. Good luck, and let me know when I should bring chocolate cake to Sunday dinner." That's how my oldest sister wins everyone over—by baking her famous cake.

"Got it. Tell them if they cooperate, Uncle Luke will bring them something fun on Sunday." We say our goodbyes before I hang up, staring at my phone and dialing Cassie's number to set her straight.

THIRTEEN

-Cassie-

CASSIE: THANK YOU VERY MUCH FOR MOVING MY CAR AND replacing my tire. Please send an invoice to my assistant, and I can process payment to you.

Done. I place my phone on my desk after sending the message to Luke. Now I can concentrate on work. Opening an email from a potential new client, I start to read it.

Five minutes later, I try to ignore the fact I've been staring at the screen of my computer the entire time and not a single word has registered in my brain. *What the fuck.* This isn't like me at all. I love my job. Love my clients. A new one in my inbox, looking to spend $600 to be matched, should excite me. But my mind is still...

My phone vibrates from where I placed it, the screen lighting up and flashing the name of what's keeping me so distracted. It's probably because I feel guilty. Not only did he fix my car without payment, but I was utterly unprofessional during our first meeting. Lifting the phone, I glance at Gabrielle's desk to see her deep in conversation on a call.

"Hello?"

"You're not paying me." His voice is gruff and annoyed and instantly sends a traitorous chill down my spine.

"What?"

"For the tire. You're not payin' me." Something told me it wouldn't be that easy.

"You provided me a service. I know I needed a new tire. That wasn't without a cost. Any reputable mechanic shop—"

"The shop didn't do it. I did." I'm silent, trying to process what he's saying.

"What?"

"It wasn't a job, Cass. It was a favor. You needed your tire fixed. I did it."

"But... Why?"

"It's not safe for you to drive around on your spare. I didn't like the idea of you doing it." He stops there, but my mind fills in blanks it has no right to fill in as unexpected warmth floods me. But still...

"Did you steal from the garage?"

"What?"

"Tires aren't free, Mr. Dawson—"

"Luke. We're past that shit." I sigh and roll my eyes.

"Fine, Luke. Tires aren't free. So either you paid for the replacement yourself or you stole it. And if you stole it, I'm not sure I want to be driving on stolen property." His laugh has me forcing my lips not to tip up and join in.

"I didn't steal it. I get a generous employee discount. Consider it a thank you for a great night."

"I can't accept that. I'd be much more comfortable paying—"

"You push it, I'm gonna be mad. Please, don't fight me on this. I'm exhausted, sure you are too. You can pay me back by being a good sport." Guilt fills me, knowing he's at work, exhausted because of me. As much as I want to argue, it doesn't feel like the right thing to do. So instead, I sigh, resigned.

"That's very... kind of you."

"That's me, kind." He says it with a laugh, like he thinks I'm cute instead of annoying.

"You are. Well. Thank you for clearing that up. And for... the tire. I won't take up more of your time."

"I have time."

"What?" I ask in confusion.

"On my lunch."

"What?"

"Is your phone broken?"

"What?" *Can I say anything else besides what?!* The uptight librarian shakes her head at me, arms crossed over her chest as she watches me continue to make a fool of myself in front of this man.

"Can you hear me?"

"Shit. I mean, shoot. I mean. Yes. Yes, I can hear you." What is going on with me right now? I spend every day doing phone interviews, talking, and analyzing. Then, I get this one man on the phone and what, I revert to goofy college girl? "You're on your lunch?"

"That's why it took me a bit to call you after you texted. Had to clock out, get to the break room."

"Oh, well. Enjoy your lunch. I'll... speak with you later."

"I took my lunch to call you."

"What?" He laughs, and it takes a lot for me not to laugh at myself too...

"I took my lunch to call you, Cassie. Might as well keep me on the line a little longer, don't you think?" It made some kind of weird sense. It would actually be rude to hang up, right? I should... you know, talk to him.

"Oh. Okay. Do you normally do that? Take calls on your lunch?"

"It's not strict here. I can take calls during work hours so long as I get shit done. I was talking to my sister when you texted. But I wanted privacy. No distraction. So I took my lunch."

"Oh," I say, confused about what to say, how to interpret his words. Silence takes over the line. Then, I open my mouth because I cannot seem to talk about anything but work. "Have you planned your date yet?" *Now, why the hell did I ask that?* In fact, I should be telling him the date isn't necessary. I went so off plan for our first date, I should just add him to my system as-is. We spent the required time together, after all. And I'm 99% sure he's not a mass murderer or hiding some secret wife.

But instead, I'm *encouraging* the date.

And if I'm being completely transparent with myself, I'm really looking forward to it.

Just another reason I should cancel this date before it even happens.

"Yup."

"Oh." Another pause, and even though I can't see him, even though I can't hear the action, it's like I can feel his smile down the line. The smile he made all last night when I'd blush because I knew some random trivia or when I'd ask him a question from my sheet. "How did you get my cell number?" I don't give clients my personal number for safety reasons. Instead, we communicate on the office phone or via email exclusively.

"Jordan."

"I figured. She's nice. I... I like her. And your friends. They were very welcoming."

"They liked you." His voice softens like he's settling into a conversation where I'm not arguing with him about vehicle repairs. Like this is something we do often, sit on the phone while he's on his lunch and while I'm sitting in my office not answering emails. His words send another rush of warmth through me as if this is some new boyfriend and I just met his friends for the first time, as if their liking me mattered.

Which it does *not matter*. He is a client.

Then why does the thought of matching him make you queasy? my sex fiend asks, a curious smirk on her face.

I shake my head. Too many drinks last night. That's what it is.

"Do you forgive me for skipping the museum?" I laugh at the question.

"I was looking forward to the new modern art exhibit." That's kind of a lie.

"I'll take you next time." I pause, but there must still be liquor in my system, or maybe this man works his own kind of intoxifying magic, because the words tumble from my lips.

"I lied."

"What?"

"I lied. I wasn't looking forward to it. I actually find art museums quite boring." His laugh comes from his belly, something I noticed last night when he held me close to him in the crowded bar. He has three kinds of laughs from what I saw. The first is a chuckle he paired with a head shake when I said something he disagreed with or he thought I was being silly. The second is the fake one he used on the server when she got a bit too close and brushed her hand on his arm. And a third—a big belly laugh accompanied by the happiness which shone from his eyes and a huge, genuine smile. All three brought out the dimple in his left cheek.

Jesus, now I'm dissecting the man's laughs?

"Then why were we going there?" I sigh, not really wanting to answer this. It feels like a weird industry thing, like a dirty secret making me less authentic or manipulative.

"My job is to find the true feelings and actions of the people I'm setting up," I say, giving him time to process.

"Got that. What does it have to do with an art museum?"

"So, you bring a man to an art museum, and there are a few ways he'll act. One, he's excited. There are two subreactions to this. One, he'll mansplain every piece, even if you know more about it. That's a flag for me. The other subreaction is he'll be excited and enjoy the experience alongside you. That's a good mark. Perfect to match with another lover of the arts. The next is he'll clearly be hesitant. The subreactions for this are, A. He makes it verbally clear he's not enjoying it but goes along with it. That's kind of like a yellow flag and can be neutral or bad, depending on how the rest of the night goes. Or B. It's clear art museums aren't his thing, but he goes for it with a smile because it's the polite thing to do. Usually a green flag." He laughs. It's the chuckle.

"You've really thought about this art museum thing, haven't you?"

"It's my job. To be fair, your application said," I shuffle through papers to find the application I now know his sister filled out, "ahem, you enjoy fine art and museums." Again, he laughs, this time the belly laugh.

"I'm gonna kill Tara."

"It's fine. I will say you're the first case that's gotten to a date without actually filling out the application. Usually, it's a mom or a grandmother, and we filter those out pretty easily. You were a surprise." He mumbles something under his breath which sounds suspiciously like, "so were you," but his next words distract me.

"So, what's option three?"

"Option three?"

"You bring a man to a museum; what's option three?" I pause, unsure if I should answer.

"Option three is new. It's when the man decides there's no way in hell he's going to a museum and takes me to a bar trivia night with his friends." My voice is low when I answer, and I'm silent for long moments while I wait for his reply.

"What's the verdict on that?" *And for some unknown reason, I answer without running the words through the filter I normally use when talking with clients. When talking with anyone, really.*

"Undecided." His laugh flows through the line and through my veins, filling it with the *warmth* he always seems to bring. My ears feel hot as I flit my eyes to Gabrielle and see she has a small smile on her lips as she watches me.

"Alright, well, when you decide, you let me know." A voice is heard in the background, then a muffle comes through the line like he's moving his phone against his shirt. "Hey, sweetheart, I gotta go, okay? Talk to you soon."

"Okay, Luke," I say, but I stay on the line after he ends the call, the silent cell held to my ear like I might learn what the hell is going on, why this man is affecting me and turning me upside down.

"Okay, spill." The voice comes from Gabrielle, standing in front of my desk, pen in her hair and an eyebrow raised. Staring at her for long seconds, I don't speak while I weigh my options, weigh wanting to remain professional to my employee and really wanting a *friend* to gab with. Finally, my decision made, I lower my phone and look her in the eye.

"What are you doing tonight?"

———

Hours later, Gabrielle is sitting in sweats on my couch while we watch one of those gushy Hallmark movies they play around every holiday to convince women they need a man in their life. This time it's a cupid retelling, where some sassy New Yorker falls in love with, you guessed it, Cupid. Perfect for Valentine's Day.

The thought reminds me I need to figure out a date for my dad's wedding. *Shit.*

"You can call me Gabi, you know." Her voice comes through a mouthful of noodles, chopsticks resting in the white container from the killer Chinese food place down the road.

"Huh?" I look over at her, missing the guy catching his first glimpse of the woman and probably deciding to marry her and have a million babies with her.

"Gabi. You always call me Gabrielle. You can call me Gabi. All of... all of my friends do."

"Oh." The word sounds confused, and, in all fairness, I am.

"Or you can call me Gabrielle if you're more comfortable with that."

"No, it's not—it's..." How do I explain to my sweet assistant that I don't really have friends and no concept for acting without sounding like a fucking loser? I'm sitting on the floor of my apartment, leaning against the couch she's sitting on. My eyes lock on the TV, but I don't see anything anymore. Before I say more, I take a huge sip of the sake I bought to go with our food. Considering the hangover I woke up with this morning, I should not be drinking again, but... "I don't have any friends."

She chokes on her food.

"Oh, my God! Are you okay?" She coughs a few times before taking a sip of her own sake.

"Yeah, sorry. What do you mean, you have no friends?"

I sigh. This is embarrassing. Ever since I met Luke on the side of the road, I've been one embarrassing overshare after another.

"It's not that I don't have friends. It's more that all of the friends I have are married, and... we drifted. So I haven't taken the time to... make new ones."

"You're very... formal with people," she says.

"Yeah, I know." I laugh. "But it's a product of my childhood. Only child. We moved a few times when I was a kid, different schools every few years. I never had the chance to connect with people. And then my dad." Gabi smiles, the look relaxed and friendly, like she's settling in for a good story. Like she's turned off the 'employee' switch and gone to 'girlfriend.'

"Okay, that's it. This might get me fired, but I've been dying to know what's going on there. What is *up* with your parents?" I've never seen this side of her, this sweatpants-and-Chinese-and-gossip side. It's... fun.

"You won't get fired," I laugh. For a moment, the uptight librarian in my mind warns me not to open up, not to tell personal details to my employee, but then I push her aside and move forward. Maybe Luke was right—perhaps I need to open up more, to have more fun. To be a human and not a robot. "It's kind of a long story. My parents were together for twenty years and had me after they married. My dad traveled for work a lot, and we moved around a bit, but we never settled until we landed a few towns from here the last five years I was in grade school... When I graduated high school, he told my mom he was leaving her, and since we'd moved there, he'd had another woman on the side. So when he was 'traveling'" — I use air quotes to tell her it's a loose term — "he was living with his mistress. Actually, *mistresses*, since our moves were less about his work and more about his side pieces. We suffered financially when I was a kid—not a ton, but enough I noticed. It turned out he actually had a good chunk of money; he just was using it for his other life."

"No way!" Gabi gasps, her eyes wide and unbelieving. I'm just realizing now this might be the first time I've told anyone the story outright, and it actually is pretty gasp-worthy. Instead of saying that, I just nod before continuing my tale.

"So my mom sued him for a ton of money and got alimony, even though the reason he stayed was so he wouldn't have to pay child support. It was messy. Now she spends her days between rehab and wellness retreats. She's my mom, but she's kind of a mess. It seems valid, considering her entire life was a lie, but still. She feels like she wasted her best years on him, which... again... valid." Gabi nods in agreement.

"Cassie, I'm so sorry. That's crazy. It had to be so hard for you. Did they make you choose sides?" My mind drifts back to my college life, where I graduated in only three years by taking classes on campus instead of going home and avoiding having to choose where to go. Working my ass off to impress my dad so he wouldn't forget me the way he forgot my mom.

What good that did.

Last I spoke with him, excitedly telling him about the successful business I've built from the ground up, he said, "So you're a matchmaker who can't find a man?"

The friends I made in college were superficial. We'd go to classes together, they'd invite me to parties, that kind of thing. But I was so wrapped up in graduating and avoiding home, and, as my therapist tells me, trying to process my own trauma after finding out about my dad's deceit, I couldn't create any bonds with my classmates. After graduation, most only reached out with requests to be matched or to invite me to lavish weddings to get a nice gift from their registry.

"Yes, and no. He left a few days after I left for college, and then during the first winter break, I stayed on campus. Most holidays, I would split, and then for summers and breaks, I just... stayed at school. That's how I graduated early. I didn't want to have to choose. Plus, he's a bit bitter with me. I look a lot like my mother, so I think when he sees me, he sees the fact he stayed for so long to hold on to his money but still has to pay her alimony. It's a mess, to be honest. When I graduated, I had an apartment and started The Ex Files. Most of the time, my mom is off on some retreat and my dad is occupied with his... wives."

"Wives?!"

"He's going for his third."

"But he was divorced, what, ten years ago?"

"Just about."

"Damn, he works quick."

"That's my dad for you," I say, lifting my drink and emptying it. I screw up my face at the taste, and she laughs at the cough.

"Little much?"

"Yeah."

"So the wedding?"

"The wedding. His third. My newest stepmom can't be more than a few years older than me."

"Ouch."

"Yup. And every time I'm with him and his family, all I hear about is how I need to find a man, how I'm getting old, how I'm clearly not very good at what I do because I can't even find myself someone."

"Well, that's bullshit. The number of happy couples who credit The Ex Files with their happiness is huge!"

"Yeah, well, it's not enough. And that's why I need to scramble to find a date before Valentine's Day."

"That's in like, three weeks." I mentally do the math and see my always astute assistant is once again correct. Shit.

"Shit. Yeah. It is." I'm silent as I crack open a fortune cookie as if inside will be the answer to all of my issues. It reminds me of Luke and making wishes on them. "' All the answers you need are right there in front of you!'" I read the message aloud to Gabi and crunch through the sugary cookie, annoyed. "Well, that's no help."

"Or is it?" I raise an eyebrow at her, already folding up the paper out of habit. "What if the answer *is* right in front of you?"

"No offense, Gabi, but my dad would not be impressed by my bringing a woman as a date."

"Not me, you dumb butt."

"Dumb butt?"

"Dumb butt." My head goes back with a laugh at her silly word, and it feels *good* to laugh with someone, to spill my guts, to lounge in sweats and eat junk food. It's similar to the feeling from last night, hanging out with Luke and his friends, giggling with Jordan, and rolling my eyes at Chris. "What about Luke?"

"Luke?" The name sends a thrill down my spine.

"Yeah, the guy from last night."

"The client?"

"He's not a client. He's a potential match, not even on our roster yet."

"Same thing."

"No, it's not. Are you going to tell me what happened last night?"

"We went on a date."

"Stop playing games, Cassie. What on earth happened? You're frazzled. You don't *get* frazzled." A sigh escaped my chest, heavy and filled with emotion. Regret? Anticipation? *Excitement?*

"We went on a date. It was... good. Really good. We went to dinner, and I interviewed him, but..." I pause, thinking.

"But...?!"

"But he decided it should be a question for a question. He told me if I could ask questions, it was only fair if he could too."

"I mean, he's not wrong."

"That's not how it works."

"I know, but maybe... it should. You know, see if he can hold a

conversation." I glare at her, remembering that was basically his argument as well.

"Anyway, every question I asked, he asked one. Nothing big—
favorite foods and stuff. But it was... fun. And then we went to the
museum...."

"I thought you didn't go there?"

"Can I tell my story?" I say, throwing a wrapped fortune cookie at
her. She laughs, and I like this, goofing with a friend and gossiping
about boys.

"Go, sorry!"

"We went, and he said he wasn't going in. It wasn't his style.
Instead, he had a friend in town, so we went to a bar for trivia night."

"You? A bar?" Her eyes are wide with shock.

"I know. But... it was good. His friends were a blast. And he... he
was fun. I drank a bit too much—"

"You *drank on a date?!*"

"Jesus, Gabi, hush! Let me finish!"

"Sorry!" She's not, though—she's laughing at me, excitement on
her face.

"So we went to trivia night, but I drank a bit too much, and he
drove me home. He walked me to my apartment and kissed me...."
My mind floats off, remembering the kiss, those brief moments where
his lips were on mine, and I wanted so much more. "It was *good*,
Gabi. Really, really good."

She smiles at me. "And then what!?"

"That's it. Except then this morning, he brought my car to my
parking space and fixed my tire sometime between last night and this
morning. He couldn't have slept much. It was... sweet. And he won't
accept payment." Gabi's eyes go gooey.

"Cassie, that is the sweetest, cutest first date story ever." She's not
wrong. I've heard my fair share when I debrief with clients, and this
might be at the top.

"I know," I admit this, half excited, half dismayed. If only... if only he wasn't a potential match. If only I wasn't so damaged and could set aside the inevitable heartbreak and let myself enjoy this. Enjoy *him*.

"And now you're going on a date on Saturday?"

"Yes." The acid in my stomach churns at the thought of yet another rule broken, another first.

"Cassie, I'm not trying to scare you, but...." I take a deep breath, wondering what she'll say. "I don't think he's in this for a match."

"Well, no. His sisters set this up."

"No, I know that. But if your sisters set you up with a match-maker, you do the date, get it done with, and tell them it didn't work. You don't make it magical, don't kiss her, don't make her break her rules and insist on going out on the weekend." I've put blinders on so I can ignore this fact. She's not wrong, but if I look at it that way, if I start to think...

"I can't. No. This is a client. It has to stay that way."

"Why?" The question floors me. No one has ever bothered to ask.

"My father lied to my mom, kept it up for twenty years, and when it was all said and done, she was destroyed. I can't let it happen to me. I won't let anyone hold that much power over me. Not for good or bad. Because it *always ends badly*. Even the ones that seem like fairytales."

"Okay, then why The Ex Files? You don't believe a relationship can last, but you help create them?"

"I can't stop people from wanting to find love. What I can do is make sure the women who use my services are equipped with the knowledge to protect themselves." Gabi stares at me, nods, but then keeps on digging.

"Well, who said it has to be forever? Who said it has to be seri-ous? Couldn't you just... have fun with him? Enjoy spending time with someone?" I don't tell her I've been asking myself the same all day because yesterday was fun. And tonight, gossiping with a friend after spending a night out with new ones, I realize maybe I built my protective wall a little too well. But still...

"That never works, Gabi. Someone always gets hurt." She stares

at me for long moments, reading my face, but then she blinks, acceptance and... strategy coming over her expression.

"Okay, Cassie," she says before turning to focus on the TV. "You
wanna watch this or *Housewives*?"

The night continues with ease—the ease of a new friend, of
hanging with a girlfriend. But her words stay in the back of my mind
for days.

*You don't make it magical, don't kiss her, don't make her break her
rules...*

FOURTEEN

-Cassie-

LUKE: WEAR JEANS ON SATURDAY.

My phone buzzes on Thursday morning, two days after my... date with him. I stare at it like it might explode when the name I saved into my phone after the last call blinks across the screen....

Luke: Sneakers. Or boots. No heels.

That requires a response.

Cassie: I don't do flats.

Luke: I'll buy you a pair then.

Cassie: I don't need you to buy me shoes, Mr. Dawson.

Luke: Be careful with what you call me, sweetheart. I might want to hear you say it again in a much more comfortable setting.

Heat runs down my spine against my will. *This is so inappropriate!* my inner rule-following librarian shrieks. *Then why does she like it so much?* my sex fiend retorts. Rather than give in to their bickering, I reply to Luke.

Cassie: *This is inappropriate.*

He doesn't reply, and something about that adds a black cloud to my entire morning as I dig through my emails. I'm more aggressive than usual, tossing potential clients onto my waitlist with much less thought, sending snippy replies, and even glaring once at Gabrielle—I mean Gabi. Thankfully, she just laughed when I did, and that tiny glimmer of growing friendship turned the black thundercloud into a light grey one.

But it still rubbed me wrong, how annoyed I was with his lack of reply.

As I walk out of the office to grab a coffee mid-day, my phone rings.

Lucas Dawson calling.

Staring at my phone, I let it ring once, twice, three times as I stand completely still in the middle of the busy sidewalk, people bumping into me and grumbling as they walk around.

"Hello?" My words are shaky as I answer. Then, clearing my throat, I repeat myself. "Hello?"

"Hey, sweetheart." Silence. What the—I move the phone from my ear to look at it once more, to make sure it's him. Maybe he has some girlfriend he meant to call? His sisters set him up; perhaps they didn't know...

"Uh, this is Cassandra with The Ex Files. Unfortunately, I think you have the wrong number.

"I'm the one who called you, Cass."

"Yeah, but..." my voice trails off as I try to decide what to say next. "Is something wrong? Do you need to... talk about the next date or something? Reschedule?"

"Nope."

"Well, then... why are you calling me?" The words tumble out, and he laughs. Laugh number one, when I do something he thinks is silly.

"On my lunch."

"You're... on your lunch?"

"Yeah, babe."

"And you're... calling me."

"Yes."

"Why?"

"I like talking to you." In the background, there's a racket of noise, metal clanging and men laughing, but it's not distracting. In fact, it just reminds me who I'm talking with, this normal, every day, down-to-earth man who I'm supposed to be setting up.

"But we're... you're a client. We're not..."

"I'll let you keep thinking that." What the hell does that mean? "How's your day goin'?"

"Uh. It's uh... okay?"

"Mine's been shit." I move again when a large man with killer B.O. smacks into me.

"Oh, I'm sorry, why?"

"Mind is all over the place, can't concentrate on anything."

"Yeah, I know the feeling," I say, thinking about the blinking line on the email I opened this morning and still haven't written. "Seems to be an ailment that's going around."

"Pretty brown-eyed girl runnin' through my mind non-stop." Once again, I stop in my tracks. This time it's a pretty woman in a business suit smacking into my back.

"Learn to walk!" she shouts at me as she moves around me.

"What was that?"

"I uh, I tripped." The scoff in his voice tells me he might not believe me, but he lets me have it.

"So you're wearing boots tomorrow?"

"I told you, I don't own boots. I wear heels."

"Flats?"

"Heels, Luke."

"Why do you only have heels? That sounds like a terribly uncomfortable life to live." My mind flits back to a conversation I overheard my dad having with stepmom number one while I visited them not long after my parents split.

. . .

"New shoes?"

"They're the ones you bought me," she had purred in a way that made my stomach churn.

"Love a woman in heels. Makes her look feminine, gorgeous. A woman not in heels says she doesn't care."

Instantly I'd thought about my mom, who spent most of my childhood wearing cute but comfortable clothes that fit the life of a stay-at-home mom whose life revolved around the PTA and volunteering.

I threw out all of my flats when I got back to school.

"I wear heels. I date people for a living. Heels make a woman look feminine. Pretty." The words come out tasting of the acid in my stomach, but I persevere, the coffee shop now in my line of sight.

"That's stupid."

"No, it's not."

"A woman in flats says she's comfortable with who she is. Not trying to impress anyone."

"So you don't like a woman in heels?" I ask.

"Oh, I love when a woman wears heels."

"Then why—"

"A woman in heels is sexy as fuck. A man looks at a woman in heels, he instantly thinks about wrapping them around his back or bending her over to fuck her from behind while she's still wearing them—"

"Luke! Not every—"

"Every man, sweetheart. And I guaran-fuckin'-tee every man who has seen you in your heels with your pretty skirts and your tight dresses has thought the same thing."

"There's no way—"

"I sure as fuck did that first time, side of the road. Bending you over the hood of your car, eating you while they dug into my back."

Any remaining drive to argue his point, to cut him off, has completely evaporated in the heat of unexpected lust running through me. For a split second, a reel of images runs through my mind, images that are absolutely filthy staring this all-American man whom I never in a million years would have pictured saying this to me. I bite my lip as the center of my panties grows suspiciously damn.

"But a woman in flats?" His voice is lower now, growly and untamed, similar to how he said goodbye after our last date. After that kiss. "A woman in flats tells me she's comfortable with me, a woman I can take home to meet my parents, a woman I can take out for a night with my friends, show off, and then take home, strip naked, and do unbelievably dirty things to."

And fuck if that stupid ho of a sex fiend doesn't speak before the straight-laced librarian can chain her in her dungeon.

"What kind of dirty things?" Am I... am I dirty talking a potential match? While standing in the middle of a busy street? That's not happening right now, right? Like... no. Not at all.

"Oh, Cassie, sweetheart, you give me the chance, and I'll show you a whole new fuckin' world." Once again, a reel of inappropriate clips pulsates through my mind, the throb mimicked in my needy clit that's been woefully neglected over the past weeks, months... years, if I'm being honest. But before the librarian or sex fiend can break through to make the situation worse, a noise on the other end of the line breaks through, and the receiver is muffled before his voice is back. "Gotta run, babe. Flats, yeah?"

That's all he says, and I should argue, tell him I need to break the date, that we can't meet up, that this is so out of my comfort zone and so far from what is acceptable, but the only words that come from my mouth are, "Okay, Luke," before the phone line goes dead. Then, I'm standing in front of the coffee shop, staring down the road, the cold biting my nose and wondering if maybe I should bronze those heels I wore the night I met him.

And then I turn around, skipping the coffee shop to head to a shoe store to buy my first pair of flat shoes other than running shoes in over 10 years.

For a man.

Because I have lost all sense of who I am.

FIFTEEN

-Cassie-

When I use Google Maps to check out the address he sends over Friday night, I get my second sign this will not be the typical date I'm used to.

In fact, it's in a Wawa parking lot.

A convenience store slash gas station parking lot.

And while I love Wawa as much as the next girl, it's not exactly where I'd envision a date whose intention is to impress me.

But still, I pull up on Saturday morning at 9:55 because I can't bear to be late and park next to the black truck that's backed into a spot in the far corner of the lot.

On the roof of the truck is a fountain drink and a pretzel. My mind flits to our first date, then to the surprisingly many text strings we've exchanged over the past few days, the daily lunchtime phone calls. Exchanges I don't normally do with clients, but I decided it was just another chance to learn the ins and out of him. For a future client, of course.

Luke: *Favorite gas station snack?*

Cassie: Diet Coke and a soft pretzel.
Luke: Bottle or can?
Cassie: Fountain. Always a fountain drink.

And there he stands, leaning against the front of his truck, arms crossing his jacket-covered chest, light jeans leading to the same pair of boots he wore last time.

With a fountain drink and a soft pretzel.

As I pull in, I give him a small wave, and he gives me a smile, dimple on display. When I park, turn off, and step out of my car, he takes me in with a head to toe before looking at his boots and shaking his head with a slight chuckle.

"Couldn't resist, could you?"

My outfit consists of a body-hugging but warm sweater dress with a small v-neck, chunky jewelry, and a warm trench coat. When I went shopping, strangely energized despite the coffee I never ended up getting, I found the perfect pair of flat, over-the-knee boots that brought the outfit together perfectly. So while I don't have the benefit of increased height, better posture, and a badass gait, I still have my badass woman armor.

At least, that's what I tell myself.

I look down my body, kicking out my foot to look at the sole. "No heel. I listened." Instead of replying, he just rolls his eyes at me before throwing a hand out and taking me off guard when the hand hits the dip in my waist and pulls me in. Right in. Right into his chest, where I collide with an oof.

"Not gonna scare me off with your hot girl armor." I look up at him with, I'm sure, shock on my face. How does he— "Two older sisters and a mom, sweetheart. You've never battled with my kind, trained by women who love me but also wanted to make sure I don't scare off the good ones, leaving them with a shitty sister-in-law they hate." My eyes widen. He's got one thing right—I've never dealt with his kind.

"Oh." It's all I can say, but I don't need to say anything else because his head is lowering, eyes on my lips, and unconsciously I tip my chin up, giving him better access to... what? Kiss me? It's the last thing I should allow to happen with the man who I'm essentially interviewing for a position. Nevertheless, my heartbeat quickens, my body tensing in preparation, my lips pressing together just a fraction...

But his lips hit my forehead instead, and goddammit if I don't feel a crushing level of disappointment I should not be feeling.

"Missed you, sweetheart." The disappointment fades as a new, different satisfaction takes its place. I stare at him, trying to decode him, to get past the facade to figure out his end game, what his goal is.

And I see absolutely nothing.

Nothing but Lucas.

And that scares me more than anything I've ever experienced in my life.

"What are we doing here?" The words come out faint and breathy like I've just run a mile, and to be honest, when they come out, I'm not sure what the actual question was. What are we doing here, in this parking lot? What are we doing....

"I'm teaching you to change a tire."

"What?"

"Tire. You said you keep meaning to learn, right?"

"Yes?" I had told him the first night, with black mascara stains and panic leaking from my pores. I'd told him I didn't know how to change my stupid flat to the spare, but I'd been meaning to learn. That I was going to the very next day so I wouldn't be stuck on the side of the road for hours contemplating life and where I've gone wrong.

"No better time than now." I stare at him. "Come on, let's go." His hand goes to mine, twining his fingers with mine and pulling me to my trunk. "So your spare and tools are here, in your truck. Pop it for me?" I dig in my pocket and press the button, watching the small trunk pop open and bob once, twice before stilling. Luke lifts it and then shows me a pull tab. "Pull this up, and you'll see the tire." I do as he asks before a shout of surprise comes from my mouth

"Oh! Look at that! A whole tire!" Luke laughs, his second, booming laugh.

"Yeah, sweetheart, and see there? That's the wrench and the jack. Grab those first. We'll practice on your rear tire." I grab the tools and place them on the ground. "Okay, so first you're taking this to loosen the nuts." He hands me a heavy piece of cold metal. I examine it, noting the sockets at the end before looking at him.

"Aren't we supposed to, like, lift the car up with that thingy?" I point to the jack.

"Yeah, eventually. But if it's lifted and the nuts are tight, it will be harder since the entire tire will rotate." I nod. That makes sense, I guess. "Squat in front of the tire." I do as he asks and freeze when his warm body comes up behind me, lining up with my own, warmth from his body leaking into mine despite at least two layers of thick jackets. Although I know it's nearly impossible, it's like I can feel the tiny muscles of his chest moving against my own.

Why is this strangely sexy?

It doesn't get better when his hands run down my arms from my elbows, a slow, gentle stroke that has goosebumps sprouting everywhere before his hands meet mine, moving them to grab the tool correctly and line it up.

"So you use this part to crank the tool and loosen the nut." His breath is on my neck, his voice low in my ear has chills rushing down my spine, chills that have nothing to do with the winter cold and everything to do with the man behind me. "Good, just like that." Fuck, his words are going into my mind and jumping, envisioning them in different situations that are so inappropriate, so wrong, I can't function, can't move as my hand slips when I try to line up the tool to loosen another nut. "Easy."

"Sorry." I've had men teach me things while on a date. Cooking classes and wine classes. I've had clients take me to football games and hockey games and race tracks. Each explained the steps to me, some acting like I was a moron who couldn't breathe air without instruction (those were deleted from my system quickly), some annoyed when I messed up (ditto), and others I had a great time with. But as Luke shows me how to loosen the nuts, how and where to place the jack and crank it (he did that part, and holy shit, the whole vision of it made me want to give in to the sex fiend begging me to jump him and the librarian who was begging me to run away), how to remove the nuts and the bolts, how to remove the tire, I'm not just enjoying myself, but also learning.

"We're not going to use the spare; just put this back on. But I'll rotate your tires in a few weeks, and we can go through your training again," I turn back to look at him behind me once again as I tighten the bolts, and he's smiling at me, pride in his eyes.

"A few weeks?"

"Need to do it every so often. When I replaced your tire, I saw they'd need it soon. Probably when it warms up. You'll come down to the shop, and I'll show you around," he says with ease, as if this isn't the last time I'm going out with him, the last time I need to meet with him.

"Oh." When we remove the jack and finish tightening, he shows me how to test the air pressure and ensure it's good. It's a well-rounded lesson over all. When we're done, he grabs the drink and pretzel and hands them to me.

"For you."

"For me?" I ask as if I didn't realize this when I pulled in.

"You said you like them."

"I mean, thank you. I do. That was very... thoughtful of you. To remember." Something gleams in his eye like a secret he's keeping. A secret he's eager to share.

"You can eat it at our next stop."

"Next stop?"

"My date. Next stop."

"Oh. That's not... I can..." I trail off as I stare into his shining eyes and take a sip of my soda.

"My date, my rules."

"What?" Once more, he laughs. Laugh number one.

"My date has many parts, sweetheart. We'll take your car, okay?" He walks over to his truck, grabbing some things before slamming the door and beeping the locks as I stand there, confused.

"I'll drive," he says as he takes my keys out of my hand, opens the passenger seat, and helps me in. The whole time I'm wondering what the hell I got myself into.

———

The first place we stop is the quiet end of the boardwalk on Ocean Ave, winding along the beachfront.

"What are we—"

"Beach or lake?" he asks, but it's less a question, more a statement.

"What?"

"When I asked you, you said beach." I squint at him, trying to understand. A couple with a stroller walks past, the wheels thumping the boards as a little girl with pigtails runs past. Seagulls caw in the background, though less than you'd see in June or July with the cold January air taking over.

And then I remember.

I'd just asked him who his biggest influence as a kid was (his dad, which was sweet but also predictable and safe), and he asked me...

"Beach or lake?" There's one of each nearby, the beach and boardwalk on one side of town and a small lake two towns over.

And I'd told him the beach because lakes creep me out with their murky waters and gooey bottoms.

"I'm not going in the water," I say instantly, thinking of those polar bear plunges they do for charity around this time of year. He throws his head back with a laugh.

"No, sweetheart. We're going for a walk." Leaning over, he presses the button on my seatbelt, grabbing my drink and snack before walking around the hood to open my door. "Come on." I obey, taking his offered hand and walking up the steps to the boardwalk. It's nice, quiet without the summer crowds.

"I should do this more."

"I try to come once a week."

"To run?" He laughs again.

"Just to walk. Take it in."

"I don't know if I could do that. I'd get... bored."

"You need to slow down. Take in the world around you. You need to stop rushing through everything, stop worrying about what's coming next, what's going to happen." I glance over at him, wondering if he has been talking to Gabi.

"Have you been talking to my assistant?" Another laugh.

"No, but it's nice to know it's not just me who sees it."

"I'm not... rushing. Or stressing."

"Bullshit. Everything you do is carefully crafted so you know the outcome." I stop walking, and he looks back at me, hand in mine.

"That's not true."

"You keep telling yourself that." His smile is genuine, not angry or demeaning, and it's that honesty that makes me think. Do I do that? Instead of answering myself, I walk again, but I'm stuck in my head now, wondering... wondering how this man can read me so well.

"Where did you go as a kid for vacations?"

"My dad was usually traveling for work." I laugh, realizing now he was probably vacationing with his mistress, playing it off like he was doing good for the family. "We didn't have a ton of money, but my mom and I would take day trips to the beach. She'd rent a room facing the water for a night, even though it was only a five-minute drive. She had contacts at the hotels, so she'd take it for cheap if there was a last-minute cancellation. We'd pretend we were on some fancy vacation and spend the day on the boardwalk. It was fun." I look up at him, the ocean breeze whipping his short, messy hair about. "What about you?"

"It changed. We all got to choose, rotating. My sisters always chose somewhere new and exciting. I always went to the beach.

Wildwood or Ocean City, Maryland. Beach, rides, boardwalk games, junk food. We'd spend days getting fried on the beach, then nights wasting money on games we'd never win and rides that probably should have gotten us killed. Living on fried food and zero nutrition."

"So basically, you went here, but just in a different city?" I ask with a laugh, bumping my hip into his. He laughs.

"Yeah, but more... family-friendly. Less city and grown-ups, more fun and games. One year, my dad got me surf lessons. Can't do that here." He tips his chin to the rocky cove, definitely not safe for surfing.

"Do you still know how?"

"Yeah. Chris and I go sometimes. When we were kids, we'd go in the cold, in winter. Great waves, then. But now we just go when it's warm and fuck around."

"I always wanted to learn."

"I'll teach you one day," he says, and my mind flashes to bare, tan skin, water, and a surfboard. It sends a shiver down my spine that has nothing to do with the weather, but he notices all the same. "You're cold. Let's go to our next stop." And I let him lead the way, never cluing him into the true source of my chill.

SIXTEEN

-Cassie-

THAT'S HOW THE ENTIRE DATE GOES. BY THE TIME WE GO TO THE little cafe I love, we've had my favorite appetizer (mozzarella sticks from the greasy corner pizza shop) and chips and margaritas from Tia Maria's. After that, we stopped at Luigi's for cannoli cupcakes (Luke agreed they are to die for) and stopped at the Tavern for burgers and fries.

All places he asked me about on our first date or in conversations since.

"So, did you know on the first date this was your plan?" I ask, stirring my latte with the tiny spoon.

"What?"

"When you asked me all of those questions. Did you know you were going to do this on your date?"

"No."

"No?"

"Nope. I just asked the important questions."

"Favorite foods aren't the important questions, Luke."

"Sure they are. I'd argue the *most* important questions. The quality of someone's favorite foods tells a lot about them."

"I guess. So what about me? Did I pass the test?"

"Mostly. A burger in a lettuce wrap? That puts you on my' potential serial killer' list," he says with a smile.

I choke on my drink with a laugh. "Shit!" I say as the warm liquid spills down my top, dripping down my cleavage and soaking my dress.

"Shit, Cass, I'm sorry." He leans over, grabbing napkins from the dispenser on the table as I watch a brown stain spread from the center of my dress like I've been shot. Except this is caramel latte instead of a searing gunshot wound. "Here, let me—" He grabs a stack of nearby napkins and starts dabbing at the stain just below my boobs before stuffing a few between my cleavage. I'm frozen, and his hand pauses once he realizes what he's doing, looking at my face with a slight look of shame.

"I swear I didn't plan this." Neither of us is moving, and just now, I realize how close our faces are, mere centimeters apart.

"I know," I say, the words a breath of air across his lips. His eyes glance down, taking in my lips that are parted, my chest rising with each breath. But then he backs up, giving me space, time to contemplate what I'm thinking, why I'm feeling this way. "Does our... does our date end here?" I ask, looking at the stain, and I'm not really sure what I'm asking. It's nearly five, and we've well exceeded my four-hour limit. Again. So many rules, completely shattered by this man. But why does the idea of this last date ending make my stomach churn?

"No. Not even close," he says the words with a surety I can't pinpoint, once again the meaning so multifaceted.

"Let's go to my place. I need to change." With a spark in his eyes and a smile on my lips, we're off. Once again, his rough hand twines with mine, fitting perfectly.

———

"So should I stay out here or..." We're standing outside the apartment, the moment bringing back memories from the last time and sending a shiver down my spine, ending suspiciously in my core. Looking him up and down, I shake my head.

"No, you can come in. The hall is freezing. Just hang out in the living room."

"Do you want to text your assistant?" he asks as I open the door, an arm out to usher him in.

"What?"

"Your assistant. Do you want to text her? Tell her I'm coming in for a moment?"

"Why would I do that?" I stare at him in confusion. Why would I tell Gabi he's here?

"For your safety, sweetheart. A strange man, a date in your apartment? Even for just a moment, that's a risk." I stare at him, floored by the thought he would think about that when I didn't. I should. I usually do, never taking risks that could put me in any kind of danger. The risks any woman dating men knows are always present. But with Luke, it's just... not on my radar. Still, I nod and type out a text.

Cassie: Gabi—I got something on my dress. Luke is coming in while I change.

Before I even close the door behind Luke and me, my phone vibrates in my hand.

Gabrielle: WHAT?

Gabrielle: WHAAAT?

Gabrielle: IN YOUR APARTMENT?

Gabrielle: YOU'RE STILL ON THE DATE?

Gabrielle: HELLO, I NEED DETAILS.

"Everything okay?" he asks, tipping his chin to my phone.

"Uh... I uh... yeah. You can sit in the kitchen; I'm going to... get changed." He smiles at me, that dimple making my belly quake as he walks into my kitchen.

Cassie: Gabi, stop. You're going to make him think I'm crazy.

Gabrielle: You are crazy!
Gabrielle: I need details.
Gabrielle: Has he kissed you again?
Gabrielle: Please tell me he kissed you again.
Cassie: What?!?

I close the door to my bedroom behind me right as my phone rings in my hand. *Gabrielle calling.* Jesus, this girl.

"Gabi, what?"

"What? Are you kidding me?! I need details!" she shouts in my ear.

"Shut up! You need to be quiet!" I whisper yell into my phone as I sit on my bed.

"Cassie, I need details."

"About what? He's a potential match. We are on a date."

"It's been seven hours, Cassie." Shit, she's right.

"It's been... enjoyable."

"What are you doing?"

"He taught me to change a tire." Silence. I stand and walk to my closet, my new flat boots clunking on the floor. The sound is unfamiliar, contrasting with my heels as I decide what to change into. Nothing seems right.

I try not to overthink how I'm so concerned about what to wear.

"Gabi?" I pull the phone from my face to check she's still on the line.

"He taught you to change your tire?" She's going to read into this.

"That first day in a panic, I mentioned it was something I keep meaning to learn. So he... taught me. So I wouldn't be caught unaware again."

"The man taught you to change your tire for your safety."

"I guess." I move hangers to find my favorite pair of jeans, the ones that hug me perfectly in all the right places, once again trying not to think about why I want to wear a pair of jeans that hug me perfectly.

"Then what?"

"Then we... went to a few places."

"Where, Cass?" She knows. She knows it was more. Because now *I* know it was more. This wasn't my normal second date, a typical second date where I'll go home after and write up some notes and match him with a woman in my file. I know now when the time comes, the decision will gut me. All the 'what ifs' will fly through my mind.

What if it were me?

What if I were brave?

What if he were mine?

No, no, no.

No man is worth that kind of stress, that kind of drama. Trauma.

"Cass?"

"Feds. For mozzarella sticks." She's silent. "And then Tia Maria's for strawberry mango margaritas. And then we drove to the other side of town to get those fries I love. I'm so going to need a trip to the gym after this."

"The ones with the parmesan and truffle oil?" I'd taken her there once.

"Yes."

"And then?"

"Dumplings."

"Let me guess, at Chao's." I stay silent. "What did you spill on your shirt?" She has to know.

"A salted—"

"A salted caramel latte." Silence again. "Cassie." This time her voice is soft. I might not have let her in much, but she orders my food enough, knows my likes and dislikes enough to know my favorites. To understand what it means for this man to do this, plan this.

"Yeah."

"I'm not going to push—"

"Then don't, Gabi."

"But I think... I think maybe he likes you, Cassie." I don't reply, instead ignoring her as I flick through my tops, landing on a pretty blush-colored one. "I know you don't date because of what you told me the other day, with your dad. It's valid. Totally. But also... you're missing out on so much."

"How's your relationship?"

"What relationship?"

"Exactly."

"You keep an open mind on this, and I'll tell you what's holding me back. I'll let you set me up." I stop, then once again pull my phone back to see who I'm talking to.

"Gabi, I can't—"

"No pressure. But when you come in Monday, I get all the details, regardless. And if it's what I hope for, then we'll get drinks after work and I'll fill you in." My psychology degree is itching to learn more about my friendly, bubbly assistant who has become a close friend seemingly overnight. To find out why she never has plans, why she loves the idea of romance and love but is single herself. I don't answer, though, contemplating why I'm even considering her proposal. He's a match. Just not for me.

"I'll talk to you Monday, Cassie. Just... keep it in mind." With that, she hangs up, and I'm left wondering what on earth I'm going to do.

But I don't have long to worry about that, because when I sit on my bed to unzip my boot, it's stuck.

I tug at it for long minutes, working up a sweat and panicking.

I knew flat boots were a bad idea.

Now I'll be stuck in these forever, stuck in this stained sweater dress forever because I won't be able to take them off. Or maybe I'll have to go to the hospital and have them cut off. Or perhaps I'll have lost all circulation to my leg because I'm incessantly tugging at them and I'll have to get my leg removed because that's the next step, right? Leg amputation?

And then forever, I'll be reminded of the one time I let my guard down and wore flat shoes for a man and thought about maybe, just maybe...

No.

I need to calm down.

My anxiety is getting the better of me.

I stop, taking a deep, deep breath and thinking about my options.

Option one: choose a different dress and head out.

But that would mean I'd still need to take these boots off later.

Option two: cut them off myself. Except, the only scissors I have are from the knife set I got when I moved into my own apartment ten years ago and are so dull they can't even open those annoying plastic security boxes. They'd break for sure. Then I'd have to buy a new pair, and I'd be out the way too high cost of these boots and a new pair of scissors. And really, how often will I use the scissors? I have a pair at the office I could use. They were kitchen shears, too, I think— what's the actual point of kitchen shears? What are you supposed to shear? Is it for food? I'm not—

Focus, Cassie.

Why is it every time I have a mini-crisis, my mind goes off on weird tangents on the most random topics? Like kitchen scissors.

Except, I know option three is the only responsible and reasonable option, so I'm avoiding thinking about it.

Because option three: go out into the kitchen and ask Luke to unzip my boot.

The thought sends a traitorous shiver down my spine.

I blame Gabi for putting the thought that I could be selfish in my mind.

Still, it's the only one that makes sense. So I straighten my shoulders, open my door, and head into the kitchen, where I catch Luke staring at the wedding invite for my father's wedding with a confused look on his face. He looks at me, still dressed in the same stained outfit, the confusion deepening.

"My boot is stuck."

"What?"

"My boot. The zipper. The dumb flat shoes you made me wear."

He smiles with recognition. "My heels would never betray me like this."

"If you changed a tire in heels, you'd fall on your ass." I roll my eyes.

"Can you help me?"

"Yeah, come here, sweetheart," he says and gestures for me to put a foot on the chair he was just sitting on. I do as he asks but wobble, losing my footing and nearly falling.

Great. Now I'm stuck in these boots, in a stained dress, and he's going to watch me fall on my ass. My luck, he'll see my panties as I fall. Kill me now.

Except I don't fall. Instead, a thick arm goes around me, catching me and pulling me into Luke's muscular chest.

"Woah, careful there." Looking down at me, his eyes are soft and sweet, but something blazes behind them. "You good?" I nod, the words no longer working in my brain or on my lips. "Where's the zip?" he asks, taking one small step back once he deems me to be stable once more.

But I'm fooling him because I'm not stable at all. Slowly, my entire world is falling apart, tipping upside down as each of my rules gets shattered, as each of my carefully placed dominos tip over with just one look from this man.

Still, I point to the back of my leg where the first of the zippers is. His fingers go there, rough, warm fingers brushing my bare skin on the back of my thigh, and my heart stops, breath hitching audibly. He looks from his hands to my eyes with a slight smirk playing on his lips.

"You good?" I nod, still incapable of words. One simple brush of his fingers on delicate skin and I can't talk. Can't think. Can't move. He smiles wide at my inability before looking back at the zip, trying to tug it down. Internally, I pray it moves easily, hoping it's just the weird angle that makes it impossible to do it alone.

Of course, that's not my kind of luck.

"Damn, you really got it stuck," he says, getting his head closer to the zipper to inspect it. His other hand moves to the front of my thigh, cupping it as a counterbalance as he tries to tug harder. I almost lose my footing again and think about how maybe I should have gone with one of the other options. Maybe added an option four where I told him to leave and just died a slow, embarrassing death in these stupid boots. It would give him a fun story to tell at bars, the matchmaker he kissed once and who utterly lost her mind after, then died alone in her room.

God, why is my brain like this?

"Hold my shoulder to keep you steady," he says, looking up at me once more. I do as he asks and urge the words to come.

"I'm so sorry. This is so embarrassing. And unprofessional. You're here to be matched—"

"I'm not. You know it." *No, I don't. That's what he's here for, to be matched. That's what he has to be here for,* I tell myself.

"Luke, I—"

"So whose wedding is that for?" He changes the subject so swiftly that it wouldn't be noticeable if it weren't part of my job to keep track of men avoiding topics.

Still, I take the lifeline for what it is and sigh before answering. "My dad's."

"You don't sound too happy about that." He grunts the words a bit as he tries to tug at the zipper, moving it this way and that.

"I'm... indifferent about it. It's his third."

"His third?"

"Yeah. And she's like, two years older than I am." He stops his ministrations and looks up at me with a raised eyebrow. "Yeah," I say, answering the unspoken question.

"That doesn't bother you?" I sigh. It should. But...

"Not anymore. I don't expect much more from him." His eyes still on mine. He's clearly trying to read into my words, but I don't let him. "I'm more annoyed about having to *go* to the wedding."

"A Valentine's Day wedding, right?"

"Yes. As cliche as it gets."

"You don't want to go?"

"Eh. Not really. My mom never got over him, so going to these things always ends... poorly for her. She'll be calling me the whole time, asking questions."

"But what about you? Will family be there? Cousins? Uncles? Aunts?" I laugh bitterly.

"None that I want to see."

"Why not?"

"My dad's side of the family... they come from money. And know it. It's kind of a long story, but I didn't know them for most of my life. And they're not a fan of my mom because she doesn't have the same pedigree, which makes me some kind of mutt in their eyes." My eyes are locked on the splash of tomato sauce on the backsplash above the stove I forgot to clean up. I don't even remember the last time I made a meal in this kitchen.

"That's stupid. You're not a dog."

"Yeah, well. Lifestyles of the rich and the famous, you know?" Except then I remember *he* comes from money, and I bite my tongue. "Shit, I didn't mean..." but he cuts me off with a laugh.

"Totally get it. My parents worked hard to shield us from that. Make sure we didn't grow up to be 'spoiled little shits,' as my dad says."

"Good for him."

"So what don't they like about you?" His head goes back down to working on the zipper.

"Mostly how I'm not from money. I add nothing to the family name, you know?" He shakes his head, but his eyes not meeting mine gives me the freedom to keep talking. "I'm not as fancy, didn't go to the etiquette classes and cotillion. Plus, I'm not skinny." His head pops up, eyes wide and about to argue. "I'm not fat, but they're all skin and bones. Their lives revolve around looking good for their husbands, perfect socialite housewives. I look like my mom, curves and all. I don't fit it." Once more, he shakes his head and goes back to work. It seems like it's working, the zipper slowly creeping down. "And I'm too old." The words fly out as the zipper goes down, his hand following, grazing down the entirety of my leg. Goosebumps cover my body.

"What?" he says with a laugh, but I'm caught up in what's happening. One hand on my inner thigh, rough calluses scraping some of my most sensitive skin, while the other runs down the back to get the shoe off. Bare skin on bare skin. "You're not even thirty."

"Basically ancient in their eyes," I say, but my voice is a whisper, and with the timbre of my words, his pupils flare. "I should have a man by now. I should be at least engaged, if not married. Maybe on my second husband. I should be social climbing instead of business building. I'm dreading it because showing up without a man on my arm will be another chance for them to tear me down." He nods and moves my legs, switching my bare one for the booted one, and begins working on the zipper.

"Got it. So why *don't* you have a man on your arm?" I laugh, but my mind is still hazy from that touch, that look.

"I study men for a living."

"Got that."

"So I see the worst of them. Hell, look at my father and his brothers. My grandfather." He nods as if he's saying that's valid.

"But you also find the good ones, right?"

"I match the ones who suck the least." The big belly laugh comes, the sound sending a thrill down my spine and warmth to my belly. I could listen to it all day.

"Are we all that bad?" he asks as he gets the second zipper down, easier this time, but the movement makes me sway. His hand goes to my hip to steady me as the other removes the boot. Is it in my head or does his hand touch even more bare flesh this time, grazing more intentionally?

It's confirmed when as he stands, hand still on my hip, the other hand skimming all the way up my bare leg, just barely dipping underneath the hem of my sweater dress. Then he's standing in front of me, one hand on my hip, one on my neck, underneath my hair, his nose just shy of mine, his breaths mingling with my own. It should scare me, knowing I'm this close to a man, knowing that he's already kissed me once before and might again.

That I could so easily picture myself giving this man it all and not walking away from the wreckage he'd leave in one piece.

But then his eyes soften, his lips brushing mine as he asks once more, "Am *I* that bad?"

I should answer yes.

Yes, he's that bad.

Or, no, he's worse.

He's worse because I can't find that flaw. I can't find the one thing that would turn off this attraction to him. I can't find a single reason to push him away, protect myself, and ask him to leave. The one reason to put him in my files and set him up with someone else. To walk away and never see him again until it's in a wedding announcement sent to the office.

Instead, I just say, "No." It comes out in the breathiest voice, nearly silent, but when I answer, his breath hitches sharply, his pupils blowing out before burning with fire, and then it happens. His hand presses on my neck, bringing my lips to his, and he kisses me.

It's not like the last time, soft and sweet.

I mean, it is. I'm sure everything about Lucas Dawson is tinged in sweetness. But... this is rough. And needy. His mouth crushes to mine, the hand on my neck going up into my hair and tugging slightly, the hand on my hip pulling me closer to him until I can feel he's enjoying this kiss just as much as I am. When I press my body further into his, into his hardness, he groans, the sound reverberating through my entire body, making the hairs on my bare legs raise, and my inner sex fiend wakes up before clapping and cheering. The uptight librarian, who might talk some sense into me, is missing, probably locked in a closet by the sex fiend.

But that's why, when Luke lifts me, forcing my legs around his waist and my center to right where his cock is, I grind down, loving the thrill that runs through me and the groan I pull from him again.

"Shit, Cass. Bedroom?" I stare at him for long moments. "You say no and this ends. You say no, I'm out that door, and you won't have to deal with me again. But you say yes, and I'm carrying you to your room and fucking you until you don't have any headspace left to over-think how fuckin' good this is between us."

And maybe it's the stress of getting my boot off or the emotions close to the surface from talking about my dad or the feel of him beneath me. Maybe it's realizing I've been lonely for years and shut-ting myself off. Or maybe it's just *Luke* being *Luke*.

But no matter the reason, I nod, giving him the permission he needs. His lips press to mine hard, like he's sharing the gratitude before he breaks the kiss, carrying me to my room.

Once there, he tosses me onto the bed, and I can't help but let out a small giggle as I bounce. He follows me onto the bed, caging me in with his arms with a playful smile on his face. For a moment, a quick moment, I instantly hide away in the recesses of my mind, wondering if we keep this up, and it doesn't end, would it always be like this? If he'd always be playful, always trying to make me laugh.

But I throw the thought away quickly.

Especially when a rough hand, callused with hard, manual labor, reaches down to my knee, slowly creeping in and up, feather-light on my soft skin. Up, up, the hand trails, my breath catching with each millimeter he goes as I wonder where he'll go next, where he'll stop. His thumb dips over, grazing the very edge of my panties where they crease into my hip before continuing up, up, dragging my dress with it. Over the waistband of my panties, where he tugs them to the side and snaps them back. My pulse jumps with the move, my clit pushing with the sudden assault to my senses. His smile grows before his eyes go back down between us to watch the hand hidden under my tight cream sweater dress. Eyes going to the expanse of skin he's meticulously revealing.

The thumb hits the lacy strap of my bra, dipping under the band then moving to the under wire, softly grazing the underside of my breast. I hold my breath, anticipating... more. More of his hands on me, my back arching slightly to tell him my needs, my wants, but he just chuckles lightly before moving the hand again, leaving and moving towards my arm until he's helping me pull the fabric down my arm, over my head, and the dress off my body.

And then I'm lying on my bed in a matching pair of purple, lacy panties and bra, displayed before him for his judgment or adoration.

"You're the most beautiful woman I've ever seen," he says, eyes on me, and it could be a line, but the sincerity in his eyes tells me it's not. The best part about this man is his honesty, his clear eyes that reflect his true feelings without shame. His eyes rove down my body, taking me in, and each inch his eyes touch, inches that I've battled with hating and loving and accepting and trying to change, my body goes up in flames. Flames of need and want and desire lap at my skin. Because that's it—I *need* this man. The shock of the realization hits me so hard, and it's all I can do not to jump him and take over. But a hand goes up to the strap of my bra to take it off.

"Uh-uh," Luke says, shaking his head with a smile before gently removing my hand and moving it to my side. "That's my job."

"Then do it," I say, eager to go.

"Patience, you greedy girl." The words make my pussy throb and wet gather there.

"Luke," I say with a whine, the sound foreign to my ears, but then his thumbs are on my shoulders, gently pushing the straps of my bra down, and I'm holding my breath.

"Be patient," he whispers across my lips before his are on me, kissing again. His tongue enters my mouth, teasing and dancing with mine, and the taste of him has me groaning and lifting my hips, desperate for some kind of friction. Desperate for him. But before I can reach anything, his mouth is trailing down my neck, licking and sucking and nipping as he goes. A hand goes behind my back, unlatching the bra before removing it and tossing it into the growing pile of clothes on the floor. When he steps back once more to take me in as I lie on the bed before him, I let out another frustrated whine, a mix of a cry and a moan. But the fiery look in his eyes... stops any anger in its tracks.

"Jesus, you're fucking perfect."

"Luke, honey, I need you." My hips are moving, desperate, and I'm feeling crazy because I'm so turned on, already on the edge, but he's barely touched me. It's like his looks, his words alone are taking me closer.

"I know, don't worry. I'll take care of you." His mouth comes to mine, giving me an almost chaste kiss compared to the burning one before slowing moving down my neck again, stopping at my breasts. His tongue goes out, licking the nipple of one breast before blowing, and the shock of warmth and then cold has me moaning and arching my back as he chuckles before moving to the next side to repeat the process. As he does, one hand goes to the already wet nipple, pinching and pulling. Each tug is like a string to my pussy, cranking my pleasure and excitement, wetness pooling. Then, right when I'm about to argue, as my hands are under his shirt to remove it, he descends. That's when I start to panic.

"Luke, I don't—"

"Nothing is going to stop me from tasting you," he says, the growl in his voice causing me to clench again as his tongue circles my belly button.

"I've never... no one has ever..." His head pops up with confusion.

"Are you telling me no one has ever eaten your pussy, Cassie?" I can feel the blush burning my face, shame for being so inexperienced.

"I'm not... I mean... I've... been with—"

"Don't want to hear about that right now, sweetheart."

"It's just... no one has ever... and I know that it's not..." I trail off, embarrassed I brought this up. I expect him to agree or argue, *some- thing* to tell me where his mind is at, but a small smile plays on his lips before he licks them—yes, he *licks his lips!*—and continues down, stopping his trail of kisses right at the top of my panty line.

"So I'm going to be the first man to taste this?" A finger trails the lacy edge along my thigh, just barely grazing my wet, and we both moan at the feel. "Answer me." The order is soft, not angry, just a gentle reminder keeping his words in the forefront.

"Yes." The admission is shy and quiet, but I'm not sure why—I'm lying here mostly naked, squirming, and already on the edge of coming.

"I really fuckin' love the idea of that." He's bending down between my legs now, hot breath fanning the insides of my thighs. Then his mouth is over my panties, right on top of my clit, hot breath and a firm tongue going at me as if there's nothing between us. My back arches off the bed, but a thick hand presses on my belly, keeping me in place as he switches off, sucking and blowing the wet fabric, creating a torturous variation in temperature and feeling. My hands trail down my sides, hooking my thumbs into the waistband and trying to tug the fabric down so he can have better access.

"These stay on for now."

"Luke, no, please. I need...." But his wicked face comes up, and he smiles at me, heat and fire in his eyes.

"No. You're mine right now. You follow my rules."

"Please, I need *more*."

"I'm takin' my time with you." But when he goes back down to my pussy, he hooks a thumb into the gusset of the underwear, pulling them to the side and placing his mouth on the exposed wet flesh.

And I scream.

I scream so loud as his tongue enters me, fucking me gently while I'm still wearing those lacy underwear, the wet cotton brushing my clit. I wonder for a split second if my neighbors are going to call the cops. But then the world melts away, and all there is is this man eating me with such enthusiasm and vigor, the groans of excitement and satisfaction he's making traveling up and straight to my clit.

His face pulls back, a gleam of wet on his chin, and he smiles at me as I mewl in protest. "Fucking delicious, baby. Nothin' better than this pussy." He trails a finger up my thigh to play in my wet, entering me once before circling my clit.

"Luke, please, please, Luke," It's a chant on my lips, my eyes hazy as I look at him through slitted lids and speak through panted breaths.

"What do you need, Cass?" His thick finger is in me, pumping slowly as he watches me, looking for an answer. "God, you're fuckin' tight."

"You, I need you."

"What do you *need*, Cassie?" I'm frustrated now, yelping as he crooks that single finger in a tease. I'm on edge, so close to finding it, so close to coming apart.

"I need you, Luke!"

"Use your words, sweetheart. Tell me exactly what this greedy cunt wants." His words make me spasm, something he feels if the smirk is any indication. I have two options here—continue to beg or ask for what I want. What I need.

"I want you to lick me until I come." It's a whine. He leans forward to kiss me, his eyes locked to me as he speaks, breath brushing my own, voice low.

"Where?" This is out of my comfort zone, so far from anything I've ever done or experienced, but every moment of it feels natural.

"I want you to lick my pussy until I come on your face, Luke. Please." His smile is all the vindication I need to ignore any flutter of embarrassment before he speaks.

"Good girl," he says, his voice low and quiet, but then his hands are tugging my panties down, tossing them aside, and he's throwing my legs over his head as he devours me. His mouth is everywhere, tongue inside me, then sucking my clit, then back inside my opening. I'm so, so close, but I need...

"Your fingers!" I shout because I'm *so close*, and if he would just...

"Good job asking for what you want," he says, and then two thick fingers are inside me, pressing up to curl on my G-spot as he sucks my clit hard, and I come apart. As I come, he puts one hand under my ass, pulling my pussy closer to his face as he continues to devour me, as if I haven't just come, as if I'm not living through the most intense orgasm of my life. My body continues to quake, to twitch with each pass of his tongue. Soon I'm crawling out of my skin, already stretching towards another orgasm.

And then he stops.

And backs up.

And I'm about to whine, about to moan about him building back up without release, but then I see his eyes, full of fire and blazing with need.

It's then he undresses, quickly, revealing hard pecs and a light dusting of hair, a stomach that's toned but not frighteningly so. Like an actual human who enjoys his life. Then those hands, still wet with me, go to the button of his pants, shucking them with his underwear until his thick cock bobs out.

I lick my lips, watching the movement, and despite the need coursing through me, coming off him in waves, he laughs.

"See anything you like?" I just nod, my mind still, so lust saturated, I'm unable to string words together. He smiles again before reaching down to his pants, grabbing his wallet, and pulling out a condom. Then, right when I think he might tear it open, roll it on, and pound into me, he hands me the foil packet. I stare at him with confusion.

"You do it. Roll it on, sweetheart, then put my cock in you." Something about his words has me needing him almost more than before, despite the orgasm, so I do as he asks, scooting up the bed so there's more room. With him following me, in front of me on his knees, his cock bobbing, I lean forward to roll on the unwrapped condom.

I can't resist.

My tongue comes out, licking him from base to tip, my eyes on him the whole time before his hand goes to my hair.

"Do that again, I'm coming in your mouth." His eyes are wild, and for a moment, I contemplate it, contemplate sucking him until he comes down my throat. Contemplate feeling that power, the power to wreck him the way he destroyed me just minutes ago, but my throbbing pussy revolts. He sees the battle, though. "Another time. Roll it on, Cass." And then I do, pinching the top of the latex and rolling it down until it hits the bottom, giving him a tight squeeze to tell him I'm finished with a smile.

But he's done with games. His hands push on my shoulders until I'm lying back on the bed, my back to the fluffy duvet I love. Then, he's moving so my legs are over his shoulders, framing his face with my ankles.

I move a hand between us, remembering his order before stroking the head of his sheathed cock in my wet.

"Jesus, fuck, you're fucking dripping for me. This mine, Cass? This cunt mine?" His eyes are dark with need and possession. I nod, then, with a groan, he slams into me, filling me completely.

And it's *everything.*

Perfection.

Nothing has ever felt as right as this man in me right now.

"This greedy cunt." He growls the words as he watches himself disappear into me, each pump hitting that spot inside me no one has ever found, each graze taking my breath away and making it build again. "Is your cunt greedy for my cock, Cass?" He's gone, lost in the feeling of us too, and it's like he knows how perfect this is, and it has him absolutely wild.

"Yes, honey, yes."

"God, I've been fuckin' dreamin' of this since I saw you. Better than I ever fuckin' thought; your pussy is so fuckin' tight." He leans in further, bending my body like a skilled contortionist while still pumping into me, and I've never been more thankful that my New Year's resolution last year was to start yoga. As he bends, the thrusts get deeper, hitting the ache in my belly squarely each time until my head is thrashing from side to side. Until I'm on the brink.

"Fuck yeah, you like that? You like when I'm deep inside of you?" I mumble some nonsense, the pleasure overtaking my body, removing my ability to speak coherently. "You gonna come on my cock, baby?" I nod, knowing it's close, knowing it's going to be huge, fearing *how fucking big* this is going to be. A single drop of sweat drips from his nose to my breast, and without thinking, I take it and rub it into my skin, over my nipple, pinching tight to amplify the feelings. He growls, a feral sound in my ear, before he orders me, "Come for me

SEVENTEEN

-Cassie-

"WHAT PART OF YOUR MASTER PLAN IS THIS?" I ASK AS I SIT ON the rug on my living room floor, folding a slice of sausage and pepper pizza from my favorite delivery place down the road. I'm dressed in sweats and a matching cropped tank now, my hair pulled up into a messy bun on top of my head.

"Favorite takeout and 80s movie." I smile at him as he glances at me. He used my TV to access his account and upload *Sixteen Candles* (the best of the Molly Ringwald, Brat Pack days) when I told him it was my favorite. There was quite a long argument about watching a John Hughes movie with a man, but it seems he's really sticking to his 'Cassie's favorites' date.

"Ah, of course. Was this part of the plan all along?"

"If I say yes, I'm an asshole. So no, but I'd be lying if in some fantasy, I didn't daydream this is how it would end." His boyish smile both puts me at ease and makes me want to jump his bones, which is so far from my usual MO. So how is this one man changing my mind up so much, breaking all of my rules?

"I'm going to need to spend a week at the gym after today," I say as I snag a garlic knot off the tin foil it came in, dunking the buttery garlic masterpiece into the tomato sauce. "Totally worth it."

"Just gonna add to that fuckin' fantastic ass of yours." I roll my eyes, resisting the urge to argue. "But if you want, I'll make sure you burn off those calories a different way," he says as he waggles his eyebrows at me like some cheesy old movie. We never ended up doing whatever he'd planned for the rest of the night. Instead, I changed into comfy clothes while he ordered delivery and set up the movie. I thought I'd feel uncomfortable, leaving my armor of designer clothes and perfectly made-up hair behind in exchange for sweats and pizza, but I don't. I couldn't tell you if it's because of what just happened a few hours ago or because of something more profound I refuse to touch on.

"You're a pig," I say with a laugh as I wipe my greasy fingers on the tissue paper-thin napkins they sent before tossing it at him. His arm goes around my shoulders with a laugh before pulling me into him, pressing his forehead to mine. His huge, white smile beams at me, the dimple clear on his smiling cheek.

"I'm joking, sweetheart. May have been dreaming about tonight since I pulled over and saw you on the side of the road, but I had no expectations for this. No idea where it would go." He presses a sweet kiss on my forehead before returning to his pizza. The movie is past the midpoint, with Andie watching her sister get married, bringing my mind back to my father's wedding with dread. Luke seems to think the same.

"So your dad's wedding—you're going alone?" I sigh.

"I guess. I fucked up and RSVP'd with a plus one in a moment of weakness because I'm tired of dealing with their shit. But I'll go alone if I go at all."

"You'd skip it?"

"I shouldn't. But I want to," I say, picking at the crust of my pizza.

"I'll go with you." Looking up, I see him staring at me with a severe look, not a joking smile.

"You can't... I can't...."

"Why not?" *Because I can't spend more time with you. Because I can't get attached, can't get involved with you. Because this is not the plan and I live by my plans. When you deviate from a plan, that's when you get hurt.* But I don't say any of that. I can't let him know all of that.

"Because this is our second date," I say the words quietly. I don't want to face that reality.

I go on two dates. Two dates, then I match them. And this, although entirely out of my norm, is our second date. So this is where it ends.

"So?" He looks so adorably confused.

"So after this, I match you."

"This isn't that."

"Isn't it? I met you because your sisters are concerned about you being single. You told me that."

"So I don't get another date after this?"

"I... I can't, Luke. It's not what I do. I don't date. And you... you deserve the total package." He stares at me, contemplating what I said. Each moment is filled with dread. I want him to accept. I want him to nod, finish his pizza, leave, and accept his next date. Even though what just happened was equal parts magical and the most erotic experience of my life, part of me wants him to prove me right. To be like the other men and take what I'll give and not demand more. But the other part...

"What if I'm not okay with that?" The other part of me wanted him to say that. To ask for more, more than I can give him. More than my shields will let him take.

"That's not how this works, Luke."

"Why not?"

"Because... it's not."

"But you'd don't normally do... this, right?" For a moment, he looks panicked, and the look is kind of endearing.

"No, I don't do this." I laugh as relief covers his face.

"Got it, so you're mine. I'm taking you to your dad's wedding."

"I can't—"

"Give me this, sweetheart. Give me this. Give me the third date." I look at him, struggling to say no. Struggling to say this is it, it ends today. "And give me the time in between. Two weeks? Give me that."

"What?" I see the gears moving in his mind like he's formulating a plan.

"Yeah, two weeks. You and me. We're together, and then we have the third date. Then... then we'll see."

"Then I'll set you up."

"Then we'll see."

"Luke..."

"Sweetheart, give me two weeks."

Staring at him, looking in those green eyes that hold nothing but honesty and loyalty and a look that tells me he wants to treasure me... I make the biggest leap I've ever made.

I say yes.

EIGHTEEN

-Cassie-

"So, how does this work?" I ask over bagels, suddenly shy. After our morning activities, Luke ran down the street for one last favorite—everything bagels and cream cheese—while I brewed us up some coffee and quickly rinsed off. Now we're sitting on my couch eating, which, in itself, is a shock. I only ever eat at my kitchen table, a rule I broke for the first time since moving here with Gabi last week, but now it seems to have become the norm.

But if you'd have told my obsessive self last month I'd be eating everything bagels, with their plethora of seeds and seasonings and crumbs on my unbearably expensive designer couch, I'd have sent you to a mental hospital.

Yet here I sit, makeup free in leggings and a tee shirt, eating my bagel next to my date the morning after.

"How does what work?" He's smiling at me like he knows what I'm asking but wants me to say it out loud. He seems to do this a lot, push my boundaries and make me open up.

"This... third date thing."

"We're dating."

"What does that mean?" He stares at me, part confused, part delighted by the conversation.

"You don't know what dating means? Aren't you a matchmaker?" I roll my eyes in response.

"I know what dating is, but this is... unconventional. We're temporary. Just until the wedding."

"You can think that." I ignore him.

"So, for the next two weeks, how does this work? Am I a booty call? Do we like... do things?" My fingers tear at the napkin as I ask, trying to avoid his eyes. Why am I so embarrassed by this? He's right —I set people up for a living. This should be easy for me.

But it's not.

Nothing with this man goes as I expect it to go. Everything about him is confusing to me. A finger goes under my chin, and when my eyes meet his, there's frustration, anger in them.

"You are not a booty call."

"So we're not... going to... do this..." — my hands flit between us — "again?" Why am I disappointed I'm not sleeping with a match again? But he smiles, the full 'Cassie's being goofy' smile with the dimple before his thumb moves to brush the corner of my mouth.

"Oh, we're most definitely doing that again."

"So I'm a booty call."

"You call yourself that again, I'm gonna get pissed. You're not a booty call. This is you giving me a shot."

"Luke..."

"Call it what you want. But for two weeks, you're mine." His eyes hide nothing as they lock on mine, and he has to know, has to understand this can't... it can't be.

"Luke, we can't—"

"We'll worry about two weeks from now, two weeks from now. But, for now, live in today with me, yeah?" It's the dimple that gets me, his sweet smile and the dimple and the green eyes which tell me everything a woman wants to hear. And the uptight librarian is yelling at me, shouting at me to use my head, to remember all men are the same. Once the rainbows and sweet dates melt away, he'll be able to break my heart all the same.

Just like my dad did.

Just like every man I've ever been stupid enough to get involved with has done.

Unfortunately, the sex fiend who has been temporarily sated has decided she wants to keep getting hers and locks up the levelheaded one, so all I have is her chanting 'G-spot orgasm!' in my ear.

So for the second time in 12 hours, I make the leap of agreeing.

"Okay, Luke. I'm yours until the wedding." I say the words precisely, knowing we need to end this once the date hits. His eyes darken for a split second, and I wonder if he'll call me out, but he doesn't, instead kissing me again before moving our food and drinks to the coffee table, covering my body with his and reminding me why I said yes.

NINETEEN

-Luke-

"Are you coming to dinner tonight?" They're the first words from my sister when I answer my phone. I'm sitting in my car we left in the Wawa parking lot yesterday. Thankfully, I have a buddy who works here, so it was a safe choice. I planned to just take a cab back, let Cass stay warm in her bed, but she insisted on bundling up and driving me over, which was fine by me. More time with this woman? Yes, absolutely.

If I could, I'd spend long days with her, talking and laughing and watching shitty movies. Movies I'm shocked she knows every word too, considering she exudes class and intelligence. Knowing every word of the monologue in *The Breakfast Club* was an interesting surprise. My sisters are going to love her for that alone.

That being said, what happened last night and again this morning was so amazing. I'm already dying for a repeat, trying to plan in my head when the next time I can see her is.

"Is it Sunday?"

"Tell me you didn't forget."

"Of course not. Gotta see my favorite Bella girl."

"Good, maybe you can talk some sense into her."

"What's going on now?"

"She's going on a hunger strike." My niece is four going on seventeen, so the source could be anything. Either way, I laugh. "It's not funny."

"It's a little funny. What's the cause?"

"She wants a pony."

"A pony?"

"A pony."

"And she won't eat until she... what? Gets a pony?" I'm laughing, but also, I can totally see it, my stubborn niece swearing she won't eat another thing until she gets a damn pony. Unfortunately, I can also picture her father giving in and finding some way to make sure she does, in fact, get a pony.

"Honestly, I don't think she thought it out very well, but Chris isn't helping *at all*." But, of course, Bella has her dad wrapped around her finger so this does not surprise me.

"I'll bring those cookies she likes from the place down the road from me," I say, adding in the time it will take to stop at the packed bakery on a Sunday. I have about two hours to get home, take a shower, clean up, and head to my parent's for Sunday dinner.

"You're a saint."

"Don't I know it?" I laugh as I start my truck, navigating out of the lot and beeping the horn twice in goodbye when I see my friend.

"You sound... happier."

"I'm always happy."

"I said happier." She pauses, trying to decode me the way she always can. "You had the date last night. Is it the girl?" I sigh.

"Yeah. I, uh, I spent the night with her." I spin the dial of my radio to avoid shattering my eardrums when her shriek comes over the Bluetooth. "Jesus, Q, calm down!"

"You spent the night with a girl?"

"Yeah. And I like her. A lot. But..."

"But what!? Bring her to dinner! I want to meet her." I roll my eyes. Just the thought of bringing Cassie to family dinner makes me laugh. She's hesitant enough; she doesn't need my sisters and mom and nieces all getting in her business and scaring her off.

"Eventually. She's... spooked easily. I gotta work slow with her. She's... I don't know. Her dad's a piece of shit, and she's seen every shithole guy by dating literally hundreds of them." The thought makes my hands tighten on the wheel, and I try to ignore the clench it brings to my gut.

"Got it. So... what's your plan?" I turn out of the gas station towards my apartment, already short on time.

"I gotta run, but I'll talk to you and Tara about it at dinner. I need your expertise." Once again, my sister squeals on the other end, but before I can even tell her to stop and spare my eardrums, she's hung up, probably calling our sister to celebrate already.

But that's fine. I think I'm going to need all the help I can get.

———

Hours later, as our mom cleans up with the help of my nieces and my dad relaxes on his La-Z-Boy like he has for thirty years, my sisters and I are down in the basement that was once our playroom and hangout space. It's now part grandkid play space, part storage, but it holds memories and little signs of the childhood we lived.

As proof, Tara touches an old Transformers sheet blanketing two shelves. "Why does Mom keep this fort we made up?" Quinn laughs, and we all remember the nights we'd build a fort and bring down sheets and pillows and have a sleepover down here. While my oldest sister and I are nearly ten years apart, it never stopped the three of us from spending time together and enjoying it.

"Honestly, I think she actually cleans it and puts it back," Quinn says, inspecting the sheet, which should, in theory, be dust-covered.

"It wouldn't shock me," I agree, looking around.

"Enough about this. What's going on with you?" Tara asks.

"Quinn said you got a girl? Finally? Please tell me we'll be aunties soon." I groan.

"Jesus, T, I said play it *cool*, not freak him the fuck out."

"Please, Luke wants babies more than either of us ever did." Once again, I roll my eyes and groan at their antics.

"*Tara!* He's never going to want to talk to us if this is how you act."

"*Fine.* So, Luke, anything new and exciting going on in your life you'd just so happen to like tell us about and ask for our sisterly advice on?" She points her eyes to Quinn with a 'Happy now?' look, and Q just rolls her eyes.

"Tell us what's going on, bro."

I sigh, not sure where to start. "It's the matchmaker."

"Got that much. What about her?" I wander to the corner holding old children's books and flip through a few.

"She's it." I feel dumb saying it out loud, but it's... it's the truth. Cassandra is what my mom was to my dad. I've fought the knowledge for a week, feeling crazy all the same. But something sparked when I found her on the side of the road. When I was amused by her attitude and anxiety. It escalated on our first date when I forced her to open up to me, when she blended so well with my friends, enjoying herself once she loosened up. The final nail was our night together, learning her body and seeing how *fucking well she suits me.* But her hesitance. Her fear, regardless of how warranted it is...

"She's it?" Quinn is confused, but Tara's staring at me because *she knows.* When Tara met Chris, she didn't bother to fight it, knowing from seeing our parents it was a useless battle. She met him when she was 20, and it's been him for 20 years now. It's a family blessing and a curse to have seen that magic growing up and know it's possible—to know it's out there.

"She's it," Tara says, her eyes locked on me.

"Yeah." Something in my voice clues in Quinn, and her face softens, eyes melting with understanding.

"Oh my god, Luke!"

"She's scared. She doesn't know," I say with some frustration, running a hand through my hair and shutting the book about mother ducklings and starting to pace.

"So tell her."

"Not that easy, Q. Not everyone grew up in our house. It's crazy to anyone else. Her dad's a fuckup—left her mom for a hidden mistress when she left for college. It destroyed her mom. He's on his third wife. Her job is to meet and filter out scumbags. She's got... she has ideas of the kind of people men are."

"I mean, it seems valid. So, what? She won't date you? You're not like that at all." Quinn is getting frustrated for me, ready to go to war if needed to protect her little brother. It's sweet but unnecessary.

"Well... not quite."

"She's going to date you?" Tara asks now.

"Not quite."

"Jesus, Luke, spit it out."

"She only does two dates. She's got these rules. To protect herself or for her job, who knows. But they exist. I've made her break all of them already." I smile with manly pride, and my sisters roll their eyes at me, probably knowing already what I'm saying. "But we've had two dates."

"But she's *it*!"

"I convinced her to give me a third. In two weeks, for her dad's wedding. So we're... tentatively together for the next two weeks."

"Just two weeks?"

"I know it's going to be more than two weeks. She doesn't." My gut sinks, wondering if I'm wrong, knowing I'm going to fight for this but letting her think I'm accepting the scraps she can give me. "Is that wrong?"

My sisters simultaneously answer.

"Yes," Quinn says.

"No," Tara disagrees.

"Look, I get it. But if she's hesitant, is it smart to get caught up in that? Not to mention, she might get really pissed when those two weeks are over and you're expecting more." I nod. Because she will, undoubtedly. She's convinced herself she's fine alone, that she's happy setting others up and getting nothing for herself. But I know she feels it too.

"Yeah, but if the reason she says no is she's scared, wouldn't it make sense to ease her into it? Let her get used to it in a way she's comfortable with?" Tara asks. That's what I was thinking.

"It just seems like a situation where everyone could get hurt."

"But isn't there also the chance for everyone to win? And isn't that the point of it all? That careful balance when you're falling in love. One wrong step, and it's all over. But if you can walk the tightrope together, it's beautiful."

"But every part of this could be the mistake which ends it. I don't know. I don't know the girl. But if she's hesitant and nervous already...," her voice trails off.

"This is really not helpful at all, you guys," I say, staring at my sisters who are arguing as if I'm not there. Both heads pop up to look at me.

"Sorry, Luke. Look. I just want you to be happy. I don't want to see you hurt. And that look in your eyes... you're already in deep."

"So let's ignore the fact I could get hurt. Let's pretend that it's less a question about *if* she'll be okay with me and date me for real, but *when*." My sisters look at each other, then at me. "In that case, how do I play this?" They do some kind of mental talk I could never do, some bond I think must be formed between sisters, before Quinn nods, and they both turn to me.

"You need to try," Quinn says.

"Got that. What else."

"You need to make her feel safe and wanted." That's Tara.

"And like you'll fight for her. Let her know, but don't push it until you have to."

"Anything too much is going to scare her off for sure."

"Honestly, Luke—just be you. Be you and she'll fall for you. You're sweet, kind. You make everyone happy. And if the look in your eyes tells me anything, it says you've already shown her that. You just need to wait until that guard drops and catch her when it does." I stare at them, strangely relieved they've confirmed my fears, until Quinn speaks again.

"And Luke, when it goes bad, when you inevitably fumble it— because you're a man and that's bound to happen..." I roll my eyes, but she keeps on. "Come to us. We'll help. We'll help you win her." Staring at them, I nod, thankful more today than ever to have two older sisters who want to see me happy.

As we trudge up the basement stairs, I can't help but wonder what will happen when she realizes I never intended to let her go.

TWENTY

-Cassie-

"Good morning, Gabi," I say as I walk in with two drinks, placing one on her desk as I walk to my own as if I have no idea why she's staring me down.

"Don't you 'Good morning, Gabi' me, miss.'"

"That's what I say every morning."

"No, you usually say, 'Good morning, Gabrielle,' but now you've decided to be a friend instead of a robot, so we've dropped the formalities. But because of that, I now get to question you endlessly." I'm kind of regretting that move, thinking about it now, knowing I'll have to dish all the dirt from my weekend, the weekend I still haven't even gone over in my own mind.

I'm not reading too hard into why I'm not going over every facet of my second date with Luke in my mind. Usually every single moment would be dissected, slowly gone through with a fine-tooth comb until I've decided who he'd work with, his hopes and dreams and motivation so I could match him. But this time... I want nothing less than to start matching him.

I guess it's a good thing I have two more weeks.

Right?

"Question me about what?"

"I swear I'm going to lose my mind if you don't spill right now. What happened on that date!? What happened at your apartment? Was he creepy?"

"No, he wasn't creepy." Those words come out quickly, a defense of him. That doesn't get past Gabi.

"So what *happened*, Cassie?"

"I thought we were doing this after work? Over drinks?"

"Oh, we are. Absolutely. But I cannot sit on this info any longer. I didn't even call you yesterday when I was *dying* to. I deserve at least this much." I sigh. Looking at her, I see the same level of aggressiveness she makes when arguing the internet bill. The woman can't handle a client complaining, but when she wants something, she's a dog with a bone and won't relent until I give her something.

"Fine. I'll give you one thing, but that's it until tonight. I have work to do. *You* have work to do." Eyeing her, I glare until she nods. "He stayed the night. It was very nice." With that, she shrieks so loud a few minutes later, a neighboring office calls to check in on us.

But still, though my cheeks burn with embarrassment, I find myself smiling throughout my morning.

———

At noon, my phone rings as I'm putting the finishing touches on an email to a client asking when she can expect her first match.

Luke calling

My face breaks out into a smile, and the butterflies in my belly wreak havoc as I pick up the phone and tap the answer. *Who am I, this girl excited to talk to a man on the phone?*

"Hello?"

"Hey, gorgeous."

"On your lunch?" I may have teased him about it, but I love these break-time calls. It's a tiny blip of sunshine in my once monotonous days.

"Yeah, figured I'd call you, see how your day is going."

"So far, so good. How was Sunday dinner?"

"You remember?"

"It's my job to."

"I guess." Something is in his tone, a small smile, a hidden meaning. "Dinner was good. My sisters are very intrigued by the matchmaker I can't stop talking about." My stomach drops, and my face burns.

"You, uh... you talked about me? To your sisters?"

"They're the ones who signed me up, remember?" *Of course.* "There really wasn't any way for me to avoid the conversation." His laugh tells me he finds my anxiousness cute.

"So, uh... what did you say?"

"That I met you, and you're beautiful. We're dating for as long as you'll have me, and I'm taking you to your dad's wedding." I smile despite the fact I should really argue and tell him otherwise. "So what about tonight? Can you meet up?"

"That's against the rules."

"What rule is that?"

"You can't date more than once in three days." I feel Gabi's eyes flick to me at the mention of my rules.

"That's a dumb rule."

"It keeps men interested." My rules have been crafted from research, psychology journals, and studying what works and what gets a girl ghosted. They work. But they're not for women to share with men, so I'm not sure why I keep revealing all of my rules to him.

"You don't need to do anything to keep me interested, sweetheart. You're all I can think about." My brain is floating in a sea of endorphins and confusion. "So, what do you think? Can we meet tonight? Dinner or dessert?"

"I can't. I'm going out with Gabi tonight."

"Gabi?"

"My assistant. I mean, friend. Assistant." This man ties my tongue more than anything, and now Gabi is looking at me like she knows what's happening and she's amused. I lift a hand and flip her off, making her laugh out loud. "She's my assistant and my friend."

"Ah, so you need to gossip with her about our weekend together." *Our weekend together.* Just those words send a shiver down my spine, memories flooding my mind with the sultry tone.

"What? No, no, not at all. That would be unprofessional."

"Sweetheart, we are anything but professional. What's it going to take for you to realize that?" I'm silent on my end as those words sink in, words he keeps saying over and over in slightly different ways. "Okay, I'll let you go; my lunch is just about over. Don't forget to tell Gabi about when I bent you over the couch and ate your sweet cunt, okay? Because I know I'll be daydreaming about it myself." A heated flush runs through me, pooling in my center as he laughs, deep and sexy, before hanging up. I sit with the phone to my ear before I move it from my face.

What have I gotten myself into?

———

"Okay, let's go," I say. It's only three-thirty, but I've decided I absolutely need a drink and to get all of this off my chest. Partly because I've been staring at my computer screen nearly all day and accomplishing absolutely nothing. Partly because I just received a text from Luke.

Luke: Hope the rest of your day is going well.

Between this sweet check-in text and the calling me on his lunch, I need another woman's insight. I need to dump everything into someone else's lap. It's not something I've ever really had a chance to do, and I probably shouldn't be doing it with an employee, but somehow over the past few weeks, despite her working for me for a year, Gabi has become my closest friend.

I'm not sure if that makes me lucky or if it's super embarrassing.

Probably both,

"Go where?"

"I don't care. Somewhere where we can drink and I can dish." I stand, grabbing my things and starting to throw them into my bag. I don't have a date again until Wednesday, thankfully. I don't think I could dissect another man with this one still on my mind.

"Want to head to a liquor store and then eat take out at my place?" I look at her with a smile before nodding. "I'll drive."

———

An hour later and a glass of wine each, I'm sitting on Gabi's comfy-as-can-be couch in her boho-chic apartment on the other side of town, avoiding her eyes.

"That's it, we're here, we have wine, so you can spill."

"I don't know where to start."

"At the beginning."

"Which beginning?" I say with a laugh, and I might be insane because while I'm laughing, I also kind of feel like crying. *What is going on with me?*

"Oh, Cassie, no! I'm so sorry. I didn't mean to push!" she says, setting her glass aside and coming closer before I wave her off. I sniff, gathering myself quickly and shaking my head.

"I feel insane."

"Why?"

"This man is driving me crazy."

"Men tend to do that."

"Not to me," I say, and I mean it. I haven't truly dated since college. I tried after the fiasco with my dad, but after a few tries with college boys who only cared about one thing, I gave up. Why put yourself through that when all men bring are drama and heartbreak?

"Okay, maybe let's start there? Why are you never dating? You're gorgeous and smart. You could easily get a man. Or a woman, whatever."

I hesitate. "I don't know. This is so embarrassing."

"You show me yours and I'll show you mine." My head shoots back and my eyebrows raise before Gabi laughs so hard tears stream down her face.

"Oh, my God. Your face! No, you dummy. It's a saying. You really are uptight. It means you tell me your drama and I'll tell you mine." As she says the words, she plays with the frayed knee of her jeans, and it's clear it makes her nervous. My sweet, headstrong assistant has something she wants to tell me about. But only if I share mine.

So I do. I tell her more about my dad and his leaving my mom. About how it affected me, about how it's why I don't date, why I vet men. How I don't need that drama in my life, how my friends all got married and drifted off, and then I was left alone, just me. Me and my business.

And I told her about Luke. About meeting him on the side of the road and the way my stomach jumped, seeing him at the restaurant and the 20 questions. About how he was the first date who was actually interested in me as a person, not in impressing me. About his friends and them welcoming me. About trivia night and the texts and the calls on his lunch. About him really truly learning about me and maybe even liking me.

I tell her about our date of favorites, about the spilled coffee and the boots.

And because I've completely destroyed my usually strong barrier, I tell her about the kiss, the boots, and what happened *after*. I tell her about the morning after and bagels on the couch. But, most importantly, tell her about him refusing to end it there and proposing two more weeks.

About how he doesn't seem to think we'll end after the wedding.

By the end of it, her eyes are like saucers as she stares me down, shock across my face.

"Oh, Cassie. That is the most beautiful love story I've ever heard."

"What? No. It's not that."

"But it could be!" she says with a shout, and once again, I'm shocked by her exuberance. "I read romance. Like, a lot of it. It's a problem, but we're not talking about me yet. But Cassie, this... this is everything good. He wants you. He wants you to be his. He wants to work with you, meet you where you are, and get past your barriers. Oh my God! It was love at first sight."

"Gabi, stop, no. It's not that."

"You might know red flags, but I know green ones. And this man is a fuckin' leprechaun." I snort wine out of my nose. "Except I saw his profile picture. He does *not* look like a leprechaun. Do you have more pictures?" I shake my head in the negative. "Give me your phone." Before I can, she grabs it from the coffee table, entering the same password I use for our office phones. "You need a better password," she says quietly as she taps it a few times.

"What are you doing?"

"Nothing."

"Gabi..." I say, reaching over to grab my phone. But she stands up and runs to the bathroom. "Gabi!!" The doorknob is useless as I wiggle it. It's locked. But just a few moments later, it opens back up, and she's walking out like nothing happened, dropping the phone into my hands.

"Here you go. He's cute. Super worth it."

"Gabi, what did you do?" I ask, unlocking my phone and scrolling to find what she may have done. My texts? No, not there. Email? No, looks normal...

"I friend requested him." My blood runs cold as she sits back on the couch and sips her wine with a smile.

"You what?"

"I found him on social media. Added him on Facebook and Insta."

"Please tell me you didn't." But the smile on her face says it all. When I open the apps, his profile is still open with 'request sent' in green letters. *No!*

"I wouldn't undo it, either. He's getting the notification either way."

"Gabi, I cannot believe you did that!" But even as the words leave my lips, my phone vibrates in my hand. I close my eyes in horror but I already know.

Luke: Stalking me now, sweetheart?

"GABI! He just texted me!" I throw my phone at her, aiming for her stupid head as she laughs, but she somehow catches it.

"Oh, my God, he calls you sweetheart! That is so, *so* cute!"

"He also called me a stalker, thanks to you."

"Oh, shut up. Oh my God, his photos on Instagram are so cute. His nieces! He accepted you, by the way. Cassie, if you fuck this up, I'm taking him for myself." The woods tumble before I can filter them.

"No way, he's mine." An eyebrow raises, but she doesn't say a word. She doesn't have to. I showed my hand. "Fuck, what am I *doing?*" My head falls back to the couch with a soft squish, but I wish it were a brick wall.

"You're having fun. Which is allowed. He seems nice. Let him take you to the wedding. If he's nice, keep it going." Her voice is soft now, like she's talking to a scared kitten.

"But what if he hurts me?"

"He might. But Cassie, avoiding all human contact outside of work isn't healthy either. If you're doing that, you're letting the assholes win. Letting your dad have an even tighter grip on you than he already does, and he doesn't deserve to have that impact." Staring at her, I know she's right. But I just... "Two weeks. Play the game for two weeks. Then, once the wedding is over, you can make your decision. But don't let these two weeks go without actually trying. Why waste them? It's like the perfect test run. If it ends badly, you only have two weeks into it. No harm, no foul."

She's right, but she's wrong. Because something tells me if I let this man in for one day or two weeks or two years, he's going deep. And scraping him out is going to hurt. God, it's barely been a week and already he's changing how I see my relationships, breaking all my rules, making me question things.

But even more, she's right—I can't keep letting the assholes of the world win, keep allowing them to dictate how I live my life. Maybe it's time to do something for me. To open myself up. So instead of answering her, I grab my phone from where she placed it on the coffee table and look down at it, making a decision.

Cassie: That was my assistant, but I'm not mad about it. Cute nieces.

Luke: Glad we can be friends this way too.

Luke: Your account is boring.

Cassie: It's for business.

Luke: I like being up in your business.

My cheeks burn, and I try to block my face with the fall of my dark hair, but she knows.

"What is he saying?!" I turn my body from Gabi to try and keep my phone from her, but it's no use. For such a tiny thing, she's feisty and somehow snatches it. Her eyes scan the texts, keeping away from me as I try to take it back. She squeals as she reads. Then she's standing on a small side table like an absolute psychopath as she types back to him.

"What are you doing, Gabi?!" She just giggles. "Seriously, give me back my phone or... I'm firing you!" She looks down at me and raises an eyebrow. It's not my best threat; I can't function without her, regardless of the fact I did it for so long. She's become my right hand without question. But before I can argue, she hands me back my phone.

Cassie: When are you getting in my business again?

"*Gabi!*" I shout at her. "That is so inappropriate!"

"Yeah, I know—rule seventeen. All men should make plans. No offense, Cassie, but some of your rules suck. We're in the 21st century. Welcome. Women get to make the rules now. We don't just wait around for men to make the first move." I stand straighter with my hands on my hips.

"Oh, like you do? Who are you dating, Gabi?" I don't know for sure since we only became close recently, but I've never heard of Gabi going on a date or of a boyfriend. The blush on her face confirms my thought.

"You're just as fucked up as I am."

"No, I'm not, I just...."

"Just what? What's the secret you have?" She steps down from the coffee table, the furniture wobbling precariously, but then she sits on the couch and looks at her hands, all joking gone. She's... nervous. "You don't... you don't have to tell me if you don't want to. If you're uncomfortable." She pauses but then sighs.

"No, fair is fair... I just... I don't know where to start." I glance at my phone and see nothing, no dots pending a text, but even if there were, my gut says the right thing to do is lock my phone and toss it aside. Sitting in front of Gabi, I try and make her feel like she can talk to me. Except, I'm kind of shitty at this. Honesty is probably the way to go here.

"I'm not gonna lie... I don't have a lot of girlfriends. I'm not exactly sure how this works, but I like... this. Being friends. Gossiping and emotional dumping. If you're open to it, I'd love to... be a sounding board." There. That felt okay. Not too pushy, not too weird. Right?

Gabi laughs, eyes watering with the action. "You're the best, Cassie. Yeah, I get friends are kind of not your thing. But I like this too—friends. I don't have many either. My best friend moved across the country after school, and I'm kind of... shy." I smile at her, relieved I'm not the only weirdo in this room with minimal friends.

What no one tells you about growing up is while finding a relationship, a boyfriend, or husband, or partner might be difficult, finding friends without the forced proximity of school and classes is really, really hard. Especially when the friends you did have either move or walk down different life paths, like marriage and kids. And when you own your own business with no one you're actively working with day in and out, like I was for years, you become isolated.

Dating services for relationships exist everywhere, but what women *really* need is a dating service for friends.

"So shy, that I've never..." she pauses, and looking at her, gorgeous and petite and literally a man's dream in every way, I think there is no way. "I've never done anything. Like, at all."

"You're a... virgin?" She nods. "You've been kissed?" I'm shocked, and it comes out in my words. "*Shit.* I don't mean—"She blushes a deep red but shakes her head.

"No, I get it. I've been kissed, but not... *kissed.* You know? I was a late bloomer. Awkward and weird in high school, I grew into myself in college, but by then... boys were rude. When they found out I was a... uh..." The blush is taking over her neck, so I help her out.

"A virgin?"

"Yeah, that. Well, they'd be assholes about it. Making jokes, trying to go for more than I was ready for. I even had a few girlfriends give me a hard time like I was some kind of party trick to show off— 'The College Virgin.'" She sighs, picking at the chipped polish on her fingers, a pretty burgundy. "I stopped trying. It wasn't worth the headache. I date sometimes. First dates, but nothing really goes past that...." I stare at her, shocked.

"Wow."

"I know it's weird, but I—"

"No, not that kind of wow. Like, wow, you're gorgeous, and I would have never known. Hell, I'm the first person to understand men being jerks and wanting to avoid them at all costs. Hello, you work for me." She giggles.

"Yeah, that's why I love this job. What you're doing? Vetting and filtering out the crappy ones? You're doing God's work, girl," she says with a laugh, and I take my drink, clinking the edge to hers.

"*We're* doing God's work." My phone vibrates on the table, breaking the moment, and we both look at it and the name flashing across the screen. I pick it up.

Luke: Tell me when you're free and I'll be there.

Gabi, who's reading over my shoulder, squeals, and I nearly pass out with panic.

"What are you going to say?!"

"I don't know! I don't know when I'm even free!" My brain is in panic mode and is complete soup. Gabi grabs her one phone, swiping a few times until she finds what she wants.

"Tuesday! You're free tomorrow night. No date."

Cassie: I'm free tomorrow.

His reply is almost instant.

Luke: I'll pick you up from your office.

Gabi squeals.

Luke: Bring a bag.

"Oh my God!" The sound nearly shatters my eardrum, but the smile on my face and the glow in my soul shadows it.

TWENTY-ONE

-Luke-

WEDNESDAY NIGHT, WALKING INTO THE SMALL BISTRO CLOSE TO work to get a sandwich before I head home and daydream about Cassie, I pause.

Gleaming dark hair flying down the back of a navy blazer.

Red lips tipped up in a small, polite smile as she listens to a man who sits across from her talking.

Cassie.

Out with a man.

When she's mine.

Because two dates, three dates, two weeks... she's mine.

Except clearly, she didn't get the memo as she sits with her notepad in front of her like she's interviewing him.

It hits me then—she's on a date, but she's not. She's interviewing him. Fury and frustration and *jealousy* fight in my gut still, but I try to tamp it down, try to ignore how I want to run over there and snatch her from the chair, kiss her hard and tell him to leave, then toss her over my shoulder and take back to my place where I can eat her instead of a fuckin' sandwich.

Last night was fucking amazing. I picked her up from her office, watching her walk to the parking garage where I waited. She was smiling and giggling with a small, brown-haired girl who was introduced to me as her assistant Gabi. The one who friend requested me. The wink she gave me told me she's on my side, even though her friend and boss might be hard to win.

Then we hit the store, getting what we needed to make a quick dinner: salad and pork chops. We cooked together, her chopping vegetables, me handling the meat, and all I could do was think about how nice this would be in a small starter home, grilling out on a back patio with her. How nice it would be to spend my nights with her like that, easy and relaxed, laughing and joking and learning about each other.

And after dinner, we went to my bed where I tasted her, touched her, made her moan my name, and she returned the favor until we were both spent, passing out until my too-early alarm went off. Then, we showered together before I drove her back to her car in the office garage on my way to work, where she headed back to her place to get ready for the day.

It was perfect.

And now, she's sitting across from another man.

And I think about going over there and dragging her away for a few long, tense moments.

But my sister's words come into my mind. "You have to play it smart, Luke. You can't scare her off."

I can't scare her off. And if this is going to work, I need to get used to this. It's her job. It's not attraction or sexually based—it's essentially a boardroom meeting. But I need to figure out how to handle it and feel about it.

And I need Cassie to tell me when her dates are, what to expect, and how she expects me to be. Especially since she definitely did *not* tell me she had a date tonight.

When I walk up to the register, the cashier who knows me well from coming here a few times a week fluffs her hair and smiles at me. I'm not dumb—I know I'm not terrible to look at. And I know the too young cashier has a thing for me, especially when I've caught her more than once trying to rearrange her tits in her bra when I'm not looking. But maybe today it can work in my favor...

"Hey Luke, how are you? Your usual?" she says, leaning on her elbows to show a glimpse of the cleavage I have no interest in. But I should bring Chris here one day. He'd love this. Flashy, in your face, absolutely no shame.

"Hey, Gina. Yeah, but get it for here." She beams.

"Oh, yay! You never stay! You go pick a seat and I'll bring you a drink." I nod before sitting at a seat in the corner, in the shadows where I can watch Cass, but she can't see me right away. I don't really care if she does see me, but I want to take it in for a bit, if only to appease my anxiety.

And mere minutes later, appeased is precisely how I feel.

Unlike our date, she asks all the questions on her little sheet, glancing down to jot things with a sparkly pink pen, which makes me smile. She dodges questions he asks her expertly, proving to me if she wanted to, she could. When she laughs at something he says, it's polite, not loud with her head thrown back. There's no hand on the table in the perfect place for him to 'accidentally' brush or hold.

It's exactly as I thought. But the date we shared was different. It was not what she expected, because *there was something there*. It was not a date for work. Nothing about us has been about vetting me or screening me. At least, not to match me with some kind of client. Now I'm just fighting to get past the most obstinate barrier of them all, the one protecting her heart from being hurt like her mother's was.

Seeing it also makes me think more rationally. My blood was boiling when I saw her with another man. Your girl out with some other man, work or otherwise, isn't something you expect to see when you're grabbing your dinner. And when she's dressed like that, beautiful and smiling at him, when he's staring at her, pausing between her face and her tits like he thinks he might have a fucking chance? No. Not at all. But this is her job, the business she built. So if I'm going to convince her to give us a try, I'll have to endure this, to accept some of her nights will be spent with other men, going on dates and finding their failings.

I just need to express to her a heads up would be nice, so I don't walk into a restaurant and see my woman out with another man.

So I sit in the corner for ten minutes, watching her do her job elegantly and professionally, so fucking beautiful it takes everything in me not to interrupt, steal her, and bring her back to my place. The whole time she engages with him, questioning and interpreting, thoughts flashing past her face.

When Gina brings my sandwich, I know my cover is blown.

That's fine; I've seen enough.

"Here you go, Luke," she says as she sets down the turkey club in front of me and grazes her breasts against my arm in a way that makes me want to brush off my arm with my hand like it left residue. But instead, I smile big at her and then catch that Cassie's eyes are now locked on me.

I should feel bad. Really, I should. To surprise her this way, to catch her off guard while she's working, isn't the best move, but to be honest, the guy is a fuckwad, and if she hasn't flagged that already, I'm sure it won't take much longer.

The ever professional matchmaker's eyes get wide, almost comically so, and the look is so adorable I have to fight not walking over there to kiss her. But then she's looking back at the man and apologizing because she didn't hear what the asshat said.

Who the fuck cares.

For the last ten minutes, all he's done is talk about himself and his achievements. There was not a single moment where he genuinely tried to ask her something, encourage conversation, and showcase he cares about anything but himself.

But again, this is her job. To go on these dates, figure out who the good ones are. To find love for anyone but herself.

So I sit there. I eat my sandwich, never moving my eyes from her as it continues, as she pretends I'm not there, watching the whole thing. Again, I probably should have taken it to go, said a quick hello before telling her to call me after to meet up. But like the ass I am, I stay and watch her as I eat. I don't taste a bite. I could have been served something nasty or fuckin' cardboard, and I wouldn't have noticed. Instead, all of my attention is on my girl. The noise in the small bistro has increased as the dinner rush approaches, and it's become more challenging to hear the conversations, but that's fine. I just... I need to watch her. I need to see her and know she's okay. My gut is urging me to do so in a way I can't explain.

It happens in a split second.

Her face goes from open and interested to confused with an edge of concern.

His hand reaches across the table to grab hers, pulling it towards him. She gently fights it, still holding a polite smile, a professional demeanor.

His head tips to the left, towards the door in a 'let's go' gesture, and in response, she shakes her head no, a small polite smile on her face.

His face goes hard and frustrated.

His jaw is tight with his next words, words I can't hear.

She shakes her head again, confusion gone, taken over by concern.

My gut sinks, and my hands go to my knees to push up and stand, but her eyes flit to me, and her head shakes, the most subtle shake. She's asking me to stop, to let her handle this.

I have to fight the urge to get up, instead staying in place and watching them like hawks, reminding myself this is her business, her job. I can't interfere. I can't—

Until she tries to pull her hand back and he tugs her towards him. Hard.

Cassie tries to say something that looks like, "Please let go," but he doesn't. Instead, he tugs again.

It's not the tug that snaps me.

It's the flash of pain on her face.

Abso-fucking-lutely not.

No way.

She can be strong and independent and handle things on her own. I'll deal with men dating her, coming on to her, daydreaming of her in their bed so long as it's mine she's sleeping at night. I'll let her handle all of it until someone puts their fucking hands on her. Then the game is over.

I'm on my feet in moments and taking the few strides necessary until I'm at their table.

My hands go to the collar of his suit jacket, a cheap department store brand clashing with the undershirt he's wearing. Not her type.

And that's the problem, isn't it? He's not her type, not for her. He must know it, has to know a sweet, gorgeous, intelligent woman like Cassie would never willingly leave to go *anywhere* with him.

"What the fuck, man?" he shouts in my face as I pull him out of the chair and force him to face me. My hand grasps the lapel of his jacket until he's close to my face.

"You put a fuckin' hand on a woman?"

"Fuck off, man." He tries to push at my chest, but he's not just a douche in a cheap suit jacket—he's weak. The shove barely even moves me.

"I asked you a question." My voice has gone cold, and even in my state, I notice the sound around us has lowered, other customers quieting to watch what's unfolding.

"Who the fuck do you think you are?"

"I'm the man who watched you put your hands on a woman more than once, then when she asked you not to, you tugged on her hand, causing her pain. Now, do you want to answer my question?" I don't know if it's fear or bravado, but his eyes roll before he opens his dumb fuckin' mouth.

"Fuck off, man. She's playing hard to get. You know how chicks can be."

I. See. Red.

My ears buzz, the background of the little bistro I'm sure I won't be welcome in again blurs as I use the hand in his lapel to push him from me as I pull my arm back and hit him, square on the side of his face.

His head instantly moves to the left with my hit, flying with the force. My arm goes back, striking him again as my mind goes blank.

Playing hard to get.

The look of concern.

The pain.

Cassie holding her wrist.

With another hit, he's pushing on me, clawing at the arm holding him, trying to get free. It's no use; the tunnel vision has me singularly focused on making this man pay. *He touched her. He hurt her.*

But a single voice breaks through the chaos of my mind.

A single voice saying, *"Stop!"*

The world comes flying back.

Customers shouting, the man in front of me pushing to get free, the throbbing in my fist, it's all there.

But my eyes are locked to Cassie, her own wide, staring at me with a mix of fear and anger and a hint of pain, begging me to stop.

And her hand is holding her wrist.

I drop the man, who stumbles back a few steps before getting to his feet and moving away from me.

"Get your shit and leave." For a moment, I think he'll argue. Try to call the cops, to press charges, to fight back. But I called it—he's weak and a coward, grabbing his coat and saying something to Cassie about this being a waste of time, but he's off my radar as soon as he scurries off with his tail between his legs.

"Let me see." I put my hand out, needing to see her wrist, to see the damage.

"What the hell was that, Luke?!" Anger is clear in her voice. If I wasn't so worried about her, dying to ensure she's okay, I might laugh. But I need to check this box in my mind first, make sure that fucker didn't do any lasting damage.

"Give me your fucking wrist, Cassandra." Her mouth thins with frustration at my words. But whether she takes my order for what it is —a damn order—or just doesn't want to argue in a restaurant where we've already made a scene, I don't care because she's wincing as she hands it over to me. The skin around her wrist is pink and angry, and I know it's going to bruise. "Shit, Cass. We should go find him, press charges. This is fucked up."

"No. No way."

"Why the fuck not?"

"For so many reasons. One, this is my business and he was just assaulted during an interview."

"*After* he assaulted you first." She rolls her eyes.

"Second, if we file charges, he'll file them against you. And there's more evidence to what you did than this being from him." Her eyes gesture to my hand with skinned knuckles, blood welling at one deeper split. "You should get that checked out." Her voice goes softer, the anger still there but subdued with worry. Something warms me, knowing she's concerned about me more than she cares about her own injury.

"I don't care if he presses charges. No one would hold it against me. There's a restaurant full of witnesses." I gesture around to the full bistro, half the eyes following our every move, the other half pretending not to be watching.

"Are you okay, Luke?" the waitress asks when she comes over, a towel with ice in her hand. I take it from her, pressing it to Cass' wrist regardless of the fact Gina intended to be my nursemaid and give the ice to me. I don't have the energy to deal with her.

"Fine. Check, Gina. My tab and Cassie's and the asshole date's." The tone in my voice must communicate my frustration because she nods before scurrying off.

"Luke, no—"

"Not the time."

"What?"

"Not the time to fuck with me. Not the time to test me. I am still so on-fuckin'-edge right now, Cass. I want to go crazy, chase the fucker down, and beat his ass. The shit going through my mind? It would not take much to push me to do it. But I gotta take care of my woman right now. Please, don't make this any more difficult by fighting with me about dumb as fuck shit." I expect her to argue. I expect it to be like nearly every other interaction I have with this beautiful, frustrating woman and for her to argue on principle alone.

But instead, she looks at me, reads me, decodes what I'm showing her, and nods.

"Okay, Luke."

———

Our meals are packed, the bill paid, and I'm walking Cass the few blocks to my apartment, both of us still stewing on what just happened.

"This is my job, Luke," she says softly, breaking the silence. I look down at her as we continue walking.

"What?"

"This is my job. I go on dates. I meet men. Good, bad, everything in between. It's just another reason I don't date." Her eyes are stuck straight ahead.

"What are you saying?"

"I don't know. I'm saying... I'm saying I can't change everything because we have some kind of... arrangement." The word digs into me, grating against nerves. *Arrangement*. She and I both know this is more than some convenient arrangement. More than three dates, more than three weeks. I just need her to accept it, to understand I'm not going anywhere. I'm not the same scum she's afraid of falling for. But I also know right now is not the time to push this. To push her.

"I know your job, Cass. Know it and think it's great. Great you built it all by yourself, that people trust you." As I'm speaking, she stops in her tracks, turning to face me. We're blocking traffic on the sidewalk, but I don't care as I pull her closer to me and keep talking. "I think it's amazing you take the crappy part of dating and meeting people out of the equation for people who just want to find their person. I think you're beautiful, inside and out, and the business you've built is a sign of that." She blinks at me a few times, mouth parted, and she looks so sweet, so beautiful, all I want to do is kiss her, but she speaks before I can.

"But... you saw me tonight. On a date. And you... Luke, you lost your mind."

"It wasn't the date, Cass. Did I like randomly seeing my girl out on a date with another man?" She opens her mouth to protest, but I keep going. "Of course not. I was going to mess with you about it later, come up with a plan for how we can handle it in the future." Another attempt at interrupting me. "But I'd already settled myself. This is your business. You do it great. I will never stop you. But regardless, you need to know I'm not that guy."

"Not what guy?" The adorable crease between her eyebrows forms.

"I am not the kind of man to sit back and watch something like that happen. If you were some stranger, I'd have done the same thing. I might have had my head on a bit more straight, but it doesn't matter. That man was fucked as soon as he touched you and you said no. There is never an excuse for that shit."

"I had it handled! I—"

"No, Cassie. No. You need to know this about me now. I will protect what is mine until my last fuckin' breath. If someone says something to hurt you, I'm talkin' to them. Someone fuckin' touches you, I'm sure as fuck making sure they never do it again. I know you're proud, know you're strong. I know you can handle yourself; you've done it for long enough. But now I'm here. Three weeks, three years, or a fuckin' eternity, right now you're mine. You got that? You being mine means I take care of you."

"Luke—"

"And it's not the date, Cass. Again, I get it. I will never get between you and the business you love. It's that you didn't fuckin' tell me. We talked today, no mention of it. I get it. It's your job. This lasts the way I want it to, I'll learn to handle that. But you'll need to give me patience. My head will get the better of me if you don't. And I'll need to know you're safe. I'll need to know shit like that—" My eyes avert to her wrist. "Won't happen again."

"Luke, I—"

"Like I said, you're mine, that's what we have to do. I need you to tell me where you're goin', who you're with. I get a weird vibe, I'm coming. Won't interrupt. You won't know I'm there. It won't be forever, just until I'm comfortable, especially after tonight. But if you want to be mine, you need to know I'm sticking up for you. I'm taking care of what's mine." We're both quiet as I let it sink in. "So are you mine? You say no, I drive you home right now, no problem. No hard feelings. But you say yes, just know that's what I expect. You need to let me in, let me take care of you." The thoughts flitting through her mind are nearly visible, and for a split second, I worry I went too far, if I should have tiptoed into this. If I should have stopped and called my sisters and figured out what the fuck I'm doing.

But then her small voice speaks, her tiny hand going to my cheek as she looks into my eyes. Fear is in hers, but also astonishment and a hint of joy.

"I'll be yours, Luke." And that's all I need.

TWENTY-TWO

-Luke-

"Ma!" I shout down the hallway of my childhood home, Cassie walking in behind me. She's white as a ghost, not because she woke up with an aching wrist, but because I've dragged her here to get it checked out.

Sure, I could have taken her to urgent care or the doctor, but my mom was a nurse for twenty years and has seen every ailment over the years. Plus, she's my mom. There's no one I trust more in the world than this woman to take care of my girl.

"In the kitchen, honey!" I grab Cassie's good hand in mine, pulling her close to me and kissing her temple before we enter the kitchen.

"To what do I owe—oh!" she says as she sees us walk in. Turning off the water to the sink, she grabs a nearby towel and wipes off her hands. "Well, who's this? Goodness, Lucas, you could have called! I look a mess!" Her cheeks blush in a way I know my dad finds cute, and now that I have Cass, I get it.

"Hey, Ma. This is Cassie, my girl. Told you about her last week."

Her eyes widen and then narrow in a 'we're going to talk about this later, sir' look I've gotten nearly my entire life before she puts an arm out.

"Hi, Cassie! I'm Lucas' mom, Kerry. So great to meet you!" And then she pulls my girl into her arms in a big motherly hug, rocking her left and right. Cassie's arms stick out to her sides, unsure of what to do, and the look of shock in her eyes when they meet mine over my mom's shoulder makes me chuckle under my breath. Finally, she rounds my mom with her arms, returning the hug before the middle finger of her good hand goes up, pulling a full-out laugh from me.

"It's nice to meet you too, Mrs. Dawson."

"Oh, no, no 'Mrs. Dawson' here. Only Kerry or Mom." Her face blushes, and my mom's head tips back in a tinkly laugh that used to fill the halls when I was a kid.

"Sorry to do this, Ma, but Cass hurt her wrist yesterday, and it's pretty sore. Figured I'd just bring her here and skip the urgent care."

"I'm really so sorry to barge in here like this, Mrs.—uh, Kerry. There's no need. I'm totally fine. Luke is just overreacting." Cassie tries to get out of it, but my mom has smelled the blood, and she's about to go full-on mama bear. I'm pretty sure this is something Cass hasn't ever experienced, or at least not in some time, and I'm kind of excited to give her that, in some sick way.

"No, no! Let me see it! You sit right here, okay?" She pulls out a kitchen table chair for Cassie and practically pushes her down, forcing her to sit in it. "And then I'll take a look! Luke, honey, can you go get my kit really quick?" I nod, walking to the hall closet where she keeps her packed-to-the-brim first-aid kit before bringing it back to her. When I return, my mom's cradling the injured wrist, inspecting it, and Cassie is laughing, at ease. Well, that didn't take very long.

"What's so funny?" I ask, setting down the kit and pressing a soft kiss to Cassie's head. She looks up at me with a small smile, and Mom looks my way with shock and excitement. I try to tell her to chill out with my eyes before she rolls her own.

"Oh, Cassie was just telling me this is all your fault, with your incessant hot head. I always tell you it's going to get you into trouble, that temper, but now look, you've hurt this beautiful girl!" My mom ticks at me before moving to her kit.

"Oh, Mrs. Dawson, it wasn't Luke's fault, really. It was some guy—"

"Yeah, yeah, I know what you told me. But I also see a split knuckle on my son's hand that tells me I'll be needing to put some butterfly stitches there as well." I look at my hand and see she's not wrong—the knuckle on my middle finger is red and painful. Somehow, even though I've been in her presence less than five minutes, my mom has seen, diagnosed, and is mentally healing my injury. "Okay, Cassie, so it doesn't look like anything major, just a sprain. Obviously, I have no X-ray machine, but I've seen this many times before. We're gonna wrap it up, but if it's still bothering you much in a day or so, you'll need to go to a true doctor, okay?" She grabs the tan stretchy bandage from her bag and Cassie nods before she wraps it around and around. "There! All better. Be easy on it and you should be good in no time."

"Thank you so much, Mrs.—" My mom glares at her. "I mean, Kerry." She starts digging in her bag before pointing to me.

"Your turn, get in the chair."

"Ma—"

"Don't 'Ma' me, Lucas Andrew Dawson. You get in that chair and let your mother clean out that cut. Then you need to tell me what on earth were you thinking, assaulting someone in a *restaurant!*" Her indignation is apparent, and I wonder how they could chat so much in the few minutes I was gone.

"I was at the restaurant. Cass was there with a client. I had an eye on them." I wince as she not so gently scrubs the cut. "I saw he touched her. She didn't like it. Then he tugged her, and I don't know... I lost it."

"You know, his father is just like this," my mom says, looking Cassie's way, and I roll my eyes, knowing what's coming. "We met when I was a young girl, love at first sight. He hooked me and never let go." My eyes meet Cassie's, and a blush creeps over her face, but I'm surprised when her eyes stay locked on mine. I'm trying to tell her things gently, things I know will scare her off without actually *saying them*. Because while I can't say I *love* Cassandra Reynolds just yet, I can say I am so enamored and wrapped up in her in a way I don't want to come out. "One day when I visited him at college, we went to a party. It was dumb, I shouldn't have been there, but we were, all the same. Some boy tried to get me to dance with him. I declined, but by then, Jack had already seen it. He brought that boy outside and taught him a lesson. Almost got kicked out of school for it. His father was so furious with him. But every time I came to see him after that, no one tried to even look at me sideways." I smile, having heard the story multiple times, in various ways, with both parents having their own spin. But it's also the reason I knew if I hit a man for touching my girl and ended up in hot water, my dad would back me.

"Yeah, I know, Ma. I've heard this story before."

"But your Cassie hasn't." Cass' eyes drift to me at being called 'my Cassie,' and I just smile because what else can I do. Eventually, she's going to see this for what it is. She's *my Cassie*, and she'll look back at this with a different lens.

Just as my mom finishes up, the front door opens with a loud bang as it slams into the wall. "Mom!"

My mom rolls her eyes.

"Quinny," she says under her breath, but it's unnecessary because Bella comes running in, arms open and shouting, "Uncle Lukey!" I pick her up and twirl her before setting her on my hip.

"Hey, Bells!"

"Mommy said we're having breakfast with your new *girlfriend*." Cassie freezes again, but I ignore it. *And again*, how was my mother able to talk to my sister so quickly?

"Grandma's making pancakes," I say, even though I don't know it as fact. If I ask my mom to make pancakes, a stack will be on the table within the hour.

"PANCAKES!" she shouts the word, nearly bursting my

eardrum before I put her down with a smile as my sister Quinn walks in.

And the chaos begins.

TWENTY-THREE

-Cassie-

THE DRIVE BACK FROM LUKE'S PARENT'S HOUSE IS QUIET AS I take in everything that happened. I never ended up going into the office today, instead texting Gabi and telling her to go home whenever. Between the chaos of yesterday and today's excitement, I'm too frazzled for work.

Breakfast was wonderful. Luke's niece is adorable, his mom sweet as can be, and his sister, Quinn, was fun, making sure I didn't leave without her putting her number in my cell. It seems I'm racking up new friends and expanding my contact list, hanging out with Luke.

The entire breakfast was full of laughter, friendly teasing, and family. It's clear they're incredibly close-knit, a family who actually enjoys spending time together instead of it being a chore. It's refreshing to see.

It's also terrifying. It's clear this is what Luke wants—what he deserves. It's just another reason this would never work between us past our arrangement. This isn't my life. I can't offer anything like this to him.

"What's going on in your head?"

"What?"

"In your head. You're a million miles away." I sigh. Of course I am. How could I not be? His family is... His family is perfect. And I'm going to be dragging him into my family's chaos not long from now. And then he'll know.

"I just... I was thinking."

"This doesn't sound good. Maybe you should stop thinkin'." He looks at me, moving his eyes from the road to me for a split second. I roll my eyes at him.

"It's just... I don't know. I was thinking... Maybe I should just—"

"No."

"What?"

"No."

"I didn't even finish what I was saying."

"You don't have to. It's stupid." His eyes are still locked to the road, his brow furrowed in frustration.

"Excuse me?"

"I said it's stupid."

"That's rude!"

"Were you about to tell me not to come with you to your dad's wedding?" *How does he know these things?*

"It's just." My finger runs over the tan bandage of the wrap Kerry put on me. "Your family is awesome. Your parents are adorable. So in love. My family... they're a mess."

"Didn't grow up in a bubble. I know not everyone is as lucky as I am. What my parents have? It's a miracle. To meet young, raise kids, go through hard times and good times and come out on top. I had friends, saw their families fall apart. Look at Chris. Tanner's girl, Jordan? She had it crazy rough. I'm lucky. I know that." He continues before I can say any more. "I want that. Yes. Of course. I want the dream. But I also know it's not handed to you. You need to work for it. Your history, your past, your family? Make you who you are. It made those walls you built, but it doesn't mean you can't have something beautiful." My breath hitches with his words, with the meaning. But I don't have to decode them, don't have to guess.

"You give me the chance, Cass, I'd kill to show you how beautiful life can be when you let your walls down, when you let people in." His eyes are still on the road which I'm thankful for. I couldn't handle meeting them right now. But there's so much vulnerable emotion in his voice...

And then, for some reason, I'm crying.

Not cute, lady-like cries or a single rolling tear, but huge, body-wracking sobs. Looking over at me, confusion and worry cross his face, and he instantly hits the hazard lights button, pulling his truck over to the shoulder before slamming it into park. Then I'm unbuckled and dragged across the seats until I'm cradled in his lap, crying into his shirt.

"What's wrong, sweetheart? I didn't mean anything. I wasn't trying to upset you."

"It's not you, I just..."

"What?"

"I wish I could have this. I wish this was in the cards for me." Without asking more questions, as if he knows he won't get anywhere with me, as if he knows all I need is for him to hold me, he does it, running a hand down my hair and rubbing my back until my tears slow, my body slack from the emotional release.

"You're going to get it when you meet my family. Get how we live in completely different universes. You deserve more." Once again, it's like he knows no argument he gives will change my mind. No words at this moment are enough to help this mess I've gotten myself into.

"We're going to be fine. It's going to be fine," he says quietly under his breath, and I'm not sure who he's speaking to—himself or me.

He might be right. It will be fine. The wedding will probably just be another day that's nothing more than a nuisance. But I still can't help but wonder if after these two weeks... will I be just fine? Or will I be irreparably damaged?

TWENTY-FOUR

-Cassie-

MY STOMACH TURNS AS I WAIT FOR MY PHONE TO RING. LUKE IS on his way over to pick me up for my father's wedding. It's not the wedding I'm anxious about. The chaos, stress, and disappointment it is most definitely going to be, I've accepted.

No, it's turning from the knowledge of what's going to happen after the weekend is over.

The past three weeks have been nothing short of perfect. My nights have been filled with sweat and moans and discovery. With nips and kisses and caresses. With cuddling and getting to know each other, sharing secrets, and gently poking fun. Mornings have been giggling and teasing, getting ready together, breakfast together, and making plans for the night. It's been calls during lunch breaks and texts just to check in.

And after this weekend, it ends. It has to end before it breaks me. Because I refuse to give it the chance to break me.

But what if it's already too late? the uptight librarian on my shoulder asks, gnawing at the end of her pencil. Surprisingly, the sex fiend also nods nervously, twirling a lock of hair around her finger as if she already knows the truth. I push them aside as my phone buzzes in my hand.

Luke: I'm downstairs. Buzz me up.

I don't, though. I've already decided I need to create space for my own sanity. He can't be up here. Not any more. I'm drawing the line.

When this is over—because it *has to be over*—I'm already going to walk through my apartment and see him everywhere. On my couch, eating everything bagels and at my kitchen table, helping me with my boots. In the bathroom where he sat on the toilet and watched me do my hair in the morning. At the coffee bar where he made me a cup of coffee without my telling him how I like it. It's something I'm already going to face, but I can't let it get any worse. Those kinds of constant reminders can destroy a woman. I saw it when my mother kept the house she shared with my dad, the house she refuses to leave or sell, regardless of the fact she's rarely there and it's way too big for just her.

And regardless of the endless hints he drops, hints he wants this thing between us to continue, it *has to be over*. Luke deserves someone who brings more to the table than familial drama and commitment issues. Someone who can confidently give themselves over to another without doubt creeping in daily.

And he's a man, which means as much as it seems impossible now, one day he'll do something to hurt me. Something stupid or mean, some kind of ultimate betrayal we couldn't come back from. It would happen when I was in too deep, too far to save myself, and it would break me. And I wouldn't survive being broken by Luke.

Cassie: On my way down.

I grab my overnight bag and the garment bag holding the way too expensive dress I bought for the wedding, which said 'black tie' on the invite. My phone rings in my hand before it stops, then starts again. I ignore it. He's going to be frustrated, but I need space.

My finger is shaking as I press the 'P' button in the elevator before I shove it in the pocket of my jacket. *Get it together, Cassandra.*

When the doors ding open, Luke is standing there, waiting for me, frustration written on his face.

"What the hell, Cass?"

"Sorry, I just want to make sure we don't hit any traffic."

"We don't even have to be there for six hours," he says. I spot his truck and make my way towards it before he tugs my bag out of my hands, hefting it over his shoulder. Ever the gentleman.

"I get car sick. I don't want to be stuck in the car any longer than necessary," I lie.

"You're a liar." When I try the door handle, it's locked. I don't turn to face him, instead leaving my hand on the handle and looking through the glass of the passenger side door. "Cassie, what the fuck?" He sets my bag on the ground, and I fight the need to argue with him about it before his hand is on my arm and tugging me to face him.

"What?"

"Cassie, what is going on?"

"I don't know what—"

"Don't pull this shit on me. You can play everyone else in your life, in the world, but not me." God, I wish he were wrong. I wish I could hide it all from him: my thoughts, my feelings, my heart. But knowing this man won't let me into the car until I explain, I sigh.

"I'm anxious about this weekend." The truth. The truth in its most basic form. So long as he doesn't dig too much, we're good.

"What, with your dad?" Sure, yeah. Let's go with that. Let's go with the fact I'm anxious about seeing my dad and his family and the newest step monster and enduring all of their bullshit. I say nothing. I don't want to outright lie to him. Not to Luke. But he makes the deduction I'm praying he will, face softening with concern and comfort. "Oh, sweetheart." A hand goes to the side of my head, pushing the hair behind my ear. "It's all going to be fine. Nothing bad is going to happen."

I nod halfheartedly before he presses his lips to my forehead, unlocking the truck, and he helps me in, but he's wrong. He's so, so wrong.

Because I fucked up and I fell for this man, and I *am* going to get hurt, and I will never, ever be fine again.

––––––––––

"So this place is fancy," Luke says, walking around the luxurious room. "Your dad put you up in here?" I hum a noncommittal sound because he didn't. I called a few days ago to see if I was registered, and there was no room in my name. The entire wedding party, the entire family, has a room paid for and booked by my father except for me.

When I called my dad, he said he must have forgotten and *"if there are no open rooms left, you can always go to the Holiday Inn down the road."*

Dear Old Dad at his best.

I don't expect him to pay my way. I can afford a stay at some random swanky hotel. It's not the point. It's the fact my father once again proved I'm not even on his radar. Not even important enough to reserve a room for or to care if I'm nearby for his wedding. I shake my head to get the intrusive thoughts out of there. I learned years ago it doesn't pay to dwell on them.

With my overnight bag on the bed, I reach in and take out the outfit I chose for the rehearsal dinner. This morning the step-monster-to-be texted me a note saying they must have 'forgotten' to invite me, but I was more than welcome to come tonight. Not long after, my dad sent me a text requesting my presence. While it was phrased as an invitation, I know it was meant as an order.

Hopefully, the long sleeve, knee-length dress with a slight dip in the front is good enough since I didn't have a chance to find any other outfit. The sleeves are a pretty navy lace overlaying the entire form-fitting dress. Paired with a thin gold belt and matte gold heels I brought for tomorrow, it should work. I'm laying out a chunky neck-lace to go with it before I grab my makeup bag to get ready when warm hands go to my hips from behind, moving up under the loose sweatshirt I'm wearing to rest on the bare skin of my belly. It's not sexual, not really. I've found Luke likes to have his hands touching me in some way if I'm within reach. It still makes a chill go through my body, the same way it always does when he touches me. I don't have the time or presence of mind for that, though.

"I have to get ready." The words are low as I continue to dig in the bag like I'm looking for something, but it's all just a show, a distraction.

"We have two hours."

"I have to do my hair and makeup."

"I've seen you get ready. It doesn't take long." The hand on my belly dips, the fingertips just barely tucking under the waistband of my leggings. "We have tons of time." His voice is lower, rougher, and because he has utter control of my body, it starts to react, softening, leaning into his touch without my mind's consent. His lips dip to my neck, exposed by the slick ponytail I put in this morning.

"I need to get ready."

"You'll be gorgeous no matter what, whether you take two hours or two minutes." He means it too. Some part of him truly thinks that. But he doesn't know the lions' den we're headed into, the jackals who will want to rip me apart for any minor indiscretion. Any flaw, any imperfection. And they never fail to find them all.

"I need to get ready, Luke." His body freezes at my words, at the curtness and the brush-off. With each breath, my anxiety increases— the emotions are too much, too strong. Emotions about having to face my dad, doing it with Luke on my arm. Knowing my mom has been calling me all week having a meltdown over the fact that once again, my dad is remarrying.

And most of all, knowing I won't feel his warm hand on my skin again after this weekend.

Knowing I won't have someone telling me I'll look gorgeous regardless of how long I spend in front of the mirror.

Like always, though I try to hide, try to conceal my fear and anxiety and self-consciousness, he sees it, pushing the ponytail over my shoulder. He opens his mouth to speak, to say something, to argue with me, I'm sure, but my phone rings.

We both glance at it where it's sitting on the bed. I should have anticipated it—I don't know why I bothered to expect anything else. But because today isn't chaotic enough, the name '*Mom*' flashes.

"Shit," I say under my breath, knowing what this is. I'm not allowed to have a day stressed out about dealing with my family without my mother also having the same.

I don't talk to her often, not because I don't love my mom, but because most conversations we have seem to degrade in the same fashion. It starts out fine—how are you, how's work—before questions about my father peek in. How is he? What's new?

And I've only had to live through this specific call once before, but the call that comes when she knows he's found someone new? A different sort of pain.

When my dad left my mother after all those years, waiting until he was just past the cusp for having to pay her child support, my mom lost everything about herself. She'd spent years and years trying to please my dad, to be what he wanted. Being the doting stay-at-home mom, the PTO parent, making sure when he was home there was always a hot meal waiting for him, a sparkling kitchen. She was always on some kind of diet, some kind of insane exercise regimen to tone the curvy body I inherited, to make it more appealing to my father. Her entire self-worth revolved around being a good wife to him. And though we had little, she made it work.

But she proved to me even if you do your best to be everything for a man, there's just no guarantee he'll be yours forever.

When he left, she took him to court for alimony, getting the money she never knew existed. She now lives a shambled life of spa days and facelifts and therapy retreats to 'try and heal her broken heart.' She sees it as her due, but to any outsider looking in, it's just sad.

But truth be told, I've never questioned her long, drawn-out heartbreak. How would I know what it's like to be lied to your whole life, to live for a man only to have it all be a falsehood? But recently, I find myself wondering more and more. Because sure, her heart was broken, and my dad was the scum of the earth to her, but looking back, there were signs. Red flags. And maybe that's the reality—there are always red flags. It's just the shade of red and the size of the flag that matters. But if you put on rose-colored glasses, the shades of red all mesh together.

Maybe it's also her own fault for accepting the scraps he gave her, never demanding more.

Maybe it's her fault for not shielding you from it better, the librarian whispers, the words so soft I almost miss them as I look to Luke.

"Your mom?" I nod. "You gonna answer?"

"I don't want to."

"It's your mom." His eyes squint, confused. Of course he is. His family is perfect and normal, his mom sweet and kind and open. But instead of saying that, I nod, swiping to answer and bracing myself.

"Hello, Mom." Instantly I hear the sniffles.

"I can't believe this is happening." I sigh, plopping onto the bed and sinking into the soft mattress.

"It's not the first, Mom." I coo the words like she's a small child or a frightened bird, but I know the inevitable is upon me.

"He was supposed to be *mine*." The last word is a wail, and my eyes shoot to Luke. There's no way he didn't hear that, no way he's not listening to the other side of this conversation. Her cries are sobs now, no longer petite sniffles. "He was *mine,* Cassandra! All those years of dealing with *his shit*! Of him hiding his family and his money and his mistresses! I deserve the big wedding and the mansion! I deserve to live the good life!"

"Mom, you *are* living the good life." Once again, my voice is soft and cajoling. I need to get off the phone. I can feel the anxiety creeping up my throat, suffocating me... putting me in the center of a fight I have no desire to relive.

"It's not the same, Cassandra. It's not the same. I'm alone! I'm so lonely. I have no one, nothing at all. He left me for some younger version, and I'm here *alone*." Don't mind me here, your only daughter. Although she lives in Tucson, the last place we all lived together as a family, never once has my mother come to visit me or invited me to stay with her. I've offered multiple times, but each time she says she can't bear the idea of being so close to my father.

"I know this is hard for you, Mom."

"No, you don't. If you did, you wouldn't be going to this wedding."

"He's my father."

"And I'm your mother." This is how it's been for over ten years, this halfhearted tug of war when it's convenient, when there's something to win. But when the interest ends, when my mom doesn't have my father to bait and my father doesn't have my mother to antagonize, it's me who falls into the mud.

"I don't know what you want me to do, Mom. This is really hard for me." My throat aches now. Each word hurts as it exits, and, to my humiliation, tears are rising, tears I beg to recede. But since when do emotions obey simple human requests?

"Just like your father. Always worrying about yourself, selfish. I can't believe this," she says, and, like most of our conversations, she hangs up before I can say another word. I move the phone to my ear and look at it.

Mom: Call ended, 2:31 seconds is flashing on the screen.

Two minutes is all it took this time for her to get under my skin, to chip another chunk off, her fierce words a chisel to what remains of me.

And then they come.

The tears.

They roll up my throat, into my eyes, and down my cheeks. My elbows go to my knees, my face to my hands, my phone tumbling to the floor as I lose it, crying with the stress of this weekend, the frustration. Of my parents. The responsibilities I shouldn't have to hold, the disappointment.

I cry the way I do most any time I have to deal with one or both of them—by myself, wallowing for a few brief minutes until I can get it together, clean myself up and move on.

Except this time, powerful arms pull me into a warm lap, cradling me and holding me tight and safe.

Luke.

Luke is here, holding me while I lose it.

"What is this?" he asks once my tears calm. He tugs on my hair tie, releasing my hair before his hand brushes through it as my head lies on his chest. My cries slow to quiet sniffles and hiccups, and I don't want to explain. I don't want to sound crazy, to feel crazy.

Because I do, right now. I feel crazy. It's not even my dad or my mom or any of it, not really. Right now, I feel so out of control in my usually carefully crafted life. This man came in and completely tore up everything. And soon it will be over, our time up.

Instead, I give him the easy answer.

"Can we skip this?" The words are muffled into his shirt, but I know he hears them when he answers.

"Of course. We can do whatever you want." Such a Luke reply.

"I can't not go."

"Yeah, you can. You're an adult. He has little to no influence in your life at this point. You make those choices." I sigh, rubbing my face into the soft cotton of his shirt smelling faintly of motor oil and cedar, the smell so uniquely and perfectly Luke. Hard work and high class. He dips his knees, arms going from around me to under my knees to lift me as he moves to sit on the bed until I'm cradled in his arms like a small child he needs to care for.

This. This is why it's getting harder and harder to convince myself ending this is the right move.

It's also the reason I need to do it.

"I'm dreading this weekend."

"With your dad?" he asks, and I accept it. Telling him otherwise is too complicated.

"Yeah. And his family. It's always… hard."

"Why?"

"I don't know them. I never did, really. I didn't know most of them existed when I was younger. He's from money, but we never knew. We always struggled. When it... all came out, and I met everyone, I was the trashy first wife's kid. Not his kid. I'd hear aunts say they didn't blame him for hiding me. Cousins murmur things, you know, about my mom. About me. How I look. They're all thin and lithe and blonde. I'm... me."

"You're beautiful." He says it without hesitation.

"You have to say that." He pulls me back to look at me, and there's frustration on his face.

"I absolutely do not. Not by any means. But you are, Cassie. You're beautiful inside and out. Curves in all the right places that any man sees and instantly pictures in his bed. Hair you want to run your hands through. A fuckin' flawless face. And you're kind and sweet and hardworking. Perfect package, baby."

"I'm—"

"I have sisters." He stops there, and I move my head from his chest to look at him with confusion on my face.

"I know that, honey."

"I have sisters, so I know how easy it is for the world to make you feel less than. Saw it happen with Quinny, with Tara. I'm their brother, but from a pure bystander point of view, I know they're gorgeous. But they still struggled. And when they hit a time when they thought they weren't the everything they very much are, they had my dad reminding them they're gorgeous. Mom whispering to them late at night about how to get over it, teaching them to be confident. You..." He pushes the hair behind my ear with a sympathetic look. "You didn't have that. You've told me about how your dad wasn't there. You've told me about your mom and her diets. I'm sure she knew, in some way. Knew he wasn't loyal, was trying to keep his interest. But they were so caught up in themselves they never reminded you how beautiful you are."

'I don't—"

"That's my job now."

"What?"

"From now on, it's my job to make sure you know how fucking beautiful you are. To make sure you don't question it, and when you look in the mirror, you only see beauty. When you see spots you used to hate, you remember me kissing them. Make sure you know how fucking gorgeous I think every damn inch of you is."

I smile at him and try not to cry. No one has ever said anything like that, much less cared.

And in his eyes, I see sincerity. He really, truly believes it. Wants it, wants me to see it. And though he won't be here in a week, a month, a year to remind me, today, I'll let him. I'll let him tell me he thinks I'm beautiful, if only so I can make it through this in one piece.

"Okay, Luke," I say, and he smiles.

TWENTY-FIVE

-Cassie-

"Hello, name?" The pretty young hostess with long, straight black hair at the entrance to the private dining room in the hotel asks.

"Cassandra." Her eyes scan the sheet in front of her before squinting. Then, finally, she meets my eyes again and fuck, fuck. I know. I *know*.

"And you're with the Reynolds party?"

"Yes, Cassandra Reynolds. The groom is my father." She looks over her paper again before looking to her right.

"One second, please." I hear a giggle behind me and turn to see one of the cousins I met at the first 'family event' I was forced to attend after the divorce. I remember her being particularly cruel, making some joke along the lines of it being 'no wonder her dad didn't want anyone to know about her, now that I've seen her.' She's my age, 29, and it's clear she's working her way up the ladder of wealthy rich men, judging by how every time I see her, she has a new and older version on her arm. This one is probably in his late 50s, early 60s, and not in the hot silver fox way.

"Your dad didn't even put you on the list? Priceless." A new hostess waves my cousin forward, and she gives her name.

"Bianca Tate." The woman puts a French manicured nail down the list, stopping on a line.

"Ah, yes. Table seven." She nods and walks past me, bumping into me in the narrow hallway and giggling a mean girl laugh again.

"Still haven't tried that workout program I suggested, huh, Cassandra?" she says before striding off, but not before she does a swift head to toe over Luke and winks at him.

"What the fuck was that?" he says, the angry gleam in his eye, the same one he had when my date touched me that night. The temper rising, heat rolling off him.

"Just one of my sweet cousins," I mumble as the server comes back with someone else, a manager, it seems.

"Hi, Ms... Reynolds?" She says the name like she's not buying it.

"Yes, that's me."

"It seems that we don't have you or your date down on our list. Could there have been a mix-up? This isn't the wedding reception, just the rehearsal dinner."

"I don't believe so. He's her father." Luke says, stepping forward.

"I understand, but sometimes—"

"Go get him."

"I'm sorry?"

"Luke, we should just—" I try to convince him to go, to head to the room, order room service, anything but cause a scene. I don't want to be here, anyway. It's just another game my dad is playing, another way to make me feel less than, to remind me of who I am—and who I'm not.

"Go get her father. This is clearly a mix-up, as this is her father's wedding and she's his only daughter." The hostess looks to the manager, who returns the same 'eek!' look I'm feeling in my gut before nodding a short, concise nod. The waitress runs off.

"Just a few moments. If you'll step aside so we can help other guests?" We do as she asks, letting the small line through. Each person checks out, each finely dressed couple on the list. Some I recognize, some giving me snide looks.

"Let's go." It's a plea. A plea for him to let me leave, get out of here, not endure this new drama.

"Absolutely not."

"Why not?" I say, the whine evident in my voice. "You said we could skip it before." His face is granite when he speaks.

"I changed my mind. You need to be here to show your face. You deserve to be here more than anyone else as his daughter. Don't let this game get to you. Let it help you win. Don't let them think they won, that you ran off with your tail between your legs." I stare at him, really seeing him, and in there, I see anger—not at me, but *for* me.

"I don't care, really, honey. It's not a big deal."

"You think I'm going to let you cry in my arms over this fuckwad and the way he makes you feel and let him pull this hours later? Do you think I'm going to let him think he got to you, let him miss out on seeing you, fucking beautiful and intelligent and sweet? Absolutely not. Chin up, sweetheart. Open your eyes. I'm not backing down until you have everything you deserve. And after, I'm sticking around to make sure you keep it."

My eyes water as I try to keep my composure.

"He's coming," Luke says, eyes above my head at something behind me. I turn to look, and he is. My dad, tall and trim in a dark blue suit with a woman I vaguely recognize as his fiancée on his arm. God, she's young. But she could be the spitting image of my mom twenty years ago if I looked deeper. Same dark hair, olive skin. Curvy build. I give it a year before everyone in this room stops seeing those curves as seductive and youthful and starts making quips about new workout routines and fancy diets. I've seen it before.

"What seems to be the issue here?" The hostess looks from her manager to me to my father with a fearful expression.

"Uh, sir, this woman says she should be on the list?" He looks at me, giving me a top to toe.

"Cassandra?"

"Hi, Dad."

"I didn't know you were coming." His voice is clipped, uninterested.

"We talked this morning."

"But you're not even staying in the hotel," his bride-to-be says. Veronica. That's her name.

"We are." It's Luke, a strong arm on my waist, holding me to him and holding me up, keeping me from falling down to the ground.

"And who are you?"

"Lucas Dawson." This is the first time I've seen this side of Luke. I know he grew up with money, but his family doesn't act like it. I know his dad wanted him to go the businessman route, the way of introductions, formal meetings, and firm handshakes. Today, his clothes are similar in quality to our first date—fine brands but expensive shoes. His hand goes out to my dad's in a masculine showdown of dominance. A showdown I know my father did not expect, a showdown I'm not sure he even knows is happening.

"Dawson. Do you know Jack Dawson?" The businessman's voice has been switched on, always game for an opportunity to increase his standing, his wealth.

"My father."

"You don't say? I was just working on a project with him."

"I'll be sure to send my regards to him." My dad looks to me, another top to toe, taking in my outfit, body, hair, and makeup. As always, it's clear his mental calculations have come up short.

"What are you doing here with my daughter?"

"I'm lucky enough to be her date this weekend." His hand tightens on my waist, not for my dad's benefit and not even for my own. It's a subtle, tiny moment of frustration. Now he's seeing it. Seeing what I was dreading, dying to avoid.

"With Cassandra?"

"Yes, sir."

"I'm sure you have better things to do this weekend." God, the words cut. The fact he'd say this to a perfect stranger with me standing right here... I shouldn't be surprised, Hell. I'm not. It's not even the words that shock me—I've heard them and variations of them for years, as soon as the facade of good dad faded with 'good husband.' But having Luke hear them?

"No place I'd rather be." My stomach flip-flops at Luke's words.

"Well, there will be quite a few young, single women here. Maybe I can introduce you to one of the nieces. It would be wonderful to have a family connection to Dawson Financials." My stomach turns with embarrassment, eyes burning. I want to die, to evaporate into the air, to go into a time machine and tell myself not to come to this stupid, stupid event. But of course, none of that is possible, so I simply move my eyes to the floor, my body going slack like they tell you to do when a bear attacks. Make them think you're dead so they lose interest. Will that work in this situation?

"I'm sorry, are you not Cassie's father?"

"I am." He sounds peeved by it like he's annoyed to be reminded.

"I'm dating your daughter." His frank words shut my father up, a feat I didn't know was possible. "It's serious. She wouldn't bring me if it wasn't. I hope you understand what I'm saying." How he couldn't figure that out, I don't know, but my dad likes to hear and see what he wants to. "Now, is there a seat for us at this dinner? Otherwise, I'd be happy to take your *only daughter* to a fine restaurant befitting her gorgeous outfit." A chill runs from my head to my toes.

It feels good. Having him here. Defending my honor. Having someone on my side.

"Uh, well. Yes. Of course. Clearly, there was a, uh. Mix-up. Right, Veronica?" He turns to my almost new step mommy, and she nods, looking flustered but also, possibly just a tiny bit, intrigued, like she's wondering if maybe she can get with Luke instead of my dad before tomorrow morning. *God, maybe he finally found his match.*

"Great, looking forward to it." And then we follow them in, and even though we're placed at a dingy, dark table in the corner, I feel like we won.

―――――

When we walk back into the room, I'm feeling good.

The entire night was great, to my utter shock and delight. We were seated with the other misfits: people who were at the dinner because of work or family, people who might not have been happy about being forced to attend.

We talked and commiserated, ate and drank, and laughed. Shockingly enough, one of the couples lives not far from my apartment, and just like that day with Jordan, the woman, Sophie, asked for my number to meet up for drinks once we're back home. It's strange, meeting people and making plans after having my protective shield up for all of those years. Yet, for weeks now, it's laid in tatters at my feet.

But most of all, I spent my night sitting next to the handsome Luke Dawson, every female—and a few male—eye on him, burning with interest and jealousy. Cousins that have frowned or scoffed at me as I walked past for years, who whispered under their breath about my looks, about my clothes, about the fact I don't belong, came to our table, giving me smiling air kisses before requesting an introduction.

And each time, Luke passed with flying colors, smiling and keeping an arm tight around me. Calling me his girl, both outright to whoever asked and with his body language. Regardless of the expensive beauty filling the room, I never once found his eyes anywhere but on me.

And now we're headed back to the room, and I'm light, not because of the two drinks I had but because of the relief. Relief for the first night being over, the first task, and the fact that, at least this once, I won. I didn't let them get to me.

And I only have Luke to thank for it.

TWENTY-SIX

-Cassie-

"Tell me that's from your sister's wedding," I say with a smile, remembering the application photo of the well-groomed version of him which looks curiously close to this version. He's delicious in the perfectly tailored black tux, each edge hugging his broad shoulders and slim waist. Even his shoes are a surprise, with handsome, shiny wingtips I know will make a clicking sound to mimic my heels when he walks down the marble hallway.

"Last time I wore it was to Q's wedding."

"It still fits?" I ask with a smile. While the outfit hugs him, it's not too tight. And from those photos, in the years since Quinn's wedding, he's definitely filled out, gotten stronger and more muscular. With my question, he blushes an adorable shade of pink, making him look boyish in his man's suit, his dimple poking out.

"My mom helped me get it tailored."

"Your mom!?" I let out a huge laugh, and God, it feels good. It feels good to laugh when my stomach is in knots.

"I told her we were coming here, and she told me I might need to get it fixed. This jacket was... not a good look. She took me to 'her guy,' and he fixed it for me. I picked it up last minute, right before I came to get you."

"Your mom has a guy?"

"She goes to a lot of fancy events with my dad. And she and my sisters like nice things. I told you that. We just don't—" He looks around the room, taking in the lavish details, gold and marble and velvet. "Flaunt it." I smile, knowing what he means.

"So you really are a momma's boy, huh?" I move a hand to the tie to straighten it.

"You've met my mom. Seen how she fusses over me. Imagine that times ten as a kid. I'm the youngest and the only boy. Double whammy. Quinn and Tara hated it growing up."

"And she also makes sure your clothes are perfectly tailored?" I tease.

"Oh yeah. She also likes to drop me off cookies occasionally."

"Well, thank her for me. You look absolutely handsome."

"You can thank her yourself when you see her next." The rock in my stomach has returned.

"Luke..."

"Not now. We're not having this talk now, but soon." I sigh, but it's not worth the argument. "Now step back, let me see you," he says, moving his hand from my waist, and I do as he asks, self-consciously allowing his eyes to roam my body.

The dress is dark green with a tight fit from the chest, which has a sweetheart neckline and two dainty straps, through the knees where it flares out. Not too much, just enough to give you a bit of a twirl if you swing your hips back and forth. It fits like a glove and did right off the rack, but the real showstopper is the low, low back stopping just above my ass. It's almost risque with the amount of revealed, bare skin. My hair is curled into big waves and loose except for the small bit on one side pinned back with gold clips.

I feel... pretty.

I feel... acceptable.

I feel... that regardless of how long I spent on this, someone will have *something* to say about it.

"Jesus, sweetheart. You're fucking gorgeous." His words are laced with awe, like he can't even process what he's seeing.

"Thanks." The words come out unsure, self-conscious, because it's how I feel. He hears it, as always, and reaches a hand out to pull me close to him.

"Cassie, you are the most beautiful thing I've ever seen. You're going to walk in there and all eyes are going to be on you. Everyone is going to wonder how on earth I scored a fuckin' eleven." I laugh at his words, humoring him. His hands push me back once more, just enough to look into my eyes. He stares at me for long moments, like he's decoding my thoughts and the emotions written on my face. "We're gonna work on this."

"On what?"

"This fucked-up idea you have of yourself."

"I don't have—"

"You do, Cass. And it's fine. Gives me somethin' to do. I'll spend as long as I need to show you how beautiful you are. Run to the ends of the earth. Tell you every day you're gorgeous, remind you how damn hard you make me. Whatever it takes until you see what the rest of the world sees."

"I've got a belly and—"

"Shut up. You shut up and you kick those assholes out of your head. You don't let them get to you, don't let them tell you how to feel about yourself when you're the most beautiful person, inside and out, I've ever met. And after tonight? Fuck those assholes. This is it. Unless you really, truly want to, we are not seeing your scumbag of a dad. Not goin' out of your way to make time for a man who doesn't treat you like a damn princess, for a man who doesn't think you make the world turn."

"Luke, I—" My eyes are watering, his words breaking the shell of the heartbroken little girl inside of me, shattering any reserve I made to protect myself from falling harder.

"No, not talking about this anymore. You're not gonna shed a single fuckin' tear. Not now. Not with me. We're going to walk down those stairs, sit in the stupid fuckin' ceremony room, and watch your scumbag father marry a gold digger. Then we're going to drink and eat and dance on their dime, have a blast, and then I'm going to come back here, strip you down, and remind you you're the sexiest woman I've ever had the pleasure of knowing."

And like always, when he sets down the law, I agree with a soft, craggy, "Okay, Luke."

———

The ceremony is beautiful, as is to be expected. They spared no cost with celebrating the new Mr. and Mrs. Reynolds, from expensive flowers to flutes of the finest champagne to drinks before the ceremony. The vows are beautiful if clearly not written by my father, and Veronica looks... happy.

I almost pity her.

When we enter the reception, the hall has been transformed into a magical fairy garden, full of fragrant flowers which, in the dead of winter, must have cost a pretty penny. A DJ in the corner is playing songs way too young for my mid-sixties father, but Veronica and her friends seem to be enjoying themselves.

The night is going well as they make their rounds from table to table. Luke and I eat and dance, drink and chat with my newfound friends from the night before, giggling over the older attendees attempting to dance to Kanye and Beyoncé or the younger guests struggling to figure out the Electric Slide. It's a great night.

When my dad and Veronica round our table, my body begins to tense. We, of course, weren't at the family table, instead in a cold, drafty corner far from any excitement.

"Hello, Cassandra."

"Hi, Dad. Congratulations. You look stunning, Veronica." And she does in a huge, princessy ball gown suitable for any cake topper.

The top is completely bedazzled, shining in the DJ's lights, and her jewelry is all glinting diamonds I'm sure were a wedding gift. We found out during last night's dinner Veronica comes from a well-known family with huge connections. It makes me wonder if maybe this will be the marriage that lasts, if only because the connections will be worth enough to at least hide his infidelities.

Veronica smiles at me, a forced thing, before she looks back at the dance floor where her friends are waving to her, urging her to come join them.

"Lucas, nice to see you were able to escort my daughter again." As if he's doing some kind of charity work. Luke's thigh tenses under my hand, and I grip harder. He can't go all defensive-Luke here. No way.

"I'm honored to be her man." That's it. Punch delivered, intent clear. My dad's thick eyebrows come together in confusion like he can't put these facts together, despite their conversation yesterday. Because it's so hard to believe *Luke* would be here with *me*. On purpose.

"I thought you were her date to this event?"

"I am because she's my girlfriend." My hand once again clenches, this time at his words. The confusion stays on my dad's face, but when his eyes dip to my cake plate, empty of everything but crumbs, a small smirk plays on his lips. New target found, like questioning my date's motives weren't enough. I dip back almost unnoticeably into my seat.

Even when I was a child, when he was playing doting father and waiting out the years until he wouldn't have to reveal his worth and pay for it, he always made it clear how he felt about my sweet tooth. We'd get ice cream, and he'd suggest low fat or sugar-free. I developed late, going from an overweight child to a curvy developed teen at fifteen, but there were about five or six years where my dad never let a day go by without mentioning my weight. Slight digs like, "Do you really want another serving?" Or, "No dessert tonight, you can spare to skip a day."

His eyes on my plate, the smirk on his lips... shit. I should have said something to Luke. Should have prepared this protective man.

"Enjoyed the cake, Cassandra?" I don't respond, don't give him what he's looking for. "Seems you did." Again, nothing. "Maybe you should have skipped it. All things considered." Even though I'm expecting the blow, my face burns with embarrassment. Not in front of Luke, who has already seen me, my body, my insecurities. Who has seen me cry, heard my story. "Some things never change, huh? I'm surprised you chose such a fitted dress." I never know why he does this. Why he feels the need to be cruel to his only daughter.

"Excuse me?" Somehow, in my embarrassment, I missed Luke leaning in to listen, his body tense, the heat roiling off him.

"Luke—"

"You must know. She's not, well... built for indulging."

"I must have heard you wrong."

"Luke—"

"Are you saying your daughter shouldn't be wearing this gorgeous dress or eating cake because *you* are judging her body?"

"Not judging, just stating the obvious." Even Veronica is now trying to flee, trying to pull my dad away. I have to wonder how much he's been drinking to be this obviously cruel in front of his peers.

"I see nothing but a gorgeous woman. Fucking beautiful." Luke's eyes are burning, but my dad, too wrapped up in himself, too oblivious to notice, just keeps going.

"I see she's got you too. Fooled you. It's nice now, the curves. A nice handful." I feel sick to my stomach, the cake roiling and churning. But, once she locks you down, that ends. She'll have kids and get fat, and then what? You're stuck with a bitchy wife with nothing to offer. You divorce her and she'll get child support or alimony for as long as she can. Don't fuck up like I did. Get the prenup, son." He winks at Luke like he's divulging some genius father-son advice.

"You're out of your fucking mind." Luke stands, and I follow, unsure of what else to do, wanting to end this, wanting to interrupt but also...

Also, a part of me wants to see what happens.

Eyes are on us. Not just the family, who looks on with small smiles and quiet chuckles, the family who have all said the same behind my back and to my face since I was 18. But also business partners and friends are watching, their faces a mix of shock, awe, and disgust.

For years, ten long years, I thought maybe this was just how it was with money and class. Constant barbs and subtle digs. Mean words. Maybe my father didn't know any better; he was so inundated in the lifestyle he couldn't see around it. But meeting Luke's family, equally well off... Seeing the business partners shocked and horrified...

"Now, Dawson—"

"The fact you cheated on her mother for years is your business. Even the fact that you barely talk to your daughter—your own business. The fact you clearly invite her to these events to use as a punching bag, to get a laugh? Fucked. But the fact you look at your daughter, the most beautiful woman I've ever seen, and say *that*, make a young girl feel shame in her own body, fuck with her confidence, fuck with her emotions and how she sees the world? You're scum." My dad stutters, trying to find the words. It seems no one has ever thrown this kind of thing in his face. But the whole time, flashes of Luke punching my date poke through, mixing with the images in front of me, and I fear it might go too far. My hand reaches out, grabbing Luke's, squeezing hard to remind him I'm here, where we are.

"You're done here, Cass." His hand goes to grab the small gold clutch I brought with me. "Done with this wedding, done with this man. I'll spend my last breath keeping you from him. You don't deserve this. His only daughter he treats like this? Kind and beautiful, inside and out." He helps me with the thin jacket I wore from our hotel room. "You want to change your shit, you come to *me*. You come talk to *me* and I'll decide if you get that chance. Any business dealings with Dawson Financials? Consider them done." He puts on his own jacket before grabbing my hand again, curling strong fingers around my trembling ones.

"You can't—"

"I can and I will. My father is a family man." Looking around, a few shocked couples are also getting on jackets, leaving. This isn't happening. It can't... not for me... "He finds out you treat blood like this, any ties you have are severed. I'm a lot like my father, cuttin' ties easy."

"This is ridiculous—"

"What's ridiculous is you neglected a little girl and still fuck with her head as a grown woman. What's fucked is she is absolutely terrified of hitching herself to any man because all she's ever seen is the shit you handed her and her mother. She's so fuckin' scared, so sure all men are are hiding things like you did, festering garbage within a pretty Trojan horse, she built a business around helping women avoid it."

"You should leave." He's angry now, my dad glaring at me and face red with anger. But instead of feeling disappointment or fear or anxiety, I feel...

Free.

Free of this man. Luke cut the tie I needed to snip years ago for my sanity, and now I'm free of it.

"Goodbye, Dad," I say, taking Luke's hand and walking out, and I don't even wonder for a moment if my dad knows I meant it more than just for tonight.

TWENTY-SEVEN

-Cassie-

WHEN WE ENTER OUR ROOM, I'M FLOATING. LUKE CLOSES AND locks the door behind us, and I stand in the center of the room, smiling.

Smiling.

After the crazy scene with my dad, the ending of a chapter, I'm standing in a pretty dress, smiling.

"You okay?" he says, leaning a shoulder to the wall.

"I'm great."

"Great?"

"I feel... I feel like I'm free. You're right—I don't need to put up with this. I let him rule me for way too long. I let his thoughts dictate my life for the entirety of it, and... I'm done with it. Done. It feels... good." He stares at me before reaching for my wrist, grabbing it, and pulling me to him. He plants a soft kiss on my lips, and I smile through that too. I have a lot to work on. Things I'm just now realizing might have been problems, things which have been holding me back. But with one of the major tethers holding me down snapped, I don't feel like worrying about it. Instead, I feel light and airy, like dancing.

I release myself from his hold, and he continues to watch me as I dance off to sit on the edge of the bed facing the large mirror and bend to start on my strappy shoes.

"Leave them." Luke strides to me with an expression I can't read on his face.

"What?" His hand is going to the tie he's wearing, tugging to loosen it as he reaches me, putting a hand on my shoulder. Looking up at him, his eyes hold fire and determination, a bit of frustration but also... awe. Or something similar to it.

"Leave the heels on." Fire runs through me.

"What? Why?"

"You know why." *Oh.* I get the fun Luke tonight, it seems. The tie is off, his hands working to unbutton the shirt before he tosses it over a loveseat in the corner. Then his hands go to his belt, my mouth going dry as I watch those hands, the hands that can do wicked things to me, move and undo the belt, slipping it from the loops and tossing it to the floor where the buckle makes a loud clunk. "Stand up."

I do as he says, turning and instinctively knowing he wants to help me with my dress. He unzips it, knuckles brushing down my back in a slow, warm caress, sending a shiver down my spine. The finger comes back up, stopping at the top of my back before he undoes the three small buttons there. Then he uses a single, callused finger to brush one strap, then the other over my shoulders. The dress falls to the floor in an emerald green puddle, leaving me completely naked.

"Jesus, Cassie." His breath brushes my ear, running down my neck as a rough hand gently ghosts down the curve of my side, over my hip. To my front, over my belly, to the spot I'm most self-conscious about.

"Luke," I say, trying to move his hand from where it rests, right under my belly button, to somewhere more comfortable, more interesting.

"Stop." His words are fierce, almost angry. "Stop this. You're fucking gorgeous, head to toe. I see you, I instantly get hard, want to hide you away so no one else can watch you. Every man in that room, every single one watched your every move, watched your ass move in this dress, watched you walk, you laugh. Watched you eat and drink and smile at me, only me. Every single man wished like fuck he was in my shoes, getting that smile from you."

"Luke—" I try to cut in, to tell him to stop, to move from the subject, but another hand comes to my hip, bringing me up against him. When I wasn't watching, wasn't paying attention, his pants came down, his hardness pressing into my back.

"Makin' it my mission to show you how fucking beautiful and sexy you are, sweetheart." Lips are on my neck, gruff 5 o'clock shadow scratching my skin and making me shiver. "Go sit on the edge of the bed. Face the mirror." My gut drops. I don't want to... I don't... but the tight, reassuring grip of his hands blocks out my thoughts, and I move, doing as he asks, resting my ass on the bed and my heels on the floor. I look at the carpet, with its pretty, if not garish, design that seems to be in all hotels. The bed presses, and soon the heat of Luke is behind me as he kneels behind my body.

"So fucking pretty, Cassie." A hand moves my hair behind my shoulder, his lips running up and down my neck, nipping. "Look." I don't. I don't look at the mirror where my body is on display in front of us. Instead, I work on steadying my breathing. His hand comes around, going to my full breast and lifting its weight, a thumb brushing over the already tight peak. "These. Fuckin' love them." His fingers pinch the flesh, and my back bows, mouth dropping open slightly. "God, look at you." It's not an instruction this time, more a reverent whisper to himself. The hand trails down, once again landing on my belly. My eyes close.

"Beautiful. All woman." His thumb grazes the skin, the skin I hate, before moving down, a thumb moving through my short curls to where I know I'm wet. My hips buck, and a finger drifts through the wetness, spreading it over my clit. "God, always so fuckin' wet for me. Is this for me, Cassie?"

"Yes, God. Yes." Chuckles against my neck, the breath hot and stimulating as a single finger enters me, thick and stretching me.

"Yeah, Cassie. This is all mine. All fuckin' mine. I'm keeping it, you hear me? Keeping you. Keeping this fuckin' beauty for myself." I shake my head, be it from his words or the pleasure ratcheting through me, I'm not sure, But now his thumb is strumming my clit, building me higher. "I am, Cass. You keep fooling yourself, telling yourself what you need to. But I'm keeping you. This is mine, not letting any other man have it." I moan his name, and he sinks his finger deeper, harder.

"Look." My eyes, still closed, remain so, regardless of his clear demand. He's no longer gently asking. "*Look*, Cassie. Look at you." I shake my head, keeping my eyes closed, my mind locked on the shards of pleasure shooting through my body with the movement of his hands. My head falls back to the shoulder behind me, his warm, bare chest a wall keeping me from collapsing under the pleasure. *"Look, Cassie."* The words this time come with the pausing of his hands, the final straw to make me open my eyes.

It takes a bit for my vision to focus, but once it does, my eyes lock to Luke's in the mirror, the dim lights of the room casting devious shadows on his face. He is handsome and wrapped in a mix of determination and lust.

"Look at yourself, Cassie."

"I need your hand, Luke."

"You need to look at yourself." I spend an eternity staring at him, his fingers moving on me, his eyes encouraging me to be brave. Finally, my eyes break from his, grazing over the image in the mirror. My naked body perched on the edge of the bed, long legs ending in strappy gold heels sprawled wide. My core exposed, covered only by the strong fingers pressing on my clit once again, rolling. I focus there, my concentration returning, the heat rising one again at the sight of those strong fingers.

"What do you see?"

"What?" My words are breathy, my mind scrambled.

"What do you see, Cassie?"

"I see... you. Touching me."

"What else?" His breath is heavy, the other hand now running from my hip to my ribs, back down, over and over, a thumb grazing my soft belly. His pinky finger caresses the roll where my hips meet belly, the spot I work endlessly to cure. Up, up to the ribs where I constantly check to see if my bra is bulging. Rough fingers graze over my breast, too large and awkward and striped with stretch marks from growing too fast. Nipples I've thought in private to be too dark and too wide. His breath reaches my neck again. "What else, Cassie?" I don't say anything, trying to figure out what he's asking, what answer he's really searching for.

Watching his hand, tanned and rough, scarred and stained from hard work, I'm seeing myself in a different light. A match. Together, it's like a gorgeous photo, a glorious depiction of opposites fitting together.

"Don't you see it? Don't you see how fucking beautiful you are? Absolutely perfect, the sexiest woman I've ever seen. All of this, fucking perfect." The words catch at the small tear in my heart, one of thousands, catching it like a tiny threaded needle, adding a single stitch to the tear. Not enough to repair it —no, that's my job. Only I can do the repairs, but a single stitch, a splint to keep it safe while I do the work.

"You see it," he says, his voice so low, so quiet I almost don't hear it, almost don't hear him speak, but it still plants itself in me where it will never leave. My eyes lock to his, and he presses a small kiss to the back of my head before he begins once more, this time in earnest.

Two thick fingers enter me, forcing me to press down and try to get them deeper as his thumb continues to manipulate my clit, continues to drive me higher.

"Ride my fingers, beautiful," he orders, and I do as he asks, using the heels on the ground to give me traction as I move up and down, eager to get his fingers deep into me as I moan and twist and grind on his hand. "God, just look at you. Look at you doing so fucking good. You gonna get yourself there? Are you gonna watch yourself come on my hand? It's fucking gorgeous, Cass. Watching you come apart, I could watch it every day." My eyes hood, his words sending me higher with each moment, each swipe of his thumb threatening to detonate me.

"Now, Cassie. Come, watch yourself come for me."

As seems to be the way, my body ignores my own pleasure to make this last, to draw it out, and obeys Luke as I shatter around his fingers.

But I don't look at myself when I come. I don't watch how my body reacts or the way it contorts. I also don't close my eyes, not screwing them shut in ecstasy.

No, the entire time, as my mouth falls open, a low, loud moan falling from my lips, my eyes remain locked to his.

He holds them until the aftershocks leave my body, long seconds which feel like a life-changing eternity before he grabs my waist and tosses me up the bed as if I weigh nothing more than a pillow.

And then he's on me, eyes locked to mine as he slides in, soft and deep in a way we've never done before. I lie on my back, staring up at him, legs cocked as he pumps into me, braced on his forearms. Slow thrusts, quiet grunts, but I don't register any of that. Instead, what has my body building once more, working to crest that hill again with him this time, is the look of desire and lust and something else I refuse to touch glowing in his eyes, telling me everything in both a million words and none at all with just one look. All of it written across his face, open and honest, the way he always is.

"You're the most beautiful woman I've ever met," he whispers against my lips, not kissing me, not breaking eye contact.

"I wish we could stay like this forever," I say with a moan, bucking my hips up to meet his, and something flashes in his eyes. He wants to say something, I know it, but before he can, I press my lips to his, grind my hips against him, and come around him, moaning into

TWENTY-EIGHT

-Cassie-

THE DRIVE HOME FROM THE WEDDING IS QUIET, BOTH OF US IN our own heads. We left early Sunday morning, skipping the farewell brunch before my father and his new bride went off to some exclusive resort or another. It wasn't even up for discussion, our attending. Instead, we stop at some greasy diner, getting our own buffet of breakfast delights from bacon and pancakes to eggs and pork roll.

We had a long conversation about pork roll versus Taylor ham, neither conceding on the point and laughing most of the meal the way that seems to be normal for Luke and me.

When we get back in the truck, heading back to our little ocean-side city, my stomach sinks, my hearty meal turning sour in my stomach. The entire ride, I stay in my head, dreading what will happen next, what *has to happen next*. It's our deal. It's my plan. I may have broken every single one of my rules in the last three weeks, but this is one I can't let pass.

Life goes on and so must I. As much as it is going to rip me to shreds.

The "Entering Ocean View" sign makes my breathing shallow, the bright green, cheery sign anything but. Traffic is low as Luke navigates the empty streets, residents sleeping in on the dreary Sunday and visitors avoiding the city during the cold. Eventually, we see my street, and he turns into the parking garage, driving past my car to park in a guest spot before turning off the truck.

My overnight bag is at my feet, strategically placed for an easy escape, and I reach for the wide strap.

"Thanks again, Luke." The words are curt, and they slice my throat as they leave my mouth. My eyes move everywhere but to Luke.

"I had fun, Cassie. Nothing to thank me for." I tell myself he's thanking me for the last few weeks. That it's been fun, a crazy ride, and we're going our separate ways like we agreed. That he knows, he know's this is it.

Are you sure you're not making a mistake? the sex fiend asks.

I ignore her, and I say the words I've been practicing in my mind the whole drive home.

"Right. Well. When I get to the office on Monday, I'll look in my database to find someone for your first date. I'll put you in contact, and if you both agree, then Gabrielle can help coordinate your first date time and location. If you have any questions at all, you can call her. She'll be able to answer them." I reach down to the footwell and grab my purse, moving my hand to the door handle. But before I can escape, before I can get out of this suffocating car, run to the stairs and skip the elevator, jogging the twenty flights before collapsing in my bed as this terrible feeling tears me apart, his hand is on my arm, stopping me from leaving.

No, no, no, no.

"What?" His words are angry and cold, full of disbelief. My eyes stay on my hand, gripping the black leather straps of my bag. On the nails I got done specially for this weekend, nails I want to chip off as I eat a pint of ice cream and curse my bad luck, this lousy timing.

"Monday. I need to look at my files or I'd give you more info today. I think I have a good idea of who to match you with, though. It should be easy." *You're a perfect catch.* I don't look at his face, don't look into those expressive eyes, instead digging through my bag like there's gold in there, a lifeline, something to save me from having this conversation.

Over the past few days, I've tried to convince myself he knew. That although he's been bugging me about *more*, he'd understand. We were on the same page. That when the time came, he'd gleefully leave, tires burning marks into the road as he drove off, free of my chaos. But each day, each word, each gesture... It said something else. Something he *can't be telling me*. Right?

"Cassie, what are you talking about?"

"Your first match. The Ex Files. You've more than completed your entry interview process."

"Are you telling me you're talking about *setting me up* with another woman?"

"That's how this works, Luke."

"No, it's not, and you fuckin' know it."

"I have no idea what you're talking about," I say with a lie. "You're a potential match. My job is to set you up with someone." The words churn the acid in my stomach, making me sick. Most women break up with a man and get to stalk him on social media, see who he moves on to, know the bigger, better things through a sense of distance. Not me. No, my lucky ass will be the one *choosing* the woman he spends his days and nights with. God, what kind of sick fate is this? To give me a taste of the perfect man and force me to find his perfect match?

"You're telling me the only reason we're in this car right now is so you can match me?"

"No, we're in the car because you helped me out, took me to the wedding."

"Don't play games."

"I'm not." *I am. I am because games are the only things saving me, the only things keeping me from breaking down, giving in. The only things keeping my heart safe from disappointment down the road.*

"Fine, play dumb. Are you telling me the only reason we've been together for the past three weeks has been to vet me? To find me a fuckin' match? To set me up with some other woman?"

"Of course." *Lies, lies, lies.* Even my uptight librarian is shaking her head at my dishonesty.

"There's no way you can think that, Cass. Not after these past weeks. Not after Friday, after yesterday. This is *more, Cassie.* This is not you setting me up. We talked about this. We are more. We're fucking great together."

"And I told you I can't date. That this would be over after the wedding."

"So that's it?"

"That's it."

"You're lying to yourself. Why are you lying to yourself?" His words cut, but his eyes are questioning, earnest, like he really wants to decode me and figure it out. To save this shipwreck.

"You know—"

"You're so fuckin' scared because of your piece of shit dad. And your fuckin' mother who lets you think all men are shit because it makes her feel validated. You're so fuckin' scared you block yourself out from ever being hurt. Cut people off before it's even an issue. God, Cass, you didn't even spend time with friends until recently. We didn't just open you to me, to letting me in. Look at you and Gabi. Look at you textin' Jordan, making plans to go up to some random little town you didn't even know existed. You're telling me opening yourself up doesn't feel good? Letting people in doesn't feel fuckin' amazing?"

"That's not—"

"Stop letting them rule your life. You're letting them rule you. You want to be like your dad, moving on to something new and shiny every few years, a gorgeous daughter he doesn't know? Always watching his back for gold diggers and people trying to one-up him?

Or what about your mom, always on retreats, always a mess, drinking and bitching to her rich alimony friends? Whining about the men who broke them instead of getting the fuck up, brushing off, and moving the fuck on?" I stare at him. He's never spoken to me like this, not Luke. This... this isn't who he's shown me over the past three weeks. "Normal heartbreak, Cass? Doesn't look like that. Normal men *don't act like that.* You fuckin' thinking I'd treat you that way, toss you aside? That's fucked. But are you going to tell me that you'd rather live a life of misery and loneliness to try and avoid heartbreak? Doesn't it feel better to fucking *live your life?*"

I break.

"It might, Luke. It might feel great—for now. It might be beautiful and magical and everything I ever daydreamed of, but you know what else it is? Fucking painful when it ends. And it will, Luke. Everything does. Everything ends and leaves you in pieces. So yeah, I choose to live my life on the outskirts, live life safe, because it always comes out. The man they've been hiding. It might not be another family or something worse. Sometimes it's just using things you've told them in confidence against you to try to get their way." Luke looks at me, understanding and... guilt in his eyes.

"Cassie—"

"I'll have Gabrielle send you an email on Monday. Goodbye, Luke." And before he can grab my arm again, before he can say another word to confuse me or get me to stay, I'm opening the door, hopping out, and slamming it behind me, and I walk away from him.

TWENTY-NINE

-Cassie-

THE NEXT DAY, I'M IN THE OFFICE BEFORE SECURITY EVEN GETS there, burying my head and my puffy eyes in work. My body aches, sore from the marathon cry fest all Sunday night. Let's not even talk about how my heart feels.

And I've been staring at the same paper, the same profile, for nearly an hour now, going over it, making my decision, gut churning and acid coming up my throat. I've been a bitch to Gabi all day, curt and short, and, to her credit, she's let me be. Whether she remembers what last weekend was or she just wants to give me space, I don't know. But I appreciate it.

And now I need to get this over with.

"Hey, Gabi, can you reach out to Maya Richards this morning to see if she'd be open to a date with Luke Dawson sometime this week?" The words are cut from me, and I refuse to look up at her. She doesn't answer for long moments. "Gabi?" I ask, again not looking her way, busying myself with papers.

I spent the entire morning with blinders, pouring over the women in our roster. I've met all of them, interviewed each to make sure they too wouldn't be a walking red flag before offering them a contract with The Ex Files. For each of the fifty or so women we currently have on our list, I've found an issue. A reason she wouldn't work with Luke. Too flighty. Doesn't like dogs. Follows a Keto diet. Loves art museums. Each one with tiny traits that 'aren't a match.' Qualities I'd typically overlook in any other situation.

Each one made my stomach churn. The thought of them going on a date with Luke, him learning their favorites and crafting some magic, spending the night at his place, meeting his nieces.

It killed me.

Maya is the closest to a perfect match I could find. She's sweet, quiet, loves family. Wants to build her own as soon as possible. She's looking for someone to spend her days with, someone to grow old with. Her music tastes align with Luke, her values and her hobbies—her father is even a mechanic, so there's something extra to talk about.

Eventually, I need to recognize this will be hard, and Luke needs and deserves to be matched. This is a perfect start.

"Cassie..." Gabi's words are quiet, and the low warning has me reluctantly looking up at her to meet her eyes.

In them is shock and concern.

"Email her, Gab."

"Cassie, what—"

"He's been approved for matches, and Maya is a great fit. Please reach out and see if she's interested. Send her his profile." My voice cracks on the last words, an ache there from crying all night in my living room tells me a few words more and I'll melt down. I nearly had to pry my swollen eyes apart when I woke this morning. But I did it. I got up, got dressed, moved on.

If this is how bad it hurts after only three weeks, it's a good enough reason to end things now. If we went further? If I gave him more of me, let him have even more of a hold on me, and something happened?

Well, I see why my mom never recovered.

"Cassie. This is—"

"Email her, Gabi!" I shout, scaring her and making her jolt back a bit. But it's too late; I'm too far gone. The tears are coming, breaking in great sobs from my chest as I bend forward and press my face into my hands.

Why is this happening?

"Oh my God, Cassie!" I hear her voice, but the real shock comes from her hands on me as she turns me in my desk chair to where she's squatting in front of me. "Cassie, what is going *on?*"

"I fucked up. I fucked up so bad," My tears are coming in huge, earth-shattering sobs, and I can barely breathe through them. Then Gabi is in front of me, hugging my sobbing form into her much smaller body and letting me weep there, quietly shushing me and brushing my hair back like I'm a child and she's the soothing mother.

"What happened, Cass?" she asks when my tears become manageable, sniffs and cries.

"Oh, Gabi. I fucked up so bad. I shouldn't have... Why did I?"

"You gotta use sentences, honey. Why did you do what?"

"Why did I fall for him?" My eyes meet hers finally, and through the watery wall of tears, I can see her understanding, her pity.

"Did you?"

"I don't know!" I shout, throwing my hands into the air and leaning back in my chair. "God, how am I supposed to know!? My family was as dysfunctional as they come. I vowed... When I was 18, I vowed I'd never fall for a man, always keep myself safe. But some-how... it was safe this way, you know? Meet men, vet them. Never get close enough to fall. Never fall for them. Two dates only. But he asked for three...."

"Would it have made a difference?" Her words are clear, but I still don't hear them, or at least don't understand them.

"What?"

"Would it have made a difference? If you'd stopped at two, if you'd gone to four. Would you be any less of a mess right now?" I know the answer, but I don't need to give it to her. She knows too. "That's what I thought. What happened?"

"The dates ended." I'm exhausted from my crying jag.

"And?"

"And I told him I'd keep in touch. For a date."

"Oh, Cassie..."

"I have to."

"Have to what?" Confusion masks her pretty face now.

"Have to set him up. He deserves that. Deserves love and affection and forever. You should have seen his family, Gab. So cute. Perfect. All of them deep in love. He wants that. The perfect marriage, the uncomplicated relationship. I'm... a mess. I'll second guess things forever." She sighs a deep sigh.

"Look. I don't... I don't want to step out of line. You're my boss. And I love this job."

"You're good. Nothing you say now reflects your work. We're... friends, Gabi." I remember Luke reminding me how I've opened up to people other than him. *Because of him.*

"Since that night... tire night... Since then, you've been... happier. More open. I mean, look at us. We're friends now. I always thought you were cool, a good boss, but a little..." she pauses, probably because she's afraid to say it.

"Cold." The words come out quickly, like somewhere deep inside myself, I knew.

"I was going to say professional." She smiles.

"Bullshit." A small, halfhearted laugh breaks from me.

"Whatever. But since then... Cassie, it's not just him. We're friends. We talk. I told you about being a..." Her voice goes lower. "A *virgin*, for God's sake." I laugh, and it feels foreign in my chest, like the sorrow I'm feeling is taking up too much space for there to be joy and laughter. "Seriously. Maybe... it was all meant to be. Maybe you need to open yourself up."

"I don't want to get broken."

"Aren't you broken right now?" The words ring out, echoing in my mind. *Aren't you now? Aren't you now? Aren't. You. Now?* I stare at her for long moments, long, painful moments. Moments where I think of Luke taking me to trivia night, Luke holding Bella and laughing with his sister. Luke, who wants a family, who wants a wife, who wants all the beautiful things the words can offer. Luke, who deserves all of those things.

I make my decision.

"Send the email, Gabi." My voice hurts as I say it, the words barbed and dipped in venom, but I spit them out, anyway.

"Cassie—"

"Please, Gabi." Looking in my eyes, she must see something. Resolve or acceptance, I don't know. But she nods before standing. "Thank you," I whisper, loud enough for her to hear but not too much that I'll lose it again as she walks away.

"Whatever you need, Cass. I just hope you know what you're doing."

So do I, Gabi. So do I.

THIRTY

-Cassie-

Late Wednesday night, not long before I'm about to pack up for the day, the front door slams against the wall and booted feet clump into my office, an angry man standing in them.

"What the fuck is this?" Luke is in my office, waving his phone in my face as if I can read it from there. But I don't need to read it. I know what he's angry about.

This afternoon, before Gabi left for a doctor's appointment, she sent over the request to Luke regarding setting up a date with Maya. It didn't take long after Gabi sent Maya the first request email for her to reply with a resounding 'Yes!'

Who could blame her? He's... *Luke.*

When she quietly, carefully told me Maya accepted the date request, I felt sick to my stomach, horrified I'd let this get this far. That I actually let him go. And then I remembered it's for the best. I thought of him with his family, happy with his nieces, deserving the calm and happy joy I don't think I'll ever be capable of giving him. I resigned myself to the fact he'll soon be someone else's and gave Gabi a few options for places to make a reservation. As I went on with my day, that sick feeling stayed with me all afternoon.

It's for the best.

But now he's standing here, somehow having gotten past the first-floor security, finding our office and slamming the door open with anger burning his face. Clearly, I forgot to lock it, just another of my rules I've been breaking non-stop, it seems.

I've never seen him this angry, and if it wasn't Luke in my doorway, I'd be scared.

"How did you get up here?"

"What the fuck is this, Cassie?" I sigh, trying to make it sound exasperated, as if I have no idea what he's asking about, as if I'm exhausted by him and not... broken by him.

"What's what?" He grabs his cell and brings it to his face.

"Let's see—*Good afternoon, Mr. Dawson. This is Gabrielle from The Ex Files. We believe we have found a great match for you and would love to work together to set your first date up. Please look over the resume for Ms. Richards and let me know if you'd be interested in a meeting and what days/times are best for you.'* What is this, Cassie?"

"It's a letter from my assistant asking if you'd be interested in a match." I move my eyes back to the blank piece of paper in front of me as if it's more interesting than him. His boots clunk on the tile floor until he's right in front of my desk.

"Look at me, Cass." The order is soft, and I can't ignore it. My eyes meet his and they're pleading and hurt, the look cutting through me like a blade. The look that's mirrored in my own soul right now, lost and aching. I did this. *God.*

If only he could see this is for the best, it's to *protect him.* Because he deserves perfection. "What is this? Why are you matching me?"

"Because you've been approved to be an Ex Files match. You've completed your two dates with flying colors and are now in our system."

"The fuck I am."

"I'm sorry, were you not interested in being matched? I can remove you—"

"Yeah, you'd better fuckin' remove me from your fuckin' system. It's you and me, Cass. No other fuckin' matches." *God, this is what I was afraid of.*

"Luke, we had an understanding."

"No, you had some fucked-up idea you could get rid of me after those dates. Some fucked-up thought we weren't as perfect as you fuckin' know we are, that I'd just lie down and let you set me up after what we've been through."

"That's how this works."

"You always fuck your clients?" I blanch and gasp, appalled he'd even say that.

"Of course not! I can't believe you'd—" He walks around my desk to kneel before me, holding my hands in his and twisting my desk chair to face him.

"I know. It's because I'm different. *We're different.* I knew it from the first day, when I found you cryin' on the side of the road. Walked to your car, had you yellin' at me for showing up late, and I think I knew then. You were it for me, attitude and fuckin' mascara face and all. You're so damn scared, though. I want to help, Cass. I do. But I need you to fuckin' *work* with me." I stare at him, my eyes wide, completely speechless. I can't... we can't...

The truth is, I know if I let Luke in completely, gave him everything, and it ended, I'd be like my mom, broken and alone and miserable, wondering where I went wrong. I can't live that life. I just... can't do it.

"Luke, we're not—" He stands, hands still in mine, now towering over me.

"I told you that first date I was keeping you. I'm here. I'm keeping you. You want to push me away, fine. You want to be Cassie, want to be scared and convince yourself we have nothing, fine. You need me to prove I'm not a piece of shit, that I'm real and I'm yours? I'll wake every fuckin' morning just to do that. I'll wake up and do everything in my power to prove it to you. But what we're not doing is this. You lying to me, lying to yourself. Telling yourself we're less than we are." The look in his eyes... I want to fall. I want to let myself go. I want it. *So. Damn. Bad.* But I...

When he tips forward, the words are gone as they always are, lips pressing to mine in a soft, sweet kiss.

Soft and sweet until it isn't, it isn't because a small moan slips from my lips, and something in him snaps. The restraint he's always holding like a tight leash unravels, and his hands are under my armpits as he drags me up to his body until I'm face to face with him, my heels making us nearly the same height.

-Luke-

In an instant, I decide we're doing this here, now. It may have only been three days since I had her last, but they have been the longest, most painful days of my life. I move her to the edge of her desk so her ass presses to the edge as I continue to kiss her, deep and rough, tongues entwining and teeth nipping. As I kiss down her neck, I move a hand to her skirt, her own hands moving frantically on the buttons of her blouse, and I smile against her skin. She needs this too.

Quick work has her in her bra and underwear; white, lacy things I want to rip off with my teeth.

Next, our hands work in sync, unbuttoning my shirt and pants, kicking them low enough to get my cock free.

"Lean back," I say as I stop kissing and nipping her neck, hand undoing her bra before she flings it somewhere. My thumbs hook in the sides of her underwear, tugging down until she's stepping out of them. My cock twitches at the sight of her black pumps still on.

"Luke, I have papers."

"Fuck the papers, Cassie. I need to be in this cunt now." Her eyes glaze, and I smirk, knowing how her uptight nature dissolves when she's wet, how I'm pretty sure if I tried hard enough, I could get her off with dirty words alone. She turns around, checking to see what's there and over a few things, tossing them to the chair she just vacated before lying down.

Jesus, this woman. All curves, all soft. All fucking mine.

I get to my knees to worship the woman of my dreams.

"Luke, you don't have to—"

I cut her off with a wide tongue from the bottom to the top of her cunt, licking everything up and moaning around her clit. I missed this, her taste, the noises. "You taste so fuckin' sweet, Cassie. Be good and lie here while your man eats you." It's a demand, her pussy convulsing in front of me at my words before I fill her with two fingers, stretching her, readying her for my cock as I suck on the hard nub, flicking my tongue back and forth as I finger fuck her.

"Luke!" My name is a shriek on her lips, and I wonder if any neighbors are still in the building, if anyone will hear. If I even care.

I don't.

My fingers curl up, hitting the spot that has her bucking and convulsing with each pass, grinding further into my face and tightening around my fingers.

Then I'm standing before her, hard cock in my hand as she whines at the loss of my fingers. I'd be lying if I say my ego didn't fucking love how she misses me as soon as I'm out of her.

But then I slam in, slam home, into her tight wet pussy that fits me perfectly, the woman who was made for me, and we moan together, both recognizing what this is.

Her hands come up, playing with her nipples as her head moves from left to right, and one of my thumbs come to play at her clit, getting her closer, closer... I'm getting there as well, my balls pulling up with the approach of my release, but I need something else. So, moving away, I use a hand on her waist to pull her up, kissing her hard before stepping back and moving carefully, boots stuck together with my pants around my legs as I lie down.

"Get on, Cassie." A flash of hesitance becomes a flash of heat in her eyes as she moves, cat-like and graceful, until she's straddling me on the floor of her office, her cunt hovering over the angry head of my cock. Still tipped in green from the wedding, her little hand comes to my dick, wrapping it and lining herself with me. Then she slams down, instantly filling herself as her head goes back, and she moans to the ceiling. My hands go to her hips, squeezing tight as we both get used to the feeling, to this position she's avoided the entire time. I can guess why, the way she's displayed, her insecurities front and center. Insecurities I find to be her more beautiful parts.

"Ride my cock, Cass." The words come deep and growly once she starts to move softly, ready for more. I watch her push her dark hair over her shoulder, leaning back with a knee on either side of my hips.

"I don't—"

"You're gorgeous. Don't worry about anything. Look at me. I've got you." Moments pass, and I wonder if maybe this is too much, if I'm asking for too much, too soon, but then a flash of determination crosses her face, and she nods, locking eyes with me. "Good girl. Now ride me, Cass." She starts to move, slow, tentative movements up then down, then up, and each stroke of her wetness down my painfully hard cock is a mix of pain and pleasure. Soon her confidence rises, and she moves faster, slams harder, filling herself with each stroke. She leans back, goddess-like as her hair tumbles back, her hand creeping up to tug a nipple and another, deeper moan filling the space as she clenches on me.

"Yeah, Cassie. Fuck me." She looks back at me, her eyes glazed, and my cock throbs at the look. I'm not sure how long I have, how long I can hold out before I need to come in this woman. "Lean forward," I demand. I could use a thumb, could have her falling in moments, but I want it to be her. I want her to do it for herself.

"What?"

"Lean forward. Trust me." Those words—mean so much more than just in this moment, but baby steps. Looking at me, there is a moment of hesitation before she does it, bracing a hand on either side of my head.

"Oh," she says, a surprised noise before another soft moan.

"Yeah, baby. Grind. Grind your clit on me and make yourself come. Use me, Cassie." God, she's so fucking hot, so perfect. I wish she could see herself now, the fucking beauty. She does as I ask, grinding her clit to my pelvis, and her cunt clamps on me. "That's it, baby. Come all over me," I say before moving a hand and smacking her ass. Once more, her pussy constricts me, the vice grip taking me closer. I do it again, eliciting a moan and another squeeze of her around me.

I'm close—too close. I need her to come. Moving my hand, I lick my middle finger, watching her with her eyes screwed up, mewling and whimpering.

"I'm so close, Luke," she says, and it's a plea like she's begging me to help her.

So I do.

That wet finger presses into her asshole, going to the second knuckle, and instantly her body starts to quake, the vice grip of her pussy sucking me in, keeping me in place, and she screams my name, coming around me. A few more grinds as she comes, and I'm following her over the edge, blissfully unaware nothing has changed.

THIRTY-ONE

-Luke-

I'M LYING ON THE PILES OF CLOTHES ON THE SMALL AREA RUG IN Cassie's office, half shocked this has happened but overwhelmingly pleased that slowly, my girl is becoming more and more confident, less uptight.

The moment is quiet with her body on my chest, my body shielding her from the floor as I play with her long dark hair, the chestnut strands sifting through my fingers to take in the different colors. My sister could make an entire color palette just from her hair —browns and golds and reds all mixing to create something so *Cassie*. Her breathing is slow and steady, and her own fingers draw shapes on my skin, eyes far away.

It's peaceful and perfect. How every moment with her should be, could be. *Will be.*

And then I go and fucking *ruin it.*

"I told you we're good together. Too good to just end things." Her body freezes on top of mine, and I hold my breath, knowing without a doubt I made some kind of fatal error, some sort of flaw I can't undo, can't unsay.

When her head picks up from my chest, her eyes dead and hollow and so far away despite her warm skin being on mine, I know. I *know* what she's going to say is going to gut me.

"You need to go on a date." I'm speechless, staring at her after what we just shared, knowing she's it, she's mine. "You need to go out with Maya."

"Are you... are you kidding me?"

"It's what you need to do, Luke." She rolls off me, refusing to meet my eyes, and stands, looking to find her bra and panties.

"The fuck I do, Cass."

"You... you deserve more. More than I can give you."

"What the fuck do you know about what I want?"

"My job is to know what you want," she says, stepping into her panties.

"Then you're shit at your job. You have no fucking idea what I want. I want *you*, Cassie. You. That's it. Told you before, I'll tell you again. *You are mine.*"

"You want someone who is going to trust you. Someone who will share your life. Someone with a family you can make your own. Someone your sisters can talk about teething and tee ball with. Someone who won't worry anytime you're out of town or when you don't text back. Someone who can handle having a man and building a life with him without panic." She lifts the dress over her head, and each word breaks something inside of me. Not something for me, but something for *her*. That she sees herself as this broken person, this unfixable being who doesn't deserve the good in the world. All because her asshole father is scum and her mother pushed all of her own issues onto Cassie. "I am not that. I'm not looking for a relationship, much less forever."

And as much as her words are breaking me, as much as I want to reassure her, my damn pride... I start to pull up my pants. "So what, that's it? You use me for a few quick fucks and a date to a wedding and we're done?"

"We had a deal, Luke." Her voice wavers.

"No. You had a deal. I always knew we were more. I fuckin' told you, time and time again."

"And every time I told you to end this or rework your expectations." I pull a shirt on, looking for my socks as she checks herself in a small mirror, trying to play it cool, like she doesn't care about what's happening.

"So what, you're just going to whore me out? You're just going to send me off to other women now that you're done with me? Now that I've served my purpose?"

"You're not being fair, Luke. That's not—"

"You're right. It's not fair. It's not fair you experienced such shit your whole life and were so betrayed. It's not fair your parents never put you first after they split so you wouldn't feel this. It's not fair your mother made you live her own heartbreak over and over again, made you experience it alongside her. Made it so painful, you now shield yourself from love because of it."

"This has nothing to do with that. We don't work. We *can't* work, Luke. Please. I'm sorry, but this ends here." Her eyes are dead, but there's a glimmer in them, a glimmer of tears that is killing me. Tearing through me like a bullet.

"Give it a shot, Cass. Give me a shot."

"I can't, Luke. I can't do it." I know what she's really saying. *I can't risk it.* But I'd risk it all for her if she would just fucking let me. And the balance of that kills me.

"You spend your whole life telling yourself everyone is deceiving you with some kind of mask, pretending to be something they're not. Look in the fucking mirror, Cassie. The only one deceiving you is yourself. You're keeping you from being happy because you're too worried about protecting yourself before you can even get close enough to get hurt." I watch her, her face hard, and I know there's emotion under there, emotion she's hiding or guarding, but all I see is cold. All I see is her not outwardly falling apart the way I am, not caring what happens next. Long moments pass as I stare at her, waiting. Waiting for her to say something, *anything*. To tell me I'm wrong, she wants to give it a chance, that she's scared. Anything.

But she says nothing, straightening the clothes she put back on at some point, staring at me like I'm a nuisance and she has better things to do.

Fuck it.

"You know what, Cass? Fuck it. Set me up. Set up something with that chick, give me her info. At least she's ready to open herself to something, to someone."

And with that, I turn and leave, already regretting every word I just spewed. Regretting them but too proud to turn around and keep trying to get through to her.

THIRTY-TWO

-Cassie-

HIS NAME MIGHT AS WELL BE HIGHLIGHTED, BOLDED, AND blown up to 100 point font with how quickly my eye finds it.

Two days later, Gabi and I are doing our Friday recap to go over all potential matches, any dates I went on over the week (none, which is a first, but in my state...), and any dates which have either occurred or will occur over the weekend.

The 'Friday Dates' roster says 'Maya Richards and Luke Dawson.'

Maya Richards and Luke Dawson

Maya Richards and Luke Dawson.

Luke Dawson.

I'm not allowed to be hurt or annoyed or frustrated. I turned him down. I told Gabi to set up the date. And then I turned him down again.

It's all on me.

But it burns.

"Cassie?" Gabi's voice breaks through my thoughts, the staring down of my paper, the molten pit in my stomach. I can't help but wonder when it will go away. It's been churning there, eating through me since Sunday night. Probably longer, if you count the three weeks I dreaded moving on from Luke.

How was I so, so stupid? So stupid to think I could keep myself out of this.

"Yeah?"

"I'm leaving, okay?" She's standing in front of me in a dark jacket, her bag over her shoulder. How long have I been zoning out on the list?

"Oh, crap, yeah. Have fun with your sister, okay?" She's going a couple of towns over to stay with her sister, hang out with her nephews.

"Yeah." She pauses, looking at me. "You okay? I can stay here if you need..."

"No, go, Gabi. I'm right behind you. Just need to clean up." She nods, looking at me once more.

"Okay, well, you have a good weekend, okay? Call me if you want... need anything. Anything at all. Work or... otherwise." She's a good friend.

"Thanks, Gabi. Now go before I kick you out." She smiles and then leaves me alone, the room painfully quiet, my lonely weekend sprawling before me with dread.

This is how I spend every weekend. Alone, getting take out, going for a run, taking a pilates class. I crafted my life to be this way, made it exactly how I wanted.

But why does it suddenly feel so damn lonely?

Sighing, I shake my head as I stand, lifting my notepad and binder, knocking over my cup of pens. They scatter everywhere.

"Godammit," I say, squatting to pick them up. My hand reaches under my desk to grab a pen, but instead of a pen, it touches paper. Feeling around, I get a good grasp on it before pulling out the small scrap, unsure of what I'll find.

It's folded into a small heart.

Red peeks out of the white paper.

I don't need to unfold to know what it is, what it says.

My mind reels trying to figure out how it got here. It's three weeks old at this point. It should be wrecked, gone through the wash, a torn-up mess. But... it's pristine. A bit crumbled, like it's traveled for some time, but...

It hits me.

Luke must have had it. It must have been on him or in his pocket the day he came here, the day he busted in and tried to convince me to change my mind. When he bent me over my desk, his jeans thrown in the corner, his wallet tumbling out and under my desk, I remember him angrily feeling around and finding it as he got dressed. As I told him no. As I broke my own heart.

That means he's kept this dumb fortune in his pocket or in his wallet for three weeks. Brought it with him everywhere. Brought *me* with him everywhere.

No man has ever done that, cared enough about me to want to carry me with him. I remember giving my dad a wallet-sized image from my school photos where I wrote 'To: Daddy, Love: Cassie' on the back in pink gel pen and finding it in a junk drawer not long after, the corner bent and crumpled.

But this man...

All this time, he's been showing me.

Showing me he's not the same. That he's real, he feels things for me, wants to try something with me. That he wants *me*.

And all this time, through the dozens of times he's told and showed me, I've ignored it. Instead, so stuck in the trap of trying to protect myself, I couldn't see there was a man in front of me willing to slay dragons for me, with me. Willing to do what it took to keep my heart safe and sound, to give me all of my girlish daydreams of family and friends and love.

And I threw it away.

But he couldn't even throw away a silly fortune from a cookie.

Oh God, what have I done?

My hands scramble, looking for the breakdown of dates Gabi makes each week for us to keep track of.

Maya Richards and Luke Dawson: 6 p.m. Valentina's.

I look at my watch—5:45.

Shit!

I need... I need to stop this like one of those goofy rom-coms where she's running to the wedding chapel or chasing a plane. I can't let him go on this date. *I can't do it.*

So I grab my keys and phone and bag and run, not even bothering to put on a coat as adrenaline takes over, and I rush to the stairs, not even waiting for an elevator, and drive my baby to go find my man before it's too late.

And the entire drive there, as I flip people off and scream at rush hour traffic, I pray I'm not too late, that I haven't fucked this up too much.

THIRTY-THREE

-Cassie-

"Hey, Cassie, I didn't know you were coming in today!" Maria, the hostess at Valentina's, another of the restaurants I frequently use for dates, says. I'm winded, panting because, *of course*, there was no close street parking. I had to park at the township lot nearly five blocks away, not even bothering to pay the meter. If I get towed, so be it. A tow truck is what got me into this mess, right?

"I'm not." She looks at me like I'm insane because, well, I am. I'm sweaty and panting and panicking. "I mean, I am."

"Sorry, babe, but you're not on my reservation list tonight, and we're booked, I—"

"No, not me. Someone else."

"Oh! You're on a date with someone else?" She looks excited for me. "How exciting!"

"No!" I shout the words because I'm literally mid-mental break-down and one step away from pushing her aside and storming in to stop Luke from falling for who, quite reasonably, would be a perfect match. *Definitely a more mentally stable one,* the snooty librarian mumbles under her breath, and the sex fiend nods in agreement.

God, I really am insane, aren't I?

"No, I have a client here tonight. He's on a date." Her brow wrinkles, and I try to drum up some semblance of professionalism. "I need to speak with him before the date begins." She looks skeptical. "It's incredibly important, Maria." My business tone is infiltrating my voice and selling her on the need.

"What's his name?" I sigh with relief.

"Luke. Luke Dawson. Gabrielle, my assistant, set it up." Her finger runs down the list, stopping on a line that's crossed out.

"It looks like he's here, but I think his date is as well?" My gut drops. I have to do it regardless, but I was definitely hoping Maya wouldn't witness this.

"Can you direct me to their table?" Maria nods, pointing behind her, but I don't hear the words. As soon as I have a direction, I blurt a 'thanks' and rush through the entryway.

Scanning the dim room, I curse the romantic lighting. It's great for a date but shit for a romantic gesture when you need to find the man of your dreams before he slips away. But it doesn't take long. Soon my eyes stop on dark hair and a huge smile, warm eyes, and the sound of his laugh as his head tips back, traveling over the sound of diners and low music.

Luke.

And in front of him is the back of a blonde head.

No, no, no!

She's here. And he's laughing with her. The comfortable belly laugh, laugh number one that he gives me when I say something silly or when Chris hit on Jordan for the third time. The one that doesn't say 'hello, stranger,' but 'hey, you're my people and I enjoy your company.'

It sucks to be so good at my job. Or maybe... maybe...

As I stand there, contemplating what on earth to do, my mind moves to dark places. Maybe he was a facade all along, the open, honest, warm man. Maybe he's like that with everyone, kind and generous. Maybe he makes everyone feel like they've found a home, makes everyone feel comfortable in their skin. Sells it with warm smiles and belly laughs. Perhaps I wasn't special to him because if I was, then how the hell is he already over me, over us, on a date and laughing like he's known her his entire life?

My anger settles before it can blossom, though, because now I know it's not true. It's some kind of deep-seated anger, a poison that's been seeping through my body for years, making it so relationships and joy and fulfillment never stick because I'm scared. It's lies I've been told my whole life, the wall I've built to protect myself. Because if there's one thing I now know, it's that Lucas Andrew Dawson is *not that*. He is not red flags hidden in sweet cotton candy, not deceit and untruths. He's just Luke, and from the first moment we met, he showed that to me. I was just too scared to see it.

Reinforced in this knowledge, I make my way through to the cozy corner, stomach a mess of butterflies and anxiety as I bump into chairs and apologize to servers just trying to do their job. I get about two-thirds of the way there when I hear the laugh, hear Maya say, "God, I'm so glad we did this. I so needed to get out."

"Yeah, me too. It's been so long since I've done this."

What the *fuck?*

I stop in my tracks, floored because what the fuck is he talking about? We just went out last week. We've been dating for three weeks. How the fuck has it been so long? Was I wrong? Was my initial fear and instinct correct? Rage flows through me, and I stop at the table, hands on my hips, fire in my eyes as I shoot Luke with the blaze. His head travels up my body, shock taking over his face laced with something I can't quite pinpoint. Fear? Relief? Joy? The thoughts flit past his face so quickly I can't stop and decode any.

"Cassie, what are you—"

"I cannot believe this," I say, my voice stern, hands on my hips, and Jesus, I feel like a jilted girlfriend. How many rom-com stereo-types can I become in one day?

"What are you—"

"Three days ago, you're in my office, begging me to give you a chance, telling me we're meant to fucking be, bending me over." My words stop as I realize we have an audience. Luke's lips tip up, a dimple showing, and I have to fight not to lose my train of thought. "Whatever. And now you're here, on a date, telling her you *haven't done this in so long? Are you kidding me?!*" I turn my face to Maya. "I'm sorry I set this up. I clearly messed up. He's obviously a *liar* and a player." Luke laughs now, as if I'm telling some grand story, and even Maya's lips tip up a bit. Rage takes over.

"I came here to apologize. I came here to stop this because *I thought I had made a mistake.* I was ready to give you a chance, to open up and let you hurt me. I know I set this up—I'm not stupid. But sitting here, cozy like you've known this *stranger* forever, saying you haven't dated in so long? Is this your shtick? How you get girls? Make them feel safe, make them feel like they're special, and when they don't cave, on to the next one?" Tears are burning my eyes, sadness and frustration battling with my anger now.

"Sweetheart, this isn't—"

"Stop it. I've heard it all. And you knew! But here I am, giving it a chance only for.... Well, thank God I found out now, right? Before I could really get destroyed? Because trust me, you could have, you know. Destroyed me." A small hand hits my arm, and I whip my head to Maya, ready to lose it. But her face is kind and clearly attempting to hold back a laugh. Not in an 'Oh, this girl is crazy' way, but in a 'This will be a great story one day' way.

What the...

"Hey, Cassie, right? I think you've got the wrong idea."

Her voice is different.

Maya has a thick Long Island accent.

And looking harder, they might have similar hair, but this woman is older than the application photo and subsequent validation photos. And her eyes are blue, not brown.

"Cass, sweetheart," Luke's warm, rough hand circles my wrist, pulling me closer to his chair as he moves his own out and stands. I look at him again and... it's there. Behind the laughter he's holding back, it's there. The same eyes. He's standing now, putting an arm around my waist. "Cassie, this is my sister. Tara."

"Oh, my..." I'm speechless as I see it now, the photos I glimpsed at in his apartment. The resemblance to Quinn and Kerry. His oldest sister. The one who set him up to be in The Ex Files.

His sister.

"*Ohmigod, ohmigod, oh my God.*" I'm hyperventilating, my face burning with embarrassment. I can never recover from this. I'll never come back from this. Bury me now. Please.

"It's so nice to meet you, Cassie," she says with a smile, and I instantly reach to the table, find Luke's drink, and down it.

THIRTY-FOUR

-Cassie-

"Seriously, there's no reason to be embarrassed. Quinn is going to love this story," Tara says as we stand outside the restaurant, Luke holding tight to me, my face still burning with embarrassment. They finished their appetizers before wrapping up as I sat there quietly, joining in the conversation in between the little mental breakdowns I was having. Apart from knowing Luke wasn't here with a date, partly because I completely made a fool of myself in front of his *sister* and partly because I let it all hang out, and Luke hasn't had his chance to respond yet. And while the fact he didn't tell me to leave, didn't give an immediate, *'Thanks but no thanks'* to my tirade, and his warm hand has been on me in some way for the past hour should comfort me, I'm anxious. "You're exactly what he needs. Don't let that smile get to you and let him get away with everything. He needs someone to keep him on his feet, keep him in line." Luke rolls his eyes at his big sister, and she winks at him.

"Alright, T, we'll see you soon," he says, kissing her cheek.

"Sunday. Bring her or mom will die. Plus, Bella keeps bragging to

Kelsey she met her, and it's starting a tense cousin feud." Luke laughs, but I can't keep up. My mind is too far gone.

"Got it. See you Sunday. I'll bring Cassie." *That's a good sign, right?* My annoying librarian and sex fiends are mysteriously missing. Tara smiles in our direction.

"See you then, Cass. It was great meeting you."

I mumble a forced, "Yeah, you too," before she walks off. I watch her go, trying to ignore Luke and the conversation to come. But of course, he doesn't let me.

"My place or yours?"

"What?"

"Where are we spending the night, sweetheart?" His face is soft as he turns me in his arms, and it feels good. It feels so damn good to be wrapped up in his arms again, feeling his heart beating on the hand I place on his chest, looking up to him and feeling small even in my heels.

"Don't we have to... talk?"

"Yeah, but no need to do it on the street, yeah?"

"Oh. I guess... uhm... I guess my place?" I mentally go over the mess waiting there, the mess of takeout containers, dirty clothes, and clutter lying around in my post-break-up cry fest. As much as I ended things to protect my heart, it's clear it didn't work. "Actually, your place." Luke looks at me, seemingly reading my thoughts as he smiles before kissing the top of my head. *Oh God, that feeling.* The feeling of safety and security. I never thought...

"Where'd you park?" he asks, and I'm pulled from my reverie.

"What?"

"Where'd you park? Or did you get a cab from the office?" He looks up and down the street, looking for my car. My gut sinks.

"Oh, shit," I say, pulling away and starting to walk briskly in the direction of the lot and my car. The lot I parked in over an hour ago and left without a paid meter on a Friday night. "Shit!"

"What the hell?"

"My car! I was so... frazzled." Out of the corner of my eye, I see Luke smile with masculine glee. "Shut up. I didn't pay the meter."

"You're so getting towed," he says with a laugh, but for some reason, he slows down, laughing, holding my hand and pulling me to slow my pace.

"Luke! This is not funny! I'm going *to get towed!*"

"Trust me. You'll be fine." I try to tug at his hand, but he won't go any faster, so I'm stuck walking the five blocks to my car at a slug's pace, looking back and forth to see if cop cars will come blazing down the street to come take my car away, as if it would actually be that dramatic.

And my fears are realized when we enter the lot and right there is a big white tow truck starting to look at my car and get it hooked up.

"No!" Luke just *laughs.*

"Calm down, Cass."

"Calm down?! Luke, they're *towing my car!*" I try to pull away, to get to the truck, to bargain my life away so he won't take it.

"No, they won't." He must be on something. Truly. Maybe I was right to say no, to push him away. Because he's clearly *out of his damn mind.* "Hey Josh, how's it goin'!" Luke shouts across the lot, and, to my shock, the tow truck driver looks at us and *waves.* We get closer, and Luke does that man-hug thing guys do before stepping back. "How are you, man?"

"I'm good! Just got a call; this one didn't pay the meter." The man hitches a thumb towards my car before reaching down towards some kind of a metal device, clearly meant to take my car away.

Except, on the side of the truck... I recognize it.

Jeff's Garage and Towing.

From that first night, the card Luke gave me.

Luke's work.

"That's actually my girl's car. She was in a rush to meet me, totally forgot." He looks at me and smiles like he finds me and my antics cute. Inside I'm freaking out over my car, over the tow, and the fact he just called me *his girl. Does that mean I didn't fuck things up beyond repair?*

"Oh, no way! You must be Cassie!" Josh takes a hand and wipes it on a rag, moving it towards me to shake my own. "I've heard a ton about you."

"Uh, thank you. Nice to meet you." I mumble the words, and he looks back at Luke.

"You won her back?" Luke smiles.

"I told you, I didn't need to win her. I needed a game plan to get her back on my side."

"Yeah, yeah, whatever. So I guess this one is a no-go. No worries, I got another right over there." He hitches his thumb back to another car, and I feel bad for the poor guy who will have to deal with the tow.

"Thanks, I really appreciate it." They say their goodbyes as I get into my car, starting it and blasting the heat as I rub my hands together. My mind is an ocean of confusion, thoughts, and insecurities floating by and leeching any remaining energy I have. Then the driver's side door opens, Luke leaning in with an arm on the roof.

"Get out, babe."

"What?"

"Get out. I'm driving us back to my place."

"I can drive. I know the way."

"Didn't say you can't do it. Just said you're not going to."

"That's stupid."

"What's stupid is me standing here in the cold, arguing with you about dumb ass shit instead of getting you back to my place so we can talk and I can peel you out of that dress I've been dreaming about since I found you on the side of the road." I sit there blinking at him.

"What?"

"That dress. You were wearing it that night you had the flat." I look at him, confused.

"It was dark that night."

"Not that dark."

"It was pitch black, Luke."

"Trust me, babe. Nothing is too dark to see your body in that dress."

"That doesn't make sense." He smiles at me, the enduring smile he gives me when I'm arguing but he thinks it's cute.

"Are you a man?"

"No."

"Then it won't make sense. But trust me." And I do because I was, in fact, wearing this dress that day. On the way here, I briefly thought I'd either have this dress bronzed or burned, depending on the night's outcome. I'm leaning towards bronzed, but I'm still not totally sure. "Now get out, Cass. Let me drive, and we'll get back sooner." I want to argue. I do. But I've learned since I've met this man, sometimes it's not worth arguing with him. Luke Dawson is the definition of 'pick your battles.'

"Okay, Luke," I say before he helps me out, walks me around to the passenger side, and helps me into the car before shutting me in and jogging around to the driver's side. And then we're off on a silent drive to his place, where my mind continues to reel.

THIRTY-FIVE

-Luke-

Walking into my apartment, I wonder if maybe we should have gone to Cassie's normally pristine place. While it isn't a disaster, breakfast dishes are in the sink, and a bag of laundry that needs to be taken to the cleaners sits near the door. The blanket for the couch is askew, pillows my mom insisted I needed tossed around. "Sorry for the mess," I say, locking the door as she hangs her coat on the hook like she belongs here, like this place is as much hers as it is mine. *Because it is.*

"God, trust me, my place is a total disaster. This is much better." I furrow my brow at her.

"You're a neat freak."

"Yeah, well, the last week or so had been a bit... trying. Cleaning hasn't been on my radar at all." She looks around, anywhere but at me, but her words bring a sick joy to me. Joy she's been as much of a mess as I have.

"You messed up over me, Cass?" I say, walking to her and pulling her into me. My arms go around her waist and she holds herself close

to her body like she wants me to wrap her up and protect her. I will. Every part of her.

"I was so wrong." It's all she says, but I know.

"You were trying to keep yourself safe." One of my hands comes up to move a hair from in front of her face. I don't even mean to, muscle memory kicking in as I tuck it behind her ear.

"But you never gave me any reason not to think you wouldn't do everything in your power to keep my heart safe."

"Old wounds go deep."

"Stop making excuses for me!" She slaps my chest with a hand, but I grab it, holding it to my heart.

"I was crazy. So mad. So angry you wouldn't even try, wouldn't even put yourself in the position to try it with me. I was mad, Cass. Then I got that email from Gabrielle and I lost it. I was a dick. I proved you right in some ways, showing parts of me I'm not proud of. I've got a temper. You know that; you've seen it. But it should never be directed at you, ever. *Ever Cassie.* You had your reasons for being careful."

"You had your reasons for being hurt."

"Cassie, I am a grown-ass man with feelings and perspective. With knowledge of what I'm working with, of whom I need to work with. You? Those wounds? It's the little girl in you, a hurt little girl with a temper masking the fact she is absolutely scared to *death* another person will let her down. It's not about men being shitheads, Cass. Yeah, that's a part of it. Your dad's a fuckup and fucked around, and you've seen some assholes, but that's not it. It's your mom who chose her own misery over helping you live your life. It's your fuckwad of a dad who chose his dick over giving his little girl every-thing she needed to be confident and glowing and *beautiful* inside and out. It's your asshole friends who you opened your heart to, gave everything to, only for them to get married and have kids and leave you behind because you were too busy making other's dreams come true to make your own life a fairytale. And somehow, despite all of that, you're the most beautiful person I know. You're kind and generous, a friend to everyone. You make me laugh, and you try to act mad when I do dumb shit, but you don't hold it against me. Watching you with Bella? Made me want to give you that, give you the world." The hand holding hers lets go to brush a tear from her eye.

"I set up that date out of spite. I was a dick about it. I shouldn't have done it. It was wrong, and the whole thing made me sick. It lasted about six hours. I called Tara and told her, then she dragged Quinn here to yell at me, talk some sense into me. You won Mom and Quinn over, by the way. And Tara, I'd assume." She blushes. "I sent a text to Maya the next morning, called it off. She was going to make a call to Gabi, tell her about it, but I guess she didn't do that?" Cassie shakes her head. "I was going to cancel my reservation, but there was a cancellation charge, so I asked Tara if she wanted to go. That's why I was there. That's it, I promise. We were actually working on a plan to win you over, get you to listen to me."

"What was your plan?" she asks, a small relieved smile on her face.

"Honestly, we didn't have one yet, so it's a relief you stepped in." Her laugh fills the room and my gut, making me lighter than I have felt since Sunday.

"I'm sorry. I—" I cut her off.

"There's no need. Stop, I get it."

"No, I need to do this." I nod. "I was scared of getting hurt. I've seen it happen, seen what happens when you let someone have any small piece of your heart. I knew from the beginning you were different. That first date, when I let you get me off my game, you *scared* me. So fucking much. You terrified me because I could see exactly how I could lose myself in you, let you take everything I am until I was gone, and when you left, you'd take it with you, leaving me a hollow shell." My hand brushes her hair back again, my gut sick knowing her asshole parents did this to her. They made her feel this way, taught her to guard herself against others like this. "But then I broke it off. I stuck to our deal even though... even though you're right. All along, you told me I was crazy, you wanted to keep it going.

I just... I couldn't see past my fear. So I broke it off, told myself it's what you'd want because I couldn't give you the easy, happy life you want—you deserve."

I try to break in. "Cassie, no—"

"No, please. I know it's messed up, but I'm not totally off base. You deserve someone who can trust right off the bat. Who won't over-think your every move for months until I make myself sick. You deserve the perfect stay-at-home mom to your kids, the one who will bake cookies and do projects. And... I'm going to work on it. I need... I need to get over this. Learn how to deal with it, to love myself. Because the way I feel when I'm with you? The person I am when we're together? You make me want to love that person. As you put it, I need to learn how to shut up the hurt little girl. To make her happy so I can move on. So I'm working on it, and it will be a journey. But honey, I'll never be a stay-at-home mom. I love this business. And I can't bake to save my life, and I'd rather buy things than make them. So you probably won't have hot homemade meals from scratch every night when you come home, and you might need to put the kids to bed without me some nights." He tries to interrupt me with a laugh, but I stop him.

"Let me finish. I know I'm not perfect. I'm not the daydream, but I'll try. I'll try every day. If you can put up with my crazy and be patient with me, I'm setting it all aside. I'm ignoring the fears and anxiety and the wall, and I'm letting you in. I want you to show me how beautiful life is, what it's like to let people in. You and Gabi and your family and your friends... you've shown me already just how beautiful life can be. I want more. If you'll take me." Her ramblings over, I stare at her for a few long moments, trying to figure out if she's done or just taking a long breath. When I determine she is, in fact, done, I start to laugh.

It's a welling of joy and relief and utter happiness that she's finally coming around, finally letting me in past her wall, past the spiky shell she puts up to keep people out. The laugh continues as I once again push her hair behind her ear, looking into her eyes as it dwindles down.

"What's so funny?"

"You."

"Me?" Even funnier, she looks angry now, the sweet, apologetic girl gone and the sassy, hands on her hips, independent and needing to prove a point one back in her place.

"Cassie, the fact you have to ask if I'll take you back is funny. But the fact you thought it was even an option for you is even more hilarious. No way in hell was I letting you get away from me. I was going to give you time to breathe, sure. But let you get away? Not a chance. I needed to sit back, lick my wounds, ask the experts for help before I took on the next part of my battle plan." I smile at her as awareness and understanding take over her pretty face, her jaw unclenching and her body melting into mine again. "The experts being my sisters and my mom."

"Oh God, *your mom!* She probably thinks I'm a terrible person! If not totally insane once your sister fills her in on what happened tonight!" She buries her head in my chest, and once again, I want to laugh. But I'm caught up in the feeling of having her back here again, in my arms, and worried about something stupid and inconsequential.

Although we haven't been together long, if at all formally, being without her for those four days? Not something I want to relive. Something about having Cassandra Reynolds in my arms, safe and sound, and looking to me to keep her that way? It's a feeling I'll fight to have for a long time coming.

"No, she probably will think I'm an idiot for letting you get away in the first place."

"You're her baby boy, though."

"I'm also a man, meaning she thinks everything I do is tinged a bit with male stupidity."

"She's not wrong," she says under her breath, and I laugh as I pinch her side, tickling her ribs in the spot I know makes her squeal and squirm.

"Luke! Stop it!" she laughs, and I do, pulling her close to me, trapping her against me the way I want her to be forever.

"This is gonna work, Cass. We're gonna have to work for it. You're going to have to trust me, and I promise to keep you safe, guard your heart, but it's going to take time, okay? And when you get scared, I need you to talk to me. There's nothing we can't get past if it's us together." Her eyes shine with moisture as she nods before I kiss her, and I know I'll do whatever it takes to keep this. Whether she knows it or not, Cassie is mine forever.

EPILOGUE

-CASSIE-

This seems like a bad idea but also a *really, really, really good one.*

Bad because if anyone but him finds me, it will be hard to explain.

Good because...

Headlights are coming over the hill, shining in the dark night sky of the thankfully now warm summer air. Headlights I can now recognize, although I'm no expert. They slow as they approach me, pulling over so I can see the lettering on the side of the truck.

A truck I recognize.

The window goes down and the interior light switches on, illuminating Luke's worried face.

"Cass, is that you? Jesus, are you okay?"

He's adorable when he's like this, worried about me, protective and slightly overbearing.

In another life, another time, I'd find it annoying. Frustrating. Suffocating. But with Luke? It's just.. him. It's us.

"Yeah, it's me." I try to make my voice sultry, but honestly, I probably landed on a weird mix of nervous and excited.

"Is everything okay? I'm on a call, gotta pick up a disabled car."

He's adorably obtuse.

"I know."

"You know?" The door to the truck pops open, and he hops out, the drop now small, and he bends to the open passenger side window and pokes his head in to see me.

"I'm the disabled car. And I really, really need your assistance." *Oh my God, cringe. That sounded way hotter in my head. Out loud, it sounds like a cheap porno.*

"What the..." His eyes roam my body, over the lacy, barely there cups of the balconette bra. The interior light I finally flicked on shows the rosy shadow of my nipples, my bare stomach. His eyes move to the curve of my waist where a garter belt sits, the straps leading to thigh-high stockings and red bottom heels so high, even I, who wears heels near religiously, almost can't walk in them. My underwear are a pretty pair of cheeky boy shorts and in the back seat is a short silky robe, just in case someone *other* than Luke stopped me. At least I *kind* of thought ahead.

It was actually Gabi's idea—sweet, innocent, *virginal* Gabi, who I found out is absolutely obsessed with trashy romance novels.

"You should totally recreate the first time you guys met."

"What?" I said absentmindedly as I swiped through the men I'd matched with on one of the many dating websites I use. Gabi is now helping me with the dates, so I have more free nights during the week and we can get more clients in the door. Every Monday night, instead of our AM session going over tasks and dates, we get Chinese and don our sweats and drink wine at one of our apartments while we chat business. Mostly. She's become my best friend, and as much as I refuse to tell him because his ego is already big enough, I know Luke is to thank for it.

"The first time you met. When you had the flat? You should recreate it." She takes a large sip of her wine before staring at me with a big, devious smile. "But sexy."

"What?"

"Like, wear lingerie or something. Then he can come to help you and boom—you can... you know. Do it."

"Do it?"

"You know—do it." Although I've determined 100% of her books are filled to the brim with complete smut, she blushes at anything even vaguely sexual in nature.

"It doesn't actually work like that, Gabs."

"But it could."

"How?" And that was how we went down a strange, giggly rabbit hole consisting of us shopping for lingerie and planning the day for my mission.

Now I'm sitting on the side of CR 324 in the dead of night while my boyfriend stares at me nearly naked.

"Surprise?" I say, suddenly self-conscious. Maybe this is an absolutely horrible idea. Actually, no maybe about it. It *is* a bad idea. Terrible, even. Perhaps my worst ever.

"Please, *please*, tell me this means I can live out the daydream of fucking you on your car out here."

Or maybe it isn't a bad idea.

"Your daydream?" He leaves the window, moving back into the truck, and I'm... concerned. This is bad, right? But then he's moving the truck, angling it so it's blocking the car, and shit, *shit*, this is a *good* sign. He hops out , jogging around to the driver's side with a mischievous smile on his face as he stops in front of my door and flings it open. He leans forward into my car and unbuckles my seat belt before he pulls me out, pressing me to the side of my car and lining his body to mine.

"Oh yeah, sweetheart. That day I found you on the side of the road? Couldn't think of anything for days but you bent over this car taking my cock." My pussy throbs, his warm body pressed to mine, scruff scratching my neck as he moves my hair aside.

"Did you really?"

"Are you gonna make that dream come true?" he whispers, ignoring my question.

Part of me wants to say no. Wants to tell him to meet me at home and we can continue this because this is a terrible idea. But the other part... I nod. He groans, deep in his chest, reverberating to my own, and his lips are on mine, kissing and nipping until I'm grinding against him, nearly nothing between us but his work pants. His hips are pressing me to the car, and he's already hard, grinding against me and making me moan with the feeling. Thirty minutes waiting in my car, all I could think about was this moment, priming me and getting more and more excited for what may come. And now...

He steps back, tugging my hand to the trunk of my car and moving me until I'm facing it before a rough hand presses into my bare lower back. I'm bent now, facing the trunk, hands on the white metal.

"This is gonna be quick, Cass. Gonna fuck you fast, you're going to come hard around me, and I'm gonna come in that tight cunt of yours, then when I get home, I can really play with you, say thank you for all of this." I hear the belt of his pants as he moves behind me. Looking over my shoulder, he's removing himself from his pants, already hard and thick, and I clench. But also...

"Luke, I don't know, this..." I'm second-guessing this. We're on the side of the road, and I'm bent over the trunk of my car in lingerie in the middle of the night. What was I thinking?

This breaks, like, at least ten laws, right? I can see the headline now: "Local matchmaker gets railed by tow truck driver on the side of the road, more details inside."

Okay, so maybe it wouldn't be *that* crazy, but you get the point.

"We're outside. What if someone—"

"Truck blocks the back. Dark enough out, I'll see any lights coming with more than enough time." A finger runs down the gusset of my panties, and he groans when he gets to the wetness. I moan as well as it goes up, a rough finger grazing my clit, so swollen I could come right here. I've been daydreaming about this all afternoon, and now...

"But what if you're too distracted to notice?" I say with a moan as he pulls the panties to the side, kneeling behind me to feel the wetness and move it around my clit. And then he's on his knees behind me, a deep moan pulling from my chest at the mere sight, the *thought,* before his tongue runs from top to bottom, licking at my arousal.

"Jesus, Cass, so wet. So fuckin' pretty, baby." It feels beyond amazing, his lips sucking and nipping at my most delicate places, begging for his attention, but still...

"Luke, really, maybe we should..." He stands, turning me to look at him, and I want to groan because even though I asked for this and know he won't do anything without my being okay with it, I don't *want* him to stop.

"Cass, you think I'd risk anyone seeing what's mine? See you in a position only I get to see you in?" His eyes, though shrouded in the dark, bore into mine, but I don't need to see his face to know the answer, the truth on his face.

"No." The word comes easy because he wouldn't. He'd never make me unsafe. He always keeps me protected.

"Good, baby. Now turn around and put your hands on the car." The moonlight glints off his white teeth as he smiles. I do as he asks, placing my hands onto the cool metal and bending so my back dips exaggeratedly, knowing the image I'm giving him is everything he loves, especially in the garters and lingerie. Proving my point, he goes to the garter straps, a thick finger running between the silky material and my thigh before moving it and snapping it against my skin. The movement brings a moan to my lips. "Like these, Cass." Once again, he's moving my panties aside before a thumb is in my pussy, his pointer and middle finger moving my wet around my swollen clit. "Like this more, though." I moan out loud, the sound swallowed by the empty night air.

"Shhh. Not too loud, got it?" he says in my ear, his breath hot again on my skin. I don't know if this is another game of his or an actual precaution, but either way, I nod before biting my lip, another moan falling from my closed mouth. His fingers continue to work me, pressing his thumb to my G-spot until I'm grinding on him, needing more.

"Luke," the words are a quiet plea, a beg. When his hand leaves the trunk, I clench, and he chuckles. Thank God this time, he's in pants and shirt uniform, not a coverall. Much easier for him to...

Then his hard cock is out, his thumb leaving me as his cock lines up with my pussy and slides in, pulling a deep moan from both of us.

"So fucking perfect, every damn time," he says, his voice a low groan that has me clamping down hard on him. He pulls out, each movement brushing sensitive nerves and swollen tissues and dragging me closer to... "Yeah, baby. You're so fucking wet for me. Feels so fucking good, you clamping on my cock"." Biting my lip, I fight a moan as he pumps in, slamming my hips into the cool metal, fucking me wild now. "Need you to come, Cassie. Need you to milk my cock." He slams in, fingers biting into my hips, and I know he's close too. Whether it's because recreating this memory is too much or because we need it to be quick, I don't know.

"Luke! Shit!" I shout, clenching around him, so close as I buck my hips back to get him deeper.

"God, taking me so deep, such a good girl, Cassie." His hips slam in, and I bend further, breasts brushing cool metal. "I need you to come right now or I'm gonna come in this cunt without you." And it's those words and his middle finger moving forward to graze my clit that has me throwing caution to the wind and screaming his name as I come around him. Luke pumps in twice more, deep, always so deep when he's getting himself there, until I feel him pulsing inside of me and hear him growl my name into the night.

———

"Jeff is going to kill me," he says as I pull on the robe, cinching it tight at my waist. Luke's eyes roam over me like he's thinking about doing it again.

"No. No way, wait until we get home," I chide, and he smiles at me, that dimple I love coming out. "And Jeff won't kill you, don't worry."

"What?"

"I told him to send you out here. He knows. You won't be in trouble." I've become friends with nearly all of Luke's friends in the past six months, including his boss and the shop owner.

"You told him to send me out here so I could fuck you on CR 324?" His eyes are wide with surprise.

"Of course not! I just asked if he could set it up, that this is where we met..." Humor now fills his shocked green eyes. "What?" He's laughing now, and dread fills my belly as he fixes his clothes. "*What, Luke!?*"

"Babe, he knew."

"No, I told him—"

"Don't care what you told him, Cass. He knew I was coming out here to get laid."

"There's no way—"

"Cassie, I'm a man. Men know. There's no way he okayed this, went along with it, and thought, what? It was going to be a romantic picnic? Love you, babe, but he knows." His eyes are sincere on mine, and I see it now, the truth.

"*No.*"

"Yes, babe." He tightens the robe I'm wearing, tugging at the bottom to cover more of me. "He knows."

"Oh, my God! I can never show my face there again."

"What? Why?"

"Uh, hello! Luke! Your boss *knows.*"

"Sweetheart, if anything, you just won the award for the best girlfriend."

"No, maybe skankiest girlfriend."

"Again, Cass, I know men. You just made me a legend, calling me out to fuck you on the side of the road." An arm goes around my waist and he laughs. "You're perfect."

"Luke, this isn't funny."

"They'll never say a word to you. Or even me, really. No need to worry. But just know, you won over every man in that shop today."

"Oh my *God*," I whisper into his chest.

"You love me?" I look up at him, a small smile still playing on his lips.

"Of course."

"That's all that matters, Cassie. You love me. I love you. That's it."

"But Luke—"

"Was it worth it?" My face burns. I know what he's asking, but I pretend I don't.

"What?"

"Me, fucking you on the side of the road. Worth it? Because it sure as fuck was worth it to me, and now I know I have to deal with all those jealous fucks at my work, thinking about you and how fuckin' lucky I am to have you." I go to argue. "Sweetheart, that was the hottest thing we've ever done. And with everything I've done to that body of yours, it's saying a lot."

He's not wrong. That *is* saying a lot. So instead of arguing, I give him a short, sweet kiss, ignoring my still-present embarrassment and saying, "Okay, Luke."

One Year Later

Walking into the apartment I share with Luke, I call out his name before bending down to unhook the leash from our yellow lab puppy's, Cooper's, collar. We got him just last month after lots and lots of begging—on Luke's end. I was against it, because fur and mess and poop, until I saw the little smushed face and melted.

But now, as I stand, my black running leggings covered in yellow fur already, I'm confused. He's not here.

He was here not thirty minutes ago when I took Coop for a run. What the...

My eye catches on the marble counter, two stacked boxes, and something small on top. Walking over, I see a fortune cookie, still in the wrapper, with a note.

"Open the cookie and get ready, then go downstairs."

It's scribbled in Luke's messy, near illegible scrawl, and I smile. He loves stuff like this. Fun outings to remind me of our first date he planned, full of surprises and twists. Opening the package and cracking the cookie, I read it:

"Your next adventure is about to begin."

My brows furrow in confusion before I set it aside, opening the top box.

Inside, nestled in white tissue paper, is a familiar dress.

A cream sweater dress with a V-neck, new tags on it, just my size.

I used to have this dress.

Well, I still do, technically—it's in a memory box on the top shelf of my closet, a coffee stain that never washed out of the luxurious fabric and all. I move to the next box.

Black over the knee boots with no heel. These aren't the same as my old ones, the ones I couldn't take off to save my life, but still...

My phone vibrates.

Gabi calling.

"Hello?" I answer, still distracted.

"Are you almost ready?"

"What?"

"We have to go. We're on a tight schedule."

"Gabi, what—"

"Rinse off, put on the dress, get ready, and let's go. Buzz me up and I'll make sure Coop has water before we leave." She clicks off and I stare at the now silent phone before the apartment buzzes with Gabi's request. Moments later, she's at my door, shooing me off.

"Go, now! We have—" She glances at her watch. "Fifteen minutes. Go!"

"Gabi, where are we—" Her hands grab my face, bringing it close to hers. "Cassie. Go get ready." There's a strange look in her eyes that

I haven't seen before, but instead of arguing, I just nod and do as I'm told. Ten minutes later, we're out the door and to our next... stop.

————

Walking into the small coffee shop I love, I'm tackled by a little body before seeing a face I recognize.

"What are you doing here?" I ask, hugging Luke's sister Quinn before kissing her daughter Bella on the cheek.

"We're your next stop!" Bella calls, nearly jumping with excitement, the look on her face priceless.

"What does that even mean!?" I ask, so confused by what has happened in the past hour.

"That's for you to find out. Here." Gabi digs in her pocket and hands me a piece of paper.

"I promise I won't make you spill this one, though I loved how that ended," the note reads in that same, near illegible font.

"What is—" Bella shoves a lidded cup in my hand.

"Here you go, Auntie Cassie!" She started calling me that a few months ago, and I never had the heart to stop her, but the twinkle in Quinn's eye...

"And a cannoli cupcake," Quinn says, handing me over the confection. "From Luigi's." She smiles, and it's sisterly and sweet and knowing.

"What the hell is—"

"No time for questions, Cassie. We have another stop to make."

————

It turns out when she says that, she meant *lots* of stops. By five, we've been to Luke's garage where I was given a soft pretzel and a fountain drink by Jeff, the owner, my tears welling with memories. Then we stopped by the best by-the-slice pizza shop, where we met up with

Kerry and Tara's daughter Jaime, eating and laughing before Cassie rushed us off.

After our lunch, we went to the small bookstore in town I could spend hours in, though I think Gabi might have had more fun than me there, followed by a stop at my favorite salon where I got a blowout, my hair perfectly coifed for... what?

Now we're sitting at Tia Maria's, eating chips and drinking margaritas with Tara, Quinn, and Jordan, who came down from Springbrook Hills, and it's been the most magical day ever. I just can't quite figure it out since there's no way...

Gabi turns to me.

"One last stop, Cassie." She's smiling, beaming really, and the girls are smiling too. My lips turn up not because I know what on earth is happening but because it's infectious, this joy and happiness and friendship. *Joy and happiness and friendship I avoided for years.*

"Okay?"

"Beach or lake?" Gabi asks, and my brows come together in confusion, trying to remember why that's familiar.

"What?"

"Which do you prefer?" *Beach or lake.* The words come to me in a whisper, everything clicking, knowing, confirming what my heart was too nervous to guess.

"Beach."

"Let's go then," Gabi says, standing up and nodding at the waitress, clearly understanding whatever is going on as we all get into our cars and drive to the boardwalk.

———

It's cold like it was that night.

The wind coming off the ocean whips my hair around as I pull my coat closer to me and semi-regret not wearing tights under this dress. Again.

But there it is, big lights, the entrance facing the ocean. My heart pounds.

Tommy's Tavern.

And on a white clapboard propped against the wall, "Tonight! Trivia Night!"

My breath hitches in my throat, a small sob dying to escape because *I know now.*

"Let's go, Cassie," Quinn says as both sisters press a hand to my back, pushing me towards the entrance. When we go in, my eyes go around the room, expecting tons of people like the first time. But instead, twenty or so come into my sight, all people I've let in since Luke changed my life. Jordan walks over to Tanner, sitting next to Ben, who smiles with a slight wave.

Chris shouts when he sees me, "She's finally here!" and I can't help but laugh. Kerry and Jack are here with Quinn and Tara's husbands. So is my friend from the wedding, Jeff and some of the guys from the shop. All here. Everyone except...

"Okay, teams, we have one final question before the fun starts!" a voice says into a microphone, the sounds reverberating through the room. It's the same MC from that night, smiling big, his eyes on me. "Are we ready?!" My friends all yell, excited, but I'm still looking around, looking for... "We have a special guest for this question, and only one of you can answer it." More cheering and then he's there.

Luke is standing in front of me, hands in his pockets. Those ever-present boots are on his feet, a huge smile on his face, directed at me. His hand goes out, grabbing mine. Those hands are so familiar to me now, every scar, every callus committed to memory.

"Cold," he says, his words soft before both hands are on my left hand, warming it.

"It's January." Those are the only words that work.

"You have fun today?" He's talking like I didn't spend the day on some wild goose hunt, ending in the bar we spent our first night in, surrounded by family and friends. It's like I just walked in the door of our apartment after a day at work and he's saying hi, dinner ready and waiting.

"What's going on?"

"You know what's going on." He says the words with surety, a smile on his lips, that damned dimple showing, and he's not wrong. I know.

"But we've only—"

"I think I knew that night I found you on the side of the road. Fell for you with makeup all over your face and bein' a bitch because you thought I was late, then feeling bad because it wasn't my fault. Your face when I came into the restaurant as your next potential match? Sealed it. You were mad. So mad and stressed and shocked. Adorable." I try to say something, to argue because even in this moment, I can't resist. But he doesn't let me. "Had to work hard to get past your wall. You were scared, with good reason. But once we got through all of that? Once I convinced you to give me a chance, give us a chance? Smooth sailing, sweetheart." I open my mouth because we fight all the damn time and—

"Love fighting with you. Love that you don't let me get away with shit and call me out, that you like to bust my balls. I love that you've learned to let people in—God, baby, look at this room, all these people. They all love you as much as I do." Sobs gets stuck in my throat, transforming from frustrated back to awed in a moment.

"You're beautiful. So beautiful, Cassie, inside and out. Everyone knows it and wants to be in your universe because of it. You're kind and dedicated, live to give people fairytales and happily ever afters and protect them from disappointment. And now it's your turn." And then it happens, and I can't control the hitch in my throat. The tears instantly start rolling.

Luke goes down onto one knee, staring up at me with his big green eyes, his dimple, and his huge smile pointed at me and only me.

"Cassie, will you do me the honor of being my wife? Let me make your life a fairytale, show you how beautiful it can be, how beautiful we can be?"

My answer doesn't take long because I already jumped the hard hurdles, learning to trust him and overcoming my own insecurities, the hurdles of worrying about if this is too good to be true or if I'm going to end up broken.

But when everyone in the room cheers before I even give an answer, it's cemented.

Because he didn't just give me himself, his love, his trust. He gave me this—people to surround me and support me, help me when I'm down and cheer with me when I'm up. I know deep in my soul he'll never lead me astray; he'll always be faithful and kind and the man I fell for. So with that in mind, knowing all he's given me, all he will give me, I say the only thing I can.

"Okay, Luke."

ABOUT THE AUTHOR

Morgan is a born and raised Jersey girl, living there with her two boys, toddler daughter, and mechanic husband. She's addicted to iced espresso, chips, and Starburst jellybeans.

Writing has been her calling for as long as she can remember. There's a framed 'page one' of a book she wrote at seven hanging in her childhood home to prove the point. Her entire life she's crafted stories in her mind, begging to be released but it wasn't until recently she finally gave them the reigns.

I'm so grateful you've agreed to take this journey with me.

Learn more about my at my website:

www.authormorganelizabeth.com

Stay up to date via TikTok and Instagram

Stay up to date with future stories, get sneak peeks and bonus chapters by signing up for my newsletter here!

ALSO BY MORGAN ELIZABETH

If you're looking for spicy small town romance, Morgan Elizabeth has you covered! Check out these releases:

Get book one, The Distraction, on Kindle Unlimited here!

The last thing he needs is a distraction.

Hunter Hutchin's success is due to one thing, and one thing only: his unerring focus on Beaten Path, the outdoor recreation company he built from the ground up after his first business was an utter failure.

When his dad gets sick, Hunter is forced to go back to his hometown and prove once and for all that his father's belief in him wasn't for nothing. With illness looming, distractions are unacceptable.

Staying with his sister, he meets Hannah, the sexy nanny who has had his head in a frenzy since they met.

When Hunter's dad gets sick, he's forced to leave the city and move back into the small town he grew up in at his sister's house. Ever since he watched Hannah dance into his life, he's finding himself drifting from his goals and purpose - or is he drifting closer to them?

She refuses to make the same mistakes as her mother.

Hannah Keller grew up watching what happens when a family falls apart and lived through those consequences. When it's time, she won't make the same mistake by settling for anyone.

But when the uncle of the kids she nannies comes to stay for the summer, she can't help but find herself drawn to the handsome, standoffish man who is definitely not for her.

Can she get through the summer while protecting her heart? Or will he breakthrough and leave her broken?

Out now in the Kindle Store and on Kindle Unlimited

He was her first love.

Luna Davidson has been in love with Tony since she was ten years old. As her older brother's best friend, he was always off-limits, but that doesn't mean she didn't try. But years after he turned her down, she's found herself needing his help, whether she wants it or not.

She's his best friend's little sister.

When he learns that Luna has had someone stalking her for months, he's furious that she didn't tell anyone. As a detective on the Springbrook Hills PD, it's his job to serve and protect. But can he use this as an excuse to find out what really happened all those years ago?

Can Luna overcome her own insecurities to see what's right in front of her? Can Tony figure out who is stalking her before it goes too far?

Out now in the Kindle Store and on Kindle Unlimited
She was always the fill-in.

Jordan Daniels always knew she had a brother and sister her mom left behind. Heck, her mom never let her forget she didn't live up to their standards. But when she disappears from the limelight after her country star boyfriend proposes, the only place she knows to go to is to the town her mother fled and the family who doesn't know she exists.

He won't fall for another wild child.

Tanner Coleman was left in the dust once before when his high school sweetheart ran off to follow a rockstar around the world. He loves his roots, runs the family business, and will never leave Springbrook Hills. But when Jordan, with her lifetime spent traveling the world and mysterious history comes to work for him, he can't help but feel drawn to her.

Can Jordan open up to him about her past and stay in one place? Can Tanner trust his heart with her, or will she just hurt him like his ex?